"F... art who-
dur... ...rs."   —*Richmond Times-Dispatch*

"Such a clever series . . . I'm on pins and needles waiting for
the next installment."   —*Book of Secrets*

"There is so much to love about this story! . . . The characters
are superb."   —*Escape with Dollycas Into A Good Book*

"*Every Trick in the Book* is, if it's possible, better than *Buried
in a Book* . . . Another fantastic cozy mystery."
                                    —*Cozy Mystery Book Reviews*

"A wonderfully crafted tome that kicked up the suspense a
notch as the pages progressed towards a finale worthy of this
terrific novel . . . [A] fabulous series."   —*Dru's Book Musings*

Buried in a Book

"Cheer up—there's no middle-aged malaise for Lila. This cozy
debut, written by a pseudonymous duo, excels at describing
bucolic North Carolina. Think Kate Carlisle for her intergen-
erational ensemble style or Mark de Castrique's series for
regional Tar Heel flavor."   —*Library Journal*

continued . . .

BOOKS, COOKS, AND CROOKS

Lucy Arlington

BERKLEY PRIME CRIME, NEW YORK

THE BERKLEY PUBLISHING GROUP
Published by the Penguin Group
Penguin Group (USA) LLC
375 Hudson Street, New York, New York 10014

USA • Canada • UK • Ireland • Australia • New Zealand • India • South Africa • China

penguin.com

A Penguin Random House Company

BOOKS, COOKS, AND CROOKS

A Berkley Prime Crime Book / published by arrangement with the author

Berkley Prime Crime Books are published by The Berkley Publishing Group.
BERKLEY® PRIME CRIME and the PRIME CRIME logo
are trademarks of Penguin Group (USA) LLC.

For information, address: The Berkley Publishing Group,
a division of Penguin Group (USA) LLC,
375 Hudson Street, New York, New York 10014.

ISBN: 978-0-425-25224-6

PUBLISHING HISTORY
Berkley Prime Crime mass-market edition / February 2014

PRINTED IN THE UNITED STATES OF AMERICA

10 9 8 7 6 5 4 3 2

Cover art by Julia Green.
Cover design by Lesley Worrell.
Interior text design by Tiffany Estreicher.

*This series never would have existed without
the friendship of two women.
Both of us, Jennifer and Sylvia, are honored
to call many of our readers friends.
Books continue to unite people. Like friendship,
they will stand the test of time.
Thank you, readers and friends everywhere.*

Chapter 1

AFTER A LONG DAY OF CONTRACT NEGOTIATIONS, PHONE calls to authors and editors, and a meeting with my fellow literary agents, the last thing I expected was to come home to find my kitchen on fire.

I knew something was wrong the moment I opened the front door. The acrid smell of burning meat assaulted my nostrils, and clouds of gray smoke plumed from the kitchen into the hall. I heard a man bark out a string of colorful expletives seconds before the downstairs smoke alarm blared.

Dropping my purse and briefcase on the floor, I rushed into the kitchen and took in the chaotic scene.

High flames were rising from a frying pan on the stovetop, police officer Sean Griffiths was holding a burning dishtowel, and a shower of sparks was spreading over the apron he wore.

I quickly grabbed the fire extinguisher from the pantry, and though I'd never used one of the devices before, I let my instincts guide my hands. Yanking out the metal pin, I aimed the funnel-shaped nozzle and covered my boyfriend, countertops, and stove with a layer of white foam.

"Are you okay?" I shouted to Sean over the shriek of the alarm.

He looked down at the smoldering towel in his hands and nodded. "I think so!"

Now that the flames had been doused I had a chance to really look around my kitchen.

The table had been set for a romantic dinner for two. I glanced from the lit candles, folded linen napkins, and the vase stuffed with bright pink roses to the handsome man wearing my apron. It was embroidered with the text *All Great Chefs Drink While They Cook*. Apparently, he had taken the motto to heart. Not only was there was an open bottle of red wine on the table, but a cognac bottle had capsized on the counter next to the stove and had emptied its contents onto the cabinets and floor.

I set the extinguisher gently on the table and picked up the bottle of wine positioned next to the roses. Eschewing a glass, I raised the bottle to my lips and took several long swallows. In light of the mayhem in my kitchen, I figured that my less than impeccable table manners could be excused just this once.

"I'm so sorry, Lila!" Sean yelled over the alarm and moved to the sink. He dropped the dishtowel in the basin, turned the water on, and began to scrub his hands.

I took another swallow, dabbed my mouth with a napkin, and opened the back door. Smoke immediately rushed outside. I darted around the first floor of my little cottage, cracking windows and turning on ceiling fans.

Mercifully, the alarm ceased its deafening ringing as I made my way back into the kitchen.

Sean had dumped the dishtowel into the garbage can and was now stuffing my ruined apron in there as well.

I got a bucket and mop from the pantry and then paused for a moment, leaning on the mop handle and surveying the mess. "What happened?"

With a remorseful expression, Sean gestured at the table. "Today's our nine-month anniversary, so I thought I'd surprise you with a delicious meal. I even bought a new cookbook from the Constant Reader. It's supposed to help beginner cooks make gourmet meals that come out looking and tasting like they were made by a professional chef." He shot a rueful glance at the book propped open near the stove. Its pages were charred and unreadable.

I couldn't help but smile. "What was on tonight's menu?"

"Chicken flambé," Sean said. "But I was behind schedule and so I didn't bother to measure the cognac. As it turned out, pouring liquor directly into the pan was a serious mistake. Cognac dribbled everywhere." He pointed at the offending bottle. "I had the gas flame set too high and once the alcohol hit . . ." He trailed off and gave me a sheepish shrug.

He looked so forlorn that I couldn't possibly be angry. After all, the only real damage was to the dishtowel, apron, and cookbook. The rest of the room could be returned to order in no time. Slipping on a pair of yellow latex cleaning gloves, I joined Sean by the sink.

"Why don't you order us takeout from Wild Ginger? Maybe some sesame chicken or beef and broccoli?" I moved closer, doing my best to avoid the fire extinguisher foam still clinging to his pants, and kissed him on the cheek. "After all, we still have a lovely bottle of wine and I don't want to waste the candlelight."

Sean's smile of relief was blinding. He cupped my chin in his damp hand and turned my face so that my lips would meet his. "I am a lucky, lucky man," he murmured and kissed me tenderly.

A moment later, I wriggled out of his arms to fill the mop bucket with soapy water. "And take your pants off, Officer Griffiths," I scolded lightly. "I don't want fire extinguisher foam to get on the hall rug."

"You want me to take off my clothes? Now that's an order I could get used to." He grinned and reached for the take-out menus I kept in the drawer below the phone.

By the time the Wild Ginger deliveryman rang the doorbell, the kitchen was clean, the windows were closed, and Sean was clad in the sweatpants and sneakers he kept in his gym bag. He insisted on plating the Chinese food at the counter while I enjoyed some wine. After placing our supper on the table, he dimmed the lights and raised his glass in a toast.

"To not setting the house on fire when we celebrate our first year together."

"Here, here!" I cried happily, clinking the rim of his glass with my own.

We dug into our meals, quite hungry by now. Both of us preferred to eat around six-thirty and it was nearly eight o'clock by the time I speared my first piece of beef with the point of my wooden chopstick.

"Learning to cook is harder than I thought it would be," Sean said after his initial hunger had been sated. "I've been getting by with frozen dinners and fast food. Maybe I should watch that TV show you love so much."

"The one with Chef Klara?" I attempted to shovel rice into my mouth using the chopsticks, but I couldn't grasp more than a grain at a time. Surrendering, I grabbed a fork from the cutlery drawer and polished off the rest of my meal. *"Tales From the Table* is the best cooking show on television. It's not just about food, but about the memories certain foods invoke."

Sean refilled my wineglass and pushed his empty plate away. "Well, I was smart enough to buy ice cream for our dessert, so if you'd like to curl up on the sofa and find an episode on the DVR, I'll bring you a big bowl of chocolate mocha chip, and we can watch Chef Klara together."

"I am lucky, lucky woman," I said, echoing his earlier sentiment. I tried to carry my dishes to the sink, but he refused to let me do the washing up. Instead, he uncorked a bottle of sweet and airy dessert wine, poured me a generous glass, and shooed me into the living room. By the time he joined me, I was feeling more than a little lightheaded.

Snuggled against each other, we ate ice cream and listened to Chef Klara talk about how invigorating it was to plant the first herbs of spring.

"To me, springtime represents the celebration of fresh colors and flavors. After a long winter, we finally get to crush some of the season's first herbs—chives and oregano— between our fingertips. How I used to love to pick these for my grandmother and then watch her sprinkle them over a lamb roast." Klara, a curvy, middle-aged brunette with sky blue eyes smiled at the camera. "Tonight, I'm going to walk you through one of my family's favorite dishes: grilled tuna and spring herb salad with marinated tomatoes. And for dessert? Ripe, juicy apricots tossed with brown sugar and honey." She grabbed a pot holder, opened an oven, and pulled out the middle rack, revealing a perfectly browned apricot tart. Karla described the heavenly smell in her kitchen and then added a conspiratorial whisper. "You don't have to be Charlene Jacques to create wonderful pies and tarts. Let me show you some of her secrets."

"Who's Charlene Jacques?" Sean asked.

"She's a famous pastry chef. Her show comes on before Klara's." I took another sip of the sweet dessert wine. "Klara is one of the agency's authors, remember? I can't believe both Klara and Charlene Jacques will be in Inspiration Valley in a few days. Our Taste of the Town is going to be amazing!"

Setting his empty ice cream bowl aside, Sean began to stroke my hair, starting at the crown of my head and pulling gently until he reached the ends. My entire body relaxed against him and I sighed in contentment.

"And how is Novel Idea involved in this festival of gluttony?" he teased.

I couldn't keep the excitement from my voice. "We've arranged for some of the country's top chefs to cook in Inspiration Valley restaurants, sign their cookbooks at the Constant Reader, and conduct classes at the new Marlette Robbins Center for the Arts. You should sign up for the 'A Chef in Your Home' class. It's all about the fundamentals of shopping, preparing, and plating simple but delicious dishes."

"If someone could teach me to scramble an egg, that would be a start," Sean said, his hands traveling down my neck and across my shoulders, massaging out the kinks. I felt like a pat of melting butter.

On television, Klara illustrated the art of rolling out a pine nut tart crust. I was too focused on Sean's touch to pay much attention, but I did hear her mention how she had seen Leslie Sterling, another celebrity chef, scorch a cream of asparagus soup once.

"This Klara woman must have a grocery list of enemies." Sean stopped rubbing my shoulders for a moment. "She's not very subtle, belittling her competition while boasting about her own skills."

I grabbed the remote control and turned the television off. Turning to face Sean, I slipped my hands under his shirt and pressed my body against his. "I think I'd rather focus on your skills, Officer Griffiths. After all, we're supposed to be celebrating."

Sean responded immediately by kissing me until I felt breathless. Then he stood up and lifted me off the sofa in a swift, powerful movement. "Speaking of skill sets," he whispered. "I'm pretty good at starting fires."

And with that, he pulled me toward the bedroom and shut the door.

THE NEXT MORNING, my short ride to work was magical. A flurry of white petals from the pear trees lining Walden Woods Circle had swirled around my yellow scooter and everywhere I looked, daffodils and tulips were bursting through the soil of my neighbors' tidy gardens. Hyacinths and forsythia perfumed the air and the pink dogwoods at the entrance to my neighborhood looked like tufts of cotton candy.

I was humming as I stepped into Espresso Yourself, my favorite coffee shop.

"Girl, I do believe you're floating on a rainbow this morning." Makayla, the coffee shop's gorgeous barista and my best friend, called out.

"I am, but I also need a serious jolt of caffeine. Sean and I celebrated our first nine months together last night and I stayed up way too late." Hearing how silly this statement sounded, I rolled my eyes. "Listen to me! I'm talking like I'm in junior high school. My son's a freshman in college and I'm going on about my nine-month anniversary."

Makayla's mouth curved into a wide smile. "I think it's right sweet. Why shouldn't a woman in her late forties have a boyfriend? Or two? Or three?" Her musical laughter was drowned out by the gurgle of the espresso machine.

I studied my friend, Makayla, who was in her mid-twenties, but had the poise and self-assurance of a much older woman. She was tall and thin with radiant skin the color of warm chocolate and the most dazzling green eyes I'd ever seen. Makayla worked long hours to keep her shop afloat and in her spare time, devoured every novel she could get her hands on. She was also tireless in her support of the local art scene. Every few weeks, she hung up a new set of photographs, paintings, drawings, etchings, or textiles created by an Inspiration Valley artist.

Now, as I took in a collection of black-and-white ink drawings of birds and butterflies, I felt a pang of sadness that my beautiful, intelligent, and generous friend had yet to find a man worthy enough of a second date.

"Hey, why'd you put on a long face?" Makayla asked, handing me a large caramel latte.

The bell above the door rang and an elderly man in a business suit walked into the coffee shop. Lowering my voice, I said, "I was just thinking that you deserve to be as happy as I am. I wish some dashing, bookish, coffee-drinking stranger would waltz in here and capture your heart."

Makayla grinned and gestured at the café table where I normally sat. "Let me get Mr. Sheehan his cappuccino and cinnamon scone and then I'll tell you about my secret admirer."

"What?" I glanced at the impatient Mr. Sheehan. "Okay, but hurry up." I checked my watch and decided that I could be a little late for work. After all, my office was right upstairs. I sipped my latte and flipped through the pages of *Inspired Voice*, Inspiration Valley's free paper, and felt another thrill of excitement about all the Taste of the Town events I'd be attending as a representative of the Novel Idea Literary Agency.

"Read this." Makayla perched on the edge of the table and handed me a scrap of paper. "This one's from yesterday. It was folded inside a two-dollar bill and stuffed into my tip jar."

I raised my brows. "You don't see these in circulation anymore."

"That's how I know it's the same guy. He always puts his notes inside a two-dollar bill." She nudged my elbow. "Go on, girlfriend. Drink in the words."

Complying, I read the following typewritten lines out loud: *"I love you without knowing how, or when, or from where. I love you straightforwardly, without complexities or pride; so I love you because I know no other way."* Putting the paper on the table, I looked at Makayla. "Wow. Who wrote this?"

"Pablo Neruda, the Chilean poet. Lord, I got weak in the knees reading his stuff." She touched my hand. "But Lila, they've all been this beautiful. My secret admirer has given me three bits of poetry so far. I didn't want to tell you until I was sure it wasn't a fluke, but this makes number four."

I shook my head in wonder. "And you have no idea who this guy is?"

"None. And it's driving me insane!" She gripped my hand. "I'm counting on your talent as a seasoned investigator to help me discover his identity. I need to find out soon, because I am not getting any sleep. I lie in bed and picture my customers' faces one by one until they're spinning around in my head like a merry-go-round on speed."

"Of course I'll help." I paused and then looked into my friend's green eyes. "But what if he's not who you hoped he'd be? What happens then?"

Makayla sighed. "If he's married, lives with his mama, or has been to jail, then I'm not interested, but if he isn't Prince Charming, that's fine by me, too. I'm no Cinderella. I want a man who appreciates stories, is a good listener, and laughs easily. It doesn't matter to me if he's black, white, bald, short, pudgy, or hairy." She gave me a sly smile. "But he's got to love books, especially since I just finished writing one."

I'd been on the verge of taking another sip of my latte when she uttered this declaration. "What?" I asked through pursed lips. "I thought it was just an idea you were fleshing out."

"I didn't want you to feel obligated to read my work in progress," she hurriedly assured me. "Besides, I wasn't sure if I'd finish it at all, but these little lines of love in my tip jar really got me going, and *The Barista Diaries* is done and ready to be submitted to an agent. Know any good ones?"

Delighted, I listened as Makayla described her collection

of short stories and then realized I was going to be noticeably tardy if I didn't zip upstairs that second. After making her promise to email me a copy of her manuscript, I scooped up my take-out cup and headed for the lobby, hoping that Vicky Crump, our agency's punctilious office manager, wasn't at her desk yet.

I SPENT ALL Tuesday morning working diligently as I wanted the tasks out of the way before Taste of the Town began that Friday. I barely stopped for a coffee break and ate my lunch of leftovers from the previous night's Wild Ginger dinner in front of my computer. Chewing on the last bite of cold broccoli beef, I placed the empty plastic containers in my tote and scooped up a package of washable markers along with my Taste of the Town folder. Thus supplied, I headed for the conference room.

As expected, no one was there, and I began to prepare for my meeting. On the whiteboard, I drew out a chart. Across the top row, I wrote in the agents' names, and in the far left column, filled in an event for each subsequent row: *Klara's Book Release*, *Books and Cooks Signings*, *Short Story Contest*, *Food in Children's Lit*, *Literary Banquet*, *TV Show*. I was so intent on my task that I didn't realize Jude had come into the room until he spoke.

"You look completely absorbed," he said in a playful tone.

His voice startled me and my hand jerked, giving the "w" on the word "show" an upturned tail. I spun around. As always, my pulse sped up at the sight of Jude. His chocolate brown eyes held a glint of amusement beneath his long lashes. Smiling at me, he ran his fingers through his dark wavy hair. "I've been watching you for five minutes and you didn't even notice," he said. "Not that I didn't enjoy the view."

I refused to respond to his flattery. I was Sean's girl, and my brief ill-advised fancy of being with Jude had dissipated long ago. Glancing at the time on the wall clock behind him, I said, "You're early. The meeting doesn't start until two."

"I know. I just wanted to have a few minutes alone with you before everyone else comes in." He stepped closer to me.

"Jude," I cautioned. "You know Sean and I—"

"Not like *that*. I know that you and the policeman are tight. My loss," he said, shaking his head. He held out a stack of papers. "I actually came here early to discuss the latest submissions for the *Alexandria Society* sequel. Not one of these has the same spellbinding, desperate voice that Marlette had, and I'm inclined to turn them all down. How did you fare with yours?"

Marlette Robbins, one of the agency's authors represented by Jude, had written an intriguing suspense novel that became an immediate bestseller. Unfortunately, he didn't live to see his masterwork in print. Now, with the book's success, his publishers were eager to put out a sequel and Jude and I had been given the task of finding a ghostwriter for the book. So far, we hadn't had any luck.

"Same here," I answered. "I wasn't impressed by any of the submissions I received. And some of them were from big-name authors."

Jude sighed and plunked himself into a chair. "I thought this would be an easy project, but Marlette's unique voice is proving difficult to replicate. Any suggestions?"

"What if . . ." I tapped the end of a marker on my chin. "Instead of focusing on seasoned authors, we expand the playing field. Go through our unsolicited queries, maybe put the word out to writers who may not have published a bestseller yet. Or published anything, for that matter. Look at Marlette. He was unknown and unpublished, and he still penned a winner."

Jude nodded. "But how do we advertise what we're looking for without seeming overanxious?"

"The Taste of the Town will bring lots of people in— maybe we could have a contest in conjunction with the first event held at the Marlette Robbins Center for the Arts."

"I like that. A ghostwriting contest to honor Marlette." Jude started writing on his notepad. "However, since we already have the Stories About Food writing contest underway, it might not be such a good idea to have two contests going at once. Should we run it by Bentley and see what she thinks?"

"Maybe we can talk to her after this meeting. Right now I have to finish this." I turned back to the whiteboard and completed the chart.

A few minutes later, the rest of the staff were seated around the conference table, gazing expectantly at me. I felt a little self-conscious standing at the front, especially with Bentley Burlington-Duke, the founder and president of Novel Idea Literary Agency, sitting to my left. She peered at me over her diamond-studded reading glasses but said nothing.

I cleared my throat and began. "I set up this meeting because the day after tomorrow the chefs arrive in Inspiration Valley and the Taste of the Town festival begins on

Friday. As you know, our agency's portion of the festival, Books and Cooks, commences at the same time. And I wanted to ensure that everything is in place so that it all runs smoothly, especially for our chef clients." Pointing at the chart on the whiteboard, I continued. "If I could get your status on the areas for which you are each responsible, we can move on from there."

Vicky spoke first. With her ramrod-straight posture and direct approach, she gave the impression that she was much taller than a mere five feet. Straightening her blue-rimmed glasses she began. "I've booked rooms for all of our celebrity guests and their entourage at the Magnolia Bed and Breakfast, although a few of the underlings have rooms at Bertram's Hotel."

"It's a good thing our Bertram's Hotel isn't like the one in the Agatha Christie story," Zach Cohen, our "Mr. Hollywood" agent for screenplays and sportswriters, interrupted. He waggled his black eyebrows. "If it was, we'd be sending those people straight into a group of criminals."

Jude chuckled. Vicky stared at Zach for a brief minute, and then continued. "I made sure that Klara Patrick's room is on an entirely different floor from Doug Corby, Leslie Sterling, and Charlene Jacques."

"Hoo boy, that was smart, Vicky!" exclaimed Zach. "The Magnolia B&B would see some fireworks if they were sleeping down the hall from Chef Klara."

"Whatever do you mean, Zach?" Bentley asked. "Aren't they all professionals?"

"Supposedly, but Klara is always undermining the other chefs, especially Charlene Jacques, who has a show on the same network. And the food critic, Doug Corby, wrote a scathing review of a meal Chef Klara prepared for the Food Fair in Baltimore last month." He feigned a throat-cutting motion with his pointer finger. "Talk about the pen being mightier than the sword. Ouch!"

"I remember that review." Flora leaned forward on the table. "He called her veal 'leather-like' and her sauce 'as heavy as cement.' Said he wouldn't feed her dish to a stray dog. Created quite an uproar at that food fair."

Bentley frowned. "Well, let's hope these people can manage to control their animosity toward each other at our events. Carry on, Lila."

I scanned my notes. "Vicky, will the chefs all be here for the introductory tour and Bentley's catered supper? Have you confirmed the pickup arrangements?"

She nodded. "Klara and her people are driving up in their limo, and three of the chefs are coming in on the train. Doug Corby will be on the Inspiration Express on Friday morning. The television crew for Klara's TV show arrived earlier this week to set up."

"Speaking of which," Zach interrupted, "the setup crew made some trouble about the stove at the Arts Center. It was wired for electric, but not for gas, and several of the chefs, including Chef Klara, insist on cooking *only* with gas. Her majesty also insisted that a stove be reserved for her use only until she has finished with her demonstration. So to keep the culinary kings and queens happy, we installed a six-burner gas stove. That cost a wad of dough." He rubbed his thumb over his fingertips. "Lila, can we bill Klara's company for that?"

I shook my head. "I doubt it. And I can certainly understand a chef preferring a gas stove to electric. Especially one as talented as Chef Klara. I find the heat on a gas stove easier to control. Franklin, is everything in place for the release party for Klara's new cookbook?"

Franklin rubbed his chin while considering my question. "Sure is. It will kick off after the filming of the television show. There'll be delectable food for people to sample and a display table for her new cookbook as well. She can sign books for her fans for as long as she likes."

"That's not to be confused with the signings scheduled at the Constant Reader," Jude interjected.

Franklin shook his head. "No, those are separate. Although, Klara expressed a desire to do a signing at the Constant Reader after her panel on Friday morning. Can we schedule that in for the early afternoon, Lila?" At my nod, Franklin continued. "The Cooks and Books chef signing session on Saturday afternoon at the Arts Center is for all the chefs other than Klara, and their latest cookbooks. The other Constant Reader signings are for books about food, but not necessarily cookbooks."

"Like Doug Corby's *A Foodie's Diary: Meals Worth Remembering (and some not so much)*," Vicky said. "I found that an intriguing read."

Flora giggled. "That man can be nasty," she said. "In a funny kind of way."

"I just hope Joel Lang's new Asian fusion cookbook won't be too overshadowed by all the focus on Klara." Franklin sighed. "It releases the same day, you know. I don't know why publishers do that."

Zach vigorously shook his head. "No way, man. There's been as much buzz about his cookbook on TV as Klara's. He's booked solid on the area morning shows for the next couple of weeks. Even with all of the prepublication hype Klara's been getting, Joel will still be a very popular dude. He might even steal her limelight."

Franklin raised his eyebrows. "Nobody needs to steal anyone's limelight, Zach. We want the pair of them to do well. Remember, they're both clients of Novel Idea."

"Then let's get two clients on the *New York Times* list at once." Zach snapped his fingers in sequence. "Batta bing."

"How about your 'Food in Children's Literature' session, Flora?" I asked after I'd updated the whiteboard data. "Is that on track?"

"Yes, dear, it certainly is. It should be a tasty exhibition, to be sure. Ed from Catcher in the Rye and Nell from Sixpence Bakery helped with the sample list. Even How Green Was My Valley got on board. Let's see." She perused her notes. "On the menu we have Stone Soup from the famous folk tale, Marilla's Raspberry Cordial from *Anne of Green Gables*, Pippi's Pancakes from *Pippi Longstocking*, Dr. Seuss's Green Eggs and Ham—"

"Whoa! How are they making those eggs green?" Zach interjected, cutting short her recitation.

Flora's cheeks flushed pink. "I'm not exactly sure, Zach. We'll have to ask the chef. Should I continue?"

"Let's leave the rest for us to discover at the event, Flora. It all sounds great." I glanced at the chart. "That about covers it, except for the short story contest, Stories About Food. We received several submissions by last week's deadline. Jude and Bentley, are you on track with the reading?"

"Of course," Bentley replied. "I'll have my assessments to you shortly."

Jude nodded. "Me, too."

"Good. Thanks for volunteering to be judges for the contest, by the way. It takes some of the pressure off me."

Bentley inclined her head in acknowledgment.

"My pleasure," Jude said. "There's always a chance we'll find a gem."

"Everything is set for the banquet as well." I passed pages around the table. "Here is the menu. And thanks for all your suggestions on which literary foods we should serve."

"Sweet!" Zach hit the table with gusto. "My suggestion to add the clam chowder from *Moby Dick* was picked as the first course! The Zachmeister rules."

"I'm glad, too," Franklin said. "I enjoy a good clam chowder. But I'm surprised you've read Melville's masterpiece thoroughly enough to remember that soup," he added with a twinkle in his eye.

Zach leaned forward. "Are you kidding? I *love* that book. Melville goes on and on for almost a whole chapter about that chowder."

"Ahem," Bentley interceded. "Back to the banquet?"

I shot Bentley a grateful smile. "We have ballots for people to guess what literary works they believe each menu item is from, and there will be door prizes, too. Should be a great evening. And at the closing ceremony we'll award the Novel Idea Best Cookbook Award as voted on by all the attendees. Vicky, you're handling the ballots, right?"

Vicky nodded. "It's all under control."

"Good. Other than that," I looked around the table, "we're good to go. The first wave of chefs arrives tomorrow and then Taste of the Town and our Books and Cooks will be underway."

"Well, Lila, you seem to have everything under control.

Remember, people, you are expected to come into work on Saturday as if it's a regular workday," Bentley said, gathering her papers together. "Let's hope that these capricious cooks behave themselves. After all, we've filled the Arts Center kitchen with an array of very sharp knives."

Chapter 2

BY THE TIME THURSDAY ROLLED AROUND, MY TO-DO list was so long that my little office at Novel Idea began to feel claustrophobic. My email was overflowing with proposals I'd requested as well as the queries Vicky had deemed worth viewing, the desk was cluttered with Taste of the Town and Books and Cooks schedules, and the coffee I'd bought hours earlier had gone cold. I don't know where the morning went, but by half past twelve I was too hungry to think straight.

Outside my window, the entire town seemed to be cajoling me to play hooky for a spell. As I stretched my arms and rubbed my sore lower back, I gazed down at the picturesque small park that stood at the heart of Inspiration Valley's business district. The grass was a lush green, daffodils bloomed in cheerful clumps along the sidewalks, and every park bench was filled with a smiling man or woman. Oh, how I envied the townsfolk and tourists their novels and paper bag lunches. Gentle sunlight fell on their shoulders, a dogwood-scented breeze tickled the ends of their hair, and a chorus of birdsong provided them with the perfect background music for reading.

The moment I spied a young woman removing a sandwich from a Catcher in the Rye take-out bag, I knew I could no more resist the temptation of an alfresco lunch on a perfect spring day than I could pass by a bookstore without going inside to browse. Grabbing my purse, I hurried out of my office before my computer chimed again, alerting me to the arrival of yet another unread email.

Vicky was at her desk sipping herbal tea from a bone china cup when I hurried by. She gave me an inquisitive glance, which I totally ignored on my way to the stairs.

"I'm taking an hour for lunch!" I called to her over my shoulder.

"Very well," Vicky replied and I swear I heard the slightest hint of reproach in her voice. Then again, it was probably my guilty conscience making me believe something that wasn't there.

I burst through the lobby doorway like a kid let out of school for recess. I felt so invigorated by my surroundings that I had to resist the urge to skip to Catcher in the Rye. But middle-aged literary agents don't typically skip down the sidewalk on their way to lunch at the local sandwich shop, so I refrained.

Maybe we should all skip more, I thought. After all, I had quite a bit to be happy about at the moment. I had the career of my dreams, my son, Trey, had matriculated as a second-term freshman at the University of North Carolina's

Wilmington campus and was doing well with his studies, and I was dating a wonderful guy.

"You look chipper today!" the cashier at the sandwich shop said when I stepped up to the counter.

"'Frame thy mind to mirth and merriment, which bars a thousand harms, and lengthens life,'" I said, quoting a line from Shakespeare's *Taming of the Shrew* and then ordered the Homer—chicken souvlaki covered with shredded lettuce, diced onions, fresh tomatoes, and Big Ed's homemade *tzatziki* sauce served on toasted pita bread.

The cashier accepted my ten-dollar bill and handed me my change with a playful smirk. "Your life won't be lengthened if you eat too many Homers."

"It's practically health food. Think of all the veggies buried under that creamy yogurt sauce," I joked, raising my voice over the din in the café. Big Ed's dining area was unusually crowded today, especially considering he had an outdoor patio section. "Is everyone in town eating here today?"

"Sure seems that way," the cashier said. "What's really happening is that no one's leaving after they're done with their food. There's some famous lady chef at the table in the back corner and she treated a whole mess of people to lunch. I swear she's made friends with half the town already."

My curiosity piqued, I accepted the name card that Big Ed would call out when my order was ready and headed for the restroom to wash my hands. However, the moment I recognized the woman holding court in the back of the eatery, I altered course. For there was Klara Patrick, dressed in tan slacks and a mint green blouse, laughing it up with a pair of Inspiration Valley bank tellers, a mail clerk, and the floral designer from the Secret Garden.

"Excuse me," I said, squeezing between the two bank tellers. "I had to come over and say hello. I'm Lila Wilkins from Novel Idea."

Klara gave me a bright smile and shook my outstretched hand. "How lovely to meet you. Have you eaten? Would you like to join us?"

I glanced at the table, noting there wasn't an empty place. Klara followed my gaze and appealed to her new friends. "We can make room for another chair, can't we?"

Everyone nodded and jumped to make room for me.

"RUMPELSTILTSKIN!" Big Ed hollered.

"That would be me," I mumbled and blushed a little.

Klara laughed. "Don't be embarrassed; my name was much worse. *I* got Morgan Le Fay!" She touched her wavy brunette locks. "I might have evil enchantress hair, but the only thing I like to make in a giant black cauldron is my grandmother's beef stew." She grinned. "No matter. Big Ed is such a wonderful sandwich artist that I forgave him for that mean old card."

I smiled at Klara, instantly warming to her. "Can I get anything for you folks while I'm up?" I asked.

"No, thanks," the mail clerk replied on behalf of his tablemates. "Ms. Klara bought sandwiches for everyone in the place. Chips and oatmeal raisin cookies, too. I don't think we're ever going to let her go back to Manhattan."

Her face the picture of contentment, Klara gestured toward the window. "This town is an oasis, a tiny utopia of art and books and food. I explored every inch of Inspiration Valley this morning and found it to be quaint, welcoming, and sophisticated." She nudged the mail clerk with her elbow. "I may just have to stay and open a restaurant, but that depends on how well my new cookbook sells." She winked at me. I returned the wink and walked over to the counter to collect my food.

Big Ed, who was one of the most cheerful people I've ever met, was especially rosy-cheeked and twinkly-eyed of late. He'd been in love with Nell, the owner of the town bakery, for years, but had never had the courage to tell her. Finally, he'd asked her on a date and a few months after that, he proposed to her by writing, "Will You Marry Me Nell?" on his daily special board. Dressed in a tuxedo, he'd knelt down beside the chalkboard, holding his mother's diamond ring in his large and trembling hand.

I'd been lucky enough to witness the proposal and had teared up watching the tender scene. I doubt there'd been a dry eye in the sandwich shop that day. Grizzled construction workers, solemn businessmen, and surly teens had all melted at the sight of Nell throwing her arms around Big Ed's neck, her cries of "Yes! Yes! Yes!" echoing through the room.

Now, Big Ed greeted me as though he hadn't seen me in ages. He asked after Sean, my family, my coworkers, and my health. Only after I assured him that everything was great did he say, "Have you had a chance to meet Ms. Klara? She's quite a doll, though I'd rather you didn't mention that to my future bride."

"I just met Morgan Le Fay and hope to join her for lunch." I examined my sandwich and wondered how I was going to eat it in front of the celebrity chef without dribbling yogurt sauce all over myself. "Big Ed, Klara called you an artist and I couldn't agree more. This looks delicious."

The sandwich maker beamed. "She bought sandwiches for at least fifty people today. And earlier this mornin' she grabbed up a whole shelf of pastries from Nell's. Raved about them all morning to everyone she met. I tell ya, that Klara's a real gem." He then shouted, "JAMES BOND!" and placed a fried fish sandwich on the counter.

I grabbed my Homer, headed back to Klara's table, and began to cut my sandwich with a fork and knife. However, Klara handed me a pile of napkins and said, "You can't eat souvlaki like a lady! Pick up that pita and have at it!"

Encouraged by a chorus of applause from my tablemates, I ate my lunch with true abandon, enjoying both the food and the company immensely. Klara regaled us with interesting television mishaps such as the time she dropped an entire carton of eggs on the studio floor or when the water she was boiling for pasta bubbled over and saturated the herb-seasoned cod sautéing in a frying pan on the front burner. "But all cooks make mistakes, even the ones on TV," she finished with a laugh. "If I didn't have my husband on set, I'd never have survived that first season. Speaking of which, he's probably wondering where I am. I should head back to that darling little B&B."

By this time, I'd inhaled my sandwich and drunk down an enormous glass of iced tea, so I offered to accompany Klara to the Magnolia. We chatted amicably and had just turned onto the cobblestone lane where the bed and break-fast was located when a turquoise pickup truck pulled alongside the curb.

Klara paused to read the magnetic sign on the truck. "Amazing Althea?" Her eyes went wide. "Oh, a psychic!"

Normally, I wouldn't have hesitated to say that Althea was my mother, but for some reason I was embarrassed to tell Klara, a famous woman whom I admired, that I was the daughter of a professed psychic. "We have all kinds of artists in Inspiration Valley," was my breezy reply.

Torn between continuing on to the hotel as though I hadn't noticed my mother's truck or saying that I needed to get back to the office right away, I hesitated. And in that moment my mother jumped out of the truck and waved. "Yoo-hoo! Lila! I knew I'd run into you if I drove into town right about now."

"Wow," Klara breathed. "Impressive."

"She probably talked to Vicky, our office manager," I murmured while my mother was still out of earshot. Then, when she got closer, I smiled and said, "Klara, this is my mother, Althea. Mama, this is Klara Patrick. We've watched her show together a few times, remember?"

Klara's eyes darted between my mother and me. "How nice that you two live so close."

My mother took Klara's hand and instantly flinched. She quickly recovered and told Klara how much she'd enjoyed her first cookbook, but I could see that something was troubling her. "Were you looking for me?" I asked.

"Thought I'd pick up that pair of Books and Cooks tickets you promised to drop off." She pouted. "Guess you've been too busy to find your way to my place."

My mother lived in a charming rustic house at the base of Red Fox Mountain. It was only a fifteen-minute ride on my Vespa, and yet I'd been so wrapped up in Taste of the Town preparations that I'd canceled our dinner plans last week and hadn't caught up with my mom since. No wonder she looked hurt. "I'm so sorry. The tickets are in my desk at the office. Do you want to come back with me now and get them?"

While my mother mulled this over, Klara fixed her gaze on a jogger racing up the sidewalk on the other side of the street. She waved and called out, "Bryce! Over here!"

Certain the runner was celebrity chef Bryce St. John, I nudged my mother. The tall, golden-haired man slowed his pace, allowing all three of us to admire his muscular body. Clad in neon orange running shorts and a formfitting Nike T-shirt, there was very little of Bryce left to the imagination.

"That's the kind of sight that'll get your blood pumpin' on a fine spring day." My mother gave the jogger a long, appreciative stare.

Klara smiled at her. "I think he looks better in a chef's jacket, but maybe I'm just thinking like a woman who's been married forever." She chuckled. "Listen, I'm going to cross over and talk to him about the first event we'll be doing together. It was nice to meet you, Althea. I'll see you tonight, Lila."

Crossing the street in an unhurried stride, Klara shook hands with Bryce and then made a show of wiping her hand off on her pants. I could hear her laughter mingle with Bryce's until the rumble of a motorcycle drowned it out. Turning back to my mother, I was about to ask her again whether or not she was going to come back to the office with me, when I saw the dark expression on her face.

I reached out and put my hand on her arm. "Is something wrong?"

Though my mother's gaze was still focused on the two chefs on the opposite side of the street, her eyes were unfocused, as if she'd drifted away to another place and time. "Mama," I whispered softly, not wanting to startle her from her trancelike state.

She blinked and I could almost see her come back into herself, gently and soundlessly, like a bird returning from flight to perch on a familiar branch. "She's no good, that one. Puts on a convincing show, but I ain't buyin' what she's sellin'."

By this time, Klara and Bryce had begun to walk toward the Magnolia B&B. I studied them for a moment and then frowned, recalling how delightful and generous Klara had been with everyone at the sandwich shop. "You don't know her from Eve. How can you pass judgment on her like that?"

My mother shook her head. "Will you ever believe in me, shug? Time after time you think the things I see and feel are nothin' but nonsense." She pulled her arm away. "I'll admit to stretching the truth sometimes, to addin' some colorful flourishes and special touches to my predictions, but when I know somethin', *I know it*."

I cast my eyes down in shame. Ever since I'd been a child, my mother's so-called gift had frightened and confused me. It was easier to view her as a performer, a harmless eccentric, than to truly believe she could sense and feel things the average person could not. However, she'd routinely proven that she was adept at reading people and that her intuition was as honed and accurate as a woodsman's ax, so why did I continue to doubt her?

"Okay, Mama." I gave her my full attention. "What troubles you about Klara? Other than you think she's insincere?"

"Her appetite," my mother answered. "That girl is hungry for money and fame. She wants 'em so bad and she'll do anythin' to get 'em. She'll step on folks, Lila. Probably already has. Just don't let yourself get caught under her boot heel. That's all I ask. Keep your guard up around that woman. Promise me that."

I sighed, but told her what she wanted to hear. "I will do my best not to be trod upon by her or any other celebrity chef this weekend."

As it turned out, that was a promise I wouldn't be able to keep.

WALKING THROUGH THE double doors of the Marlette Robbins Center for the Arts later that afternoon, I experienced both a swell of pride and a tinge of sadness. Funded by Marlette's estate, the center was a wonderful addition to our town, but it only existed because of his untimely death.

My footsteps echoed on the lobby floor. I paused at a portrait of the man, a representation of the person he'd been years before I'd met him. The vibrant expression in his eyes was very different from that which I'd experienced last summer. Below the painting, a glass case exhibited a first edition of his book, as well as a copy of the original handwritten manuscript, bits of paper bearing lines of poetry, and Marlette's leather-covered journal opened to a sketch of a wildflower. I touched the corner of the case, wishing, not for the first time, that I'd had a chance to really know him.

"Oh, there you are, Lila." Bentley's brisk voice interrupted my ponderings. "I believe Vicky has everything in order, but I need you to double-check to ensure that nothing is neglected. We can't give these celebrity chefs any reason to be critical."

"I was on my way to do just that."

"Good." Bentley headed for the exit. "I have to make a call, but I'll return in time for supper."

I checked my watch and realized I had only a few minutes

to inspect the setup in the Dragonfly Room, where the chefs, literary agents, and our guests would dine following my tour of the Arts Center. I hurried into the room and was stunned by what I saw inside. What had been an empty space yesterday was now an elegant dining hall. Four round tables were draped with white linen cloths and set with yellow and green candles in glass holders, Portmeirion botanical dishes, and glittering crystal glassware. Wildflower arrangements in crystal vases were the centerpieces and mirrors along one wall reflected the setup, adding to its glamour.

As I approached, Vicky Crump looked up from straightening a fork at one end of the table. "What do you think, Lila?" she asked. "Doesn't the spring floral theme work well?"

"It looks amazing!" I exclaimed. "Who would have imagined that a dance studio could be transformed like this?"

"It is lovely. And the theme and colors perfectly complement the meal Voltaire's has put together for us."

I picked up a printed menu from one of the place settings and read aloud. "Golden beet soup with crème fraîche and chives, grilled rosemary lamb chops with lemon caper sauce, sautéed garlic asparagus, oven-roasted new potatoes, and for dessert, a vanilla panna cotta with strawberry compote." I sighed. "I'm hungry just talking about this feast and we have hours yet before we'll be taking our first bite."

The door from the hall opened and Franklin walked in with two men.

"But you can never have enough butter," the tall man on Franklin's right declared with a slight French accent. He had sharp facial features and dark eyes, and although not a heavy man, his belly strained against his shirt.

"Yes, you can, Maurice. There should always be a perfect

blend of ingredients. A deliberate balance," retorted the slight Asian man on Franklin's left. His head was shaved, and he bore an uncanny resemblance to the chairman on *Iron Chef America*. "Too much of any one ingredient can make a dish feel heavy." He gestured at the other man's middle. "And it doesn't do your physique any good. That's why your cookbook sales were so flat. Your French decadence just doesn't cut it anymore in today's quest for lighter cuisine."

The French chef glared at him. "The *taste* is worth the indulgence, Joel. An abundance of flavor is everything. Not that *you'd* understand that."

The chef I assumed must be Joel Lang opened his mouth to respond but before he could, Franklin hastily interjected. "Gentlemen, let's save this lively and informative debate for another time. I'd like you to meet Vicky Crump, our office manager, and Lila Wilkins, another agent in our firm. These two ladies are responsible for organizing the Cooks and Books portion of Inspiration Valley's Taste of the Town festival. Lila and Vicky?" He gestured to the two men. "It is my pleasure to present Joel Lang, author of *Fusing Asian*, which is in high demand and has already received outstanding reviews." He then shifted his hand at the tall Frenchman. "And this is Maurice Bruneau. His book, *Flavor Is Everything*, was released to widespread acclaim. They are both clients of mine."

We greeted each other and shook hands, Maurice Bruneau dispatching a slight bow as he brought Vicky's fingers to his lips.

Her cheeks flushed a rosy pink. "What is the topic of your demonstration, Monsieur Bruneau?" she asked with the hint of a smile, pronouncing the French salutation with a perfect accent. Her demure tone surprised me, as I had never witnessed Vicky being anything less than confident, practical, and efficient. Had she forgotten that Maurice Bruneau was not one of the featured chefs? That he was merely in reserve should one of the other chefs cancel?

Joel Lang let loose a derisive snort. "My former mentor isn't—"

Bruneau shot a caustic look at Lang and rudely cut him off. "*Tristement*, I am not part of the program. I am merely, how you say, a standby. But"—he winked at Vicky—"I could provide a private demonstration if you desire."

As if coming out of a trance, Vicky suddenly coughed. "I believe we have a full agenda this week." She waved in the direction of the door. "Franklin, I told the other chefs to gather in the foyer for Lila's tour, so perhaps we should guide these gentlemen there . . ." The rest of her words were lost as she disappeared into the lobby. Joel Lang glared at Maurice Bruneau and hastened after her. Franklin raised his eyebrows and exchanged glances with me.

"Pardon," Maurice Bruneau apologized. "I did not intend offense."

"None taken, Maurice," Franklin said. "Come, let's catch up to the others."

I walked alongside them. "Chef Bruneau, we invited you to join us on the tour this evening so you'd be familiar with the facilities in case you need to fill in for someone. And I am truly thrilled that you are able to attend. I'm sorry there was no space in the festival schedule for your own demonstration, but we will certainly be able to highlight your cookbook during the signing sessions."

"Oh, *non, non, non*. I understand. Although I do believe I

should be taking the place of Chef Lang, for his skill is clearly inferior to mine." He stopped and leaned in toward me, lowering his voice. "You know, I taught Joel everything he knows."

"Really?" I had no desire to get caught in the middle of a chefs' feud and was relieved to see several people milling about in the lobby. "Excuse me," I said as I made my way toward Flora, who was talking to Bryce St. John. Although he had traded in his jogging clothes for khakis and a cream collared shirt, he looked just as sexy as when I'd first seen him on the street earlier that day.

"Lila, dear," Flora said when I approached. "Have you met Bryce St. John? He was telling me about different ways to cook eggplant. Bryce, this is Lila Wilkins."

"Hello. I saw you running near the B&B," I said, smiling at him.

"You did?" he asked quizzically.

"Yes, I was with Klara Patrick," I explained, a little chagrined that he hadn't noticed me.

"That's right. Sorry, but I was in the zone—completely caught up thinking about my demonstration this weekend." He reached out his hand. "Pleased to meet you, Lila." Awareness suddenly brightened his eyes. "Say, aren't you the lady who put together the program for Cooks and Books?"

"Yes, I am. And speaking of which, we need to get this tour started." I went to stand by the closed doors of the main presentation hall. Clearing my throat, I said loudly, "Could I have your attention, please?" When the din had dissipated, I continued. "Welcome to Inspiration Valley. We are honored and excited to have so many famous and talented chefs in our midst. For the first part of our evening, I will lead you on a tour of the facilities that will be available to you over the next few days, and then we will sit down to an exquisite supper prepared by one of our local chefs."

Standing by Marlette's exhibition case, Zach clapped. "Woo-hoo!"

"I think it might be a good idea if we introduced ourselves before we get started. I'm Lila Wilkins, a literary agent at Novel Idea, and the person who's been chatting with you or your personal assistants over the past few months. And over there is Vicky Crump, our invaluable office manager, with whom you've also had the pleasure of working."

Vicky dipped her head in greeting.

"I'm Zach Cohen and I'm in charge of media relations," Zach announced proudly. "I'm also *the* most awesome agent when it comes to screenplays and sports writers. You can call me Mr. Hollywood." He grinned. "Or just Zach Attack. Batta bing!"

Flora giggled as she often did in response to Zach's antics. "I'm Flora Meriweather, the agent representing children's books." She paused dramatically and placed her hands over her heart. "And historical and erotic romance as well."

"Wow," Bryce said, smiling coyly at Flora. "I am Chef Bryce St. John, but you all probably know that."

Klara had been standing beside Jude when the introductions began, but had inched her way toward Flora and Bryce. Loudly, she said, "And I'm Klara Patrick, chef extraordinaire." She pointed to a man by the watercooler. "That's my husband, Ryan, my support behind the scenes."

He saluted and smiled. "Major Ryan Patrick, United States Army, retired."

Jude smiled. "I'm Jude Hudson, and I represent thrillers and suspense novels at Novel Idea. Welcome, everyone."

Behind him, Joel Lang introduced himself, followed by Maurice Bruneau. Franklin then stepped forward.

"I'm Franklin Stafford, agent for most of the chefs gathered here today. I'd like to second what Lila said—that we are honored to have you all here to participate in our town's first food festival."

"We're the ones who are honored, Franklin," my favorite pastry chef spoke up. Charlene Jacques looked as sweet as her desserts. With voluptuous curves, a radiant complexion, and sparkling green eyes, she was beautiful. "If not for you, many of us wouldn't have our cookbooks on the shelves." She directed a pointed gaze at Klara for a second and then continued. "I'm Charlene Jacques, pastry chef extraordinaire."

Her echoing of Klara's self-introduction struck me as odd, and I recalled Sean's comment about Klara after she had criticized Charlene Jacques. I glanced around the room and began to wonder just how many of these chefs Klara had crossed in a public forum.

"And last but not least, there's little old me." Leslie Sterling was impeccably coiffed, her tailored black dress neat and classy. "I'm sure I don't need to introduce myself, but I want to declare how happy I am to be here. Although this little festival isn't a competition, I am certain that by the end of it, I will be known as the best chef in America." She raised her chin in defiance.

"A rather lofty goal, Leslie," Klara heckled. "Too bad you won't reach it."

Leslie's eyes darkened and she opened her mouth to retort, but I interceded before more could be said. "Now that we've all met, let's tour the facility. I'll show you the entire Arts Center and then we'll end up at the wing behind the main presentation hall, where you can spend some time investigating the kitchen you'll use for your demonstrations. Let's start at the pottery studio."

I held open the door leading to the first corridor while the group filed into the hall. Jude hung back, and when everyone had gone past, he leaned in toward me.

"Quite an egotistical bunch, aren't they?"

I nodded. "A little disillusioning from the personas they portray on the television screen."

Jude nodded and watched the chefs amble down the hallway. "We'll have our work cut out for us in keeping the peace at supper tonight."

"And throughout the festival, I expect," I said. I could picture the chefs at tomorrow's demonstration, squabbling over pots and pans like children fighting over toys. I wondered if, in addition to my other responsibilities, I would find myself playing referee to a bunch of egotistical maniacs.

Chapter 3

AS IT TURNED OUT, THE TOUR OF THE MARLETTE
Robbins Center of the Arts was quite entertaining. It didn't
hurt that we all carried glasses of champagne through the
facility and as I showed the chefs the main auditorium, the
pottery classrooms and kiln areas, the spacious textile work-
shop complete with weaving looms, the woodworking room,
and the smaller spaces devoted to painting, drawing, and
jewelry making, they became quite jovial.

At first, I'd wondered if I should have stopped Bryce St.
John and Maurice Bruneau from grabbing bottles of bubbly
from two flummoxed Voltaire's waiters as we left the Dragonfly
Room. But when the good-humored men passed out glasses to
their fellow chefs, I decided the sparkling wine might lend a
celebratory air to our little trip around the building.

"We've seen all of the other arts, no?" Maurice asked
me, tipping the last of the champagne into Charlene's cup.

She thanked him in French and the two of them clinked glasses and exchanged companionable smiles. "Where does the culinary magic happen in this beautiful place?"

I was pleased to hear him praise the center. The facility meant a great deal to me personally because of my connection to the man it was named after, but I knew that every Inspiration Valley resident was proud that our little town featured such a magnificent structure dedicated solely to arts education.

"The architects devoted an entire wing to the culinary arts," I told him and saw the chefs stand a fraction taller. In that brief moment, I realized it was unlikely that any member of this group had had a quick or painless rise to the top of their field. To become a renowned chef, each one of them must have paid his or her dues working endless hours, enduring biting criticism, staying on the cutting edge of the latest food trends, and continually honing their skills.

When we reached the cooking demonstration area, I turned to my followers and said, "Through the door behind me is a service kitchen where food is prepared for functions like tonight's dinner. But this kitchen is where the culinary arts are taught. It's not much bigger than some of your TV studio sets, but all the appliances are state-of-the-art. Klara, this gas stove has just been installed, and since you will be the first one presenting a demonstration, you'll be the first one to use it." I gestured at the rest of the gleaming equipment. "How different is this setting from the kitchens where you first learned to cook?" I asked, genuinely interested in how they'd gotten their starts.

"My *oma*'s kitchen was messy and wonderful," Klara answered. "She had knickknacks everywhere and her recipes were written in chicken scratch in a battered old notebook." She seemed to quickly get lost in the memory. "Food stains were on every page and she always put on this silly ruffled apron even if she was only boiling water. Oh, that woman could make anything! That's why my cookbook is called *My Grandmother's Hearth*."

Bryce St. John was listening raptly and when Klara was finished he ran his fingers through his golden hair and said, "I think your relationship with your grandmother comes through in your food, Klara. Me? I don't have any heart-warming stories to share. I learned to cook in the Navy and my skills have come a long way since the slop I used to serve to those poor sailors."

I hate to admit it, but after having seen Bryce St. John jogging earlier in the day, I spent a few pleasant seconds imagining how he'd look in uniform.

Leslie Sterling disturbed my fantasy by sliding a hand across one of the pristine butcher blocks and saying, "I got a job working for a catering company so I could pay for college. I loved the work so much that I dropped out of school and became the company's manager."

Joel Lang examined his reflection in the metal blade of a carving knife. "I was born in China. My parents were poor farmers and their dream was for me to be the first Lang to escape a life of backbreaking manual labor." He put the knife down. "When I decided to become a chef, they told me I'd dishonored my ancestors—that I should have become a successful businessman."

Everyone was silent, caught up in Lang's raw emotion.

"That's why I try to use something Chinese in every dish," he explained. "I want to pay my respects to my family's heritage and to my country whenever I cook. Thankfully, my parents lived long enough to attend the grand opening of the Purple Orchid and to see me fulfill their dream of me as a businessman, but sadly, they died shortly afterward." He dropped his gaze.

I turned my attention to Maurice, who'd once been Lang's partner at the Purple Orchid. He was staring at his former friend and co-chef with a wistful expression and for a fleeting moment, I thought I caught a glimpse of longing in the Frenchman's blue eyes. I couldn't help but wonder what had caused the rift between Joel and Maurice, his former mentor. "Although I taught Joel many, many things, he also educated me," he said after a lengthy pause. "I didn't fully appreciate the way a great chef can blend two seemingly opposing flavors to create an entire new experience for the palate. We French have great skill with the artistry of presentation and I was born with a raw talent for dreaming up beautiful dishes, but when Joel and I worked together, we made meals that had even the toughest critics swooning at our feet."

Charlene glanced at Maurice with admiration. "For me, most flavors are coaxed forth using flour, butter, and sugar. My parents owned a small café in Nice. They were famous for their light-as-air croissants and their chocolate pot de crème. My passion for all things sweet began at a very early age. It was always my dream to be the pastry chef at a famous restaurant." She dropped her arm and turned to Joel. "I'm sure your parents were just as proud of you as mine are of me."

Joel bowed stiffly in gratitude, but as he straightened, his gaze met Maurice's and I saw a shadow of hurt in his eyes.

Maurice's expression of wistfulness instantly disappeared. "They would have been more proud if you hadn't ruined everything by trying to have your finger in every pie. You should have left the finances to me. But no, you did things behind my back because you thought your way was better." His mouth tightened into a thin line of anger. "See where that got us! That's how you decided to repay me for all I've done?"

Wordlessly, Joel Lang walked away and Maurice watched him go, his fists clenched and a look of venom on his face.

"There's always a flare-up of testosterone when a bunch of chefs get together. It's like two roosters squaring off in the henhouse," Klara announced with false gaiety. I appreciated her attempt at levity and realized that there was far too much tension in the room. Before I could alter the atmosphere by reviewing Saturday's lineup, Klara's cell phone rang. The absurd sound of her yodeling ringtone made everyone giggle, successfully diffusing the tension. Klara excused herself and strode off to a corner to answer the call.

Meanwhile, Leslie and Charlene busied themselves by opening and closing drawers. Joel was also trying to become familiar with every utensil, pan, and pantry item before tomorrow's demonstration.

"That was Annie Schmidt, my assistant," Klara informed me once she'd dropped her cell phone back into her Chanel purse. "I wanted her and my sous chef to join us so they know the lay of the land. Annie keeps me organized and looking good, and Dennis is my second pair of hands in the kitchen."

"And I remember reading somewhere that your husband has never missed a taping," I said. "That's so sweet."

She sighed happily. "I've got it good, don't I? I never imagined that I'd have an entourage. And it's going to be even bigger this weekend because Ryan's kids from his first marriage are flying in from New York to be here."

I was going to need a personal assistant to keep all these people straight!

Annie arrived a few minutes later, pressing a phone to her ear with one hand and holding an appointment book with the other. A slim blonde with delicate hands and fine features, Annie wore stylish cat-eye glasses and a cotton dove gray dress. Everything about her was meticulously tidy. Concluding her phone call, she showed Klara the entries she'd made in the appointment book.

"Excellent." Klara rubbed her hands together. "I expect the new cookbook to sell out. But I'm surprised that the bookstore owner ordered so many of Joel's *Fusing Asian*. I thought *I* was the headliner at the signing." She studied Joel Lang with displeasure. "I don't know why our two books are being released on the same day anyway."

Speaking in soothing tones, Annie assured Klara that she was the true star of the event. "Your dress is laid out in your hotel room. You're going to look beautiful at tonight's dinner."

That got Klara's attention. Checking her watch, she gave a little gasp and hustled over to where I stood. "Lila, are we finished here? I need time to primp before our little get-together this evening. You and Annie can show Dennis where everything is, right?"

I nodded. "Sure." I cleared my throat and spoke loudly enough for all the chefs to hear. "I just wanted to make sure everyone was comfortable with the space, so if you'd like to change before dinner, you can head out whenever you'd like."

Most of the chefs were finished examining the space, and it wasn't long before Annie and I were the only ones left in the kitchen. She asked me a few questions about when the taped segments would air and on which television stations. As we talked, I was impressed by her thoroughness. Klara had found a real gem in Annie Schmidt.

Her sous chef, Dennis Chapman, was another matter. He stormed in the room and, without even bothering to introduce himself to me, started to complain to Annie about all the work he had to do.

"Klara barely lifts a finger." he grumbled. "And she never gives me enough time to prepare! Tonight, while she and Ryan enjoy a free meal, I'll be crushing spices and labeling bowls of ingredients."

Annie gave him a sympathetic look. "One of the head chef jobs you've applied for will come through, you'll see."

"It'd better! These high and mighty chefs—and I'm not just talking about Klara—aren't the be-all and the end-all of cooking. I have talent, too, and they know it!" Dennis growled, yanking the waist of his pants over his substantial paunch. With pallid skin and deep-set beady eyes, I couldn't help but picture the thirty-year-old man as a two-legged pig. The more he complained, the more his voice sounded like a squeal. I knew I had to say something before I threatened to blow his house down.

"Dennis, everyone at Novel Idea wants this experience to be a pleasant one. If there's anything I can do to help, let me know." I gave Klara's sous chef an ingratiating smile, though I'd taken an instant dislike to him.

Finally remembering his manners, he reached out and shook hands with me. "Sorry," he said without the slightest indication of remorse. "I get grumpy when I'm hungry." He turned to Annie. "Wanna grab a bite before we review her majesty's menu one more time?"

Annie hesitated and I got the sense she'd rather eat alone. "Let's do it now and be done for the night. Then we'll meet back here at six tomorrow morning to prep for Klara's demo." She looked at me. "That's okay, isn't it Ms. Wilkins? The kitchen will be open then?"

"Absolutely." I watched Annie take Dennis through the kitchen, showing him the equipment and food supplies. I again marveled over her people skills—how she was able to diffuse Dennis's foul mood as they discussed what he needed to do in the morning to get ready for Klara's demonstration.

When they had finished, I turned off the lights and shut the kitchen door. Without a key, I was unable to lock up, but assumed the security guard would do so on his rounds after our dinner tonight. I led Annie and Dennis through the corridors and back to the front lobby.

"Does this town have a decent barbeque joint?" Dennis asked as we stepped out into the late afternoon sun. "I'd love some shredded pork."

I managed to keep a straight face as I told him about the Piggy Bank. "But it's outside of town," I told him. "Just on the outskirts of Dunston."

"I think I'll pass," said Annie. "I'm not up for a drive, even a short one. I'll just get something from How Green Was My Valley and eat in my room."

"Suit yourself," Dennis said. I gave him directions, and he trotted off to his rental car.

Visibly relieved, Annie bid me good-bye and walked in the direction of the grocery store.

I hopped on my scooter, buckled my helmet, and murmured a Mother Goose nursery rhyme that reminded me of Dennis Chapman:

> *"The greedy man is he who sits*
> *And bites bits out of plates,*
> *Or else takes up an almanac*
> *And gobbles all the dates."*

Two hours later, I sat in the Dragonfly Room, sipping excellent wine and nibbling a heel of warm French bread. The evening felt magical. All of the Novel Idea agents and celebrity chefs were already having a good time and the meal had barely gotten underway. Gentle laughter intertwined with pleasant conversation and for a moment, it appeared as if the chefs had put aside their rivalries and were intent on enjoying each other's company.

I exchanged a contented glance with Sean and then cast my gaze around the room, noting how the soft flames of the candles on the tables caught the sparkles on the women's dresses and cast a soft sheen on the fabric of the men's tailored suits.

Voltaire's waiters moved as silently as ghosts. They cleared the soup bowls and refilled our wineglasses before serving our entrée of grilled rosemary lamb chops. The scent of lemons and garlic rose from the table and Leslie Sterling, who was seated to my left, asked the other chefs at our table to name their favorite dessert featuring the versatile yellow fruit.

"Tell us yours first," said Klara.

"Mine's not that exciting," Leslie stated. "But I do make a lemon chiffon cake that simply melts in the mouth."

Ryan whispered something into his wife's ear and she nodded and then smiled at the rest of us. "We were trying to agree on our favorite," she explained. "And I'd have to go with my *oma*'s *griesmeelpudding met bessensap*." She pronounced this as "grease meal pudding met bessen sap," and I wondered how something with the word "grease" in it could be anyone's favorite fruity dessert. "It translates to 'semolina pudding with currant sauce.' What makes it so wonderful is the boiling of the lemon peel in a pan with milk. The flavors just *fuse*, as you'd say, Joel."

The table's only male chef rubbed his chin thoughtfully. "I don't use semolina often."

"Oh, it's wonderful!" Klara exclaimed. "Tell him why, Ryan."

Klara's husband seemed delighted to participate in the discussion. "Semolina or *griesmeel* is one of the oldest of the ground grains." The way he pronounced the word sounded very different from Klara, with the "*g*" coming from the back of his throat. He sounded more Dutch than his wife. "'*Meel*' is how you say 'flour' in Dutch and '*gries*' is similar to the word 'gravel,' as semolina comes from the middlings of hard wheat. Many cultures have their own version of semolina. For example, the Italians have polenta."

"And the Moroccans have couscous," Leslie added.

"Precisely." Ryan grinned at her and then cut a piece of his lamb.

Joel Lang studied Ryan with interest. "You are very knowledgeable about food, Mr. Patrick." He dipped his chin as a show of respect.

"I spent many years traveling throughout Europe when I was stationed overseas with NATO. The base was in Brunssum, in the Netherlands, and I could hop on a train and be in another country in a few hours." He smiled, as if remembering a happy time in his life. "I became fascinated with the different cuisines of each place."

"I couldn't manage without him." Klara leaned over and kissed her husband on the cheek. "And now it's your turn to answer the lemon question, Joel. How do you make an Asian fusion dessert using lemons?"

"Lemongrass and Asian pear sorbet," he answered. "Though there is an ancient custom in China that good friends or lovers never share the same pear, for dividing the pear would lead to separation." He cast a quick glance at Jude's table, where Maurice and Franklin were laughing heartily and clapping each other on the back. "I have made the mistake of sharing a pear before."

Once again, I found myself wondering what caused the rift between the two chefs as an awkward silence settled at our table. The moment the waitstaff began to clear our plates, I hurriedly changed the subject. "Tomorrow's cooking segment should be very interesting," I said. "'Great Love Stories from Literature Interpreted Through Food.' I'm intrigued to know what each of you will be preparing for the event. Leslie, what famous couple are you representing?"

Leslie dramatically placed her hands over her heart. "Oh, just the saddest couple in the world."

We gazed at her questioningly. In my mind, I ran through famous literary couples—Jane Eyre and Rochester, Lancelot and Guinevere, Scarlett O'Hara and Rhett Butler—it seemed to me that most literary lovers were tragic.

Leslie looked at us incredulously. "Surely you know who I mean? Why, their love was so fierce and rapturous that it overpowered all their values and other allegiances." Obviously pleased that she had stumped us, she declared, "Romeo and Juliet, of course."

"Ah," we all responded simultaneously.

The server placed desserts in front of us. Leslie stared at the rich red strawberry compote flowing over the creamy vanilla panna cotta on her plate. "This looks delicious," she declared as she picked up her spoon. "To represent the passion of the star-crossed lovers, I'm making a variation of the traditional tiramisu. Rather than blending coffee with chocolate, mine will be a perfect marriage of raspberry and dark cocoa. And because there was such violence associated with their love, I've added a special ingredient to the chocolate cream." She lowered her voice and leaned in. "A hint of pepper to give it a little bite. It's remarkable how pepper and chocolate meld together."

"That sounds interesting," I said as I tried to imagine the spark of flavor in the chocolate.

"Hmph," remarked Klara as she dug in to her dessert. "I can't imagine why you'd want to ruin chocolate with pepper."

Sean laughed. "I'd say the same thing, Ms. Patrick, except that as a joke, I once tipped some pepper into a brownie mix my college roommate was baking—you know the pranks guys pull in college—and I have to say that those were some of the best brownies I'd ever eaten."

"Well, I suppose you just never know until you try," Klara said, smiling at Sean.

I gave Sean a playful nudge. "I'll have to bake them for

you sometime." I put a spoonful of the panna cotta in my mouth and almost moaned in delight at the sweet creaminess and sumptuous berry flavors. "Oh, this is divine. Klara, who are your famous literary lovers?"

"Tristan and Isolde. I was inspired by their story of the black or white sails. The story is that Tristan was in love with Isolde, even though he was already married. After falling ill, Tristan sent a ship to Isolde asking her to come to him in the hopes that she could cure him. If the ship returned with white sails, that would mean she was coming. If the sails were black, it would mean that she denied his love. Tristan's wife saw the white sails, but lied and told Tristan they were black. Heartbroken, he died of grief before Isolde arrived. When Isolde heard of her lover's passing, she died, too. So terribly, terribly sad." Klara shook her head but then immediately brightened. "I decided to do a dish that reflects their tale." She glanced at Ryan, who nodded encouragingly. "A duo of soups. I'm making a variation of my *oma*'s brown bean soup, which is very Dutch, but I use black beans instead. I'm also making her to-die-for white bean soup."

"And we were very fortunate," Ryan excitedly interjected. "We found some small black and white bowls that are shaped a little like boats. We plan to stand a cheese crisp shaped like a sail in each one."

"The cheese crisps are made with Gouda, of course, broiled under a flame for added crispness," added Klara. "They'll provide nice contrast to the color of the soup."

Leslie frowned. "So the white cheese crisp is in the black bean soup and the black one in the white?" At Klara's nod, she asked, "How do you make the black one?"

Klara seemed surprised by the question and looked at Ryan.

"With squid ink," he answered quickly. "Just a drop or two makes it very dark, and it adds an interesting flavor element as well."

Joel perked up. "Ah, squid ink. It has a very fishy flavor. I use it in some of my own recipes to great effect."

"Who are your literary lovers, Joel?" I asked, sipping the coffee that the waiter had just poured.

"I will be honoring my heritage by representing the story of *Liang Zhu*, or in English, *The Butterfly Lovers*." Joel sat back and stared off in the distance as he continued. "It's a tragic romance like Romeo and Juliet. Zhu Yingtai was a beautiful young woman from a wealthy family who lived in a time when girls were not allowed to go to school. She, however, convinced her parents to allow her to disguise herself as a young man and attend school away from home. For three years, she was the roommate and best friend of Liang Shanbo, a bookish young fellow who never discovered that she was a girl. When their studies were over, they returned to their separate hometowns and missed each other greatly. After months of being apart, Liang visited Zhu, discovered she was a woman, and they became passionate lovers who vowed that if they could not live together, they would die together."

"How beautiful," said Leslie.

"But the legend does not end there," Joel said. "Zhu's parents arranged for her to marry the son of a rich family in their neighborhood, and when Liang found out, he became ill from grief and died. On the day that Zhu was to marry, the wedding procession was halted by a strong wind as it passed Liang's tomb and Zhu left the procession to pay her respects. As she cried in front of his tomb, a flash of lightning struck it open. Without hesitation, Zhu leaped into the grave, and when the rain stopped, the sky cleared, and the spirits of Zhu and Liang turned into a pair of beautiful butterflies. They flew happily among the flowers and were never apart again."

I sighed. "What a moving story. How will you translate it into food?"

Joel sat up straighter and smiled proudly. "I am making a trio of dishes. The first dish will have two fresh spring rolls, one with basil, tofu, and fennel and the other with cilantro, chicken, and lemongrass. These represent the lovers' time at school, when they were two young men sharing a room. The second dish will be a fiery seared tuna crusted with hot Szechuan pepper and served over wasabi and lemongrass noodles and accompanied by ginger green beans. My secret to the searing is that I broil it under extreme heat. It makes for a very quick sear and increases the intensity of the Szechuan pepper. This dish, of course, represents their passion."

Klara frowned. "But don't you think the Szechuan pepper and the wasabi with the lemongrass will battle for dominance on the palate? Not to mention the ginger. There are too many different kinds of heat in one dish."

"No, there aren't." Joel's eyes darkened. "It's the perfect blend to illustrate fiery passion." But even as he made this statement, his brow creased and he looked as if he doubted his own words.

Sean exchanged a glance with me and asked, "What's the third dish of the trio, Joel?"

Joel blinked. "To symbolize the lovers as butterflies

flitting among the flowers, I will make a cilantro and lime sherbet that accentuates the floral character of the herb and sprinkle it with sugared jasmine blossoms."

I touched Joel's hand. "Your trio sounds like a very interesting mix of flavors. I can't wait to try them all."

"*I* don't think the three dishes work together, Joel," Klara said. "They seem in opposition to each other."

Joel stood, scraping his chair back. "All you do is criticize my food. What do you know about Asian fusion cuisine anyway? You're just a Dutch hausfrau cook."

As he strode out the door, Ryan put his arm around Klara's shoulders. "Don't listen to him, hon. He doesn't even know the difference between Dutch and German." He kissed her cheek. "And I think you're right about his trio. Come on, let's call it a night."

"Don't you worry, darling. I don't take a word he says to heart." Klara picked up her purse and turned to me. "Lila, dinner was lovely. We'll see you tomorrow."

I looked around the room and saw that most of the guests were leaving. Jude and Franklin were just exiting to the front lobby, so I grabbed Sean's hand and we hurried after the two agents.

"How'd things go at your table?" I asked when we caught up, keeping a safe distance between us and the celebrity chefs walking ahead of us.

Franklin grinned. "That Maurice is a card. He had me in stitches most of the night."

"But some of those chefs sure have inflated egos," Jude added quietly.

Sean nodded. "We had a couple at our table who were rather puffed up with self-importance."

"But wasn't that dinner delicious?" Flora said as she joined us, holding hands with her husband, Brian. "I think the evening was a great success."

"I agree, Flora. It was a good night." I glanced at the door of the Dragonfly Room. The last of the waiters was heading out with Zach, who flicked the light switch and closed the door. I waved him over.

Zach bounded in our direction. "Hey, people! Wasn't that totally the most—"

His words were lost in a thunderous roar that shook the room. Flora screamed. Two of the waiters bolted outside. I clenched Sean's arm. "What was that?"

"I have no idea." Sean frantically scanned the lobby and his hand went to his hip, as if instinctively reaching for a gun that wasn't there. "All of you, wait here. Jude, come with me."

The two men disappeared into the hall. Jude returned almost immediately. "Everyone get out of the building," he ordered. "There's smoke coming from the culinary arts wing. We think something exploded. The fire department is on the way."

"Oh, man!" Zach slapped his forehead as he started for the door. "Don't tell me something was wrong with that brand-new equipment."

I quickly glanced behind Jude. "What about Sean? Where is he?"

"He's checking to see if anyone else is inside. Don't worry, Lila, he'll be right behind us. Let's go." Jude herded us all to the door.

A cool evening breeze chilled me as I stood staring at the Arts Center's façade, exhaling in relief when Sean came running out alone. His hair was plastered to his head, and his suit was wet.

"The smoke was getting pretty thick and then the ceiling sprinklers came on." He ran his hand through his hair. "But I couldn't find anyone else in the building. At least no one answered when I called."

"Thank goodness," I said, expelling a pent-up breath. "I hope there's minimal damage to the center. What do you suppose happened?"

Sean shook his head. "I don't know. I'll go talk to the waiters and see if they can shed some light on the situation."

Zach glanced over to where Klara stood with the other chefs. "It better not be something to do with that gas stove that Miss Top Chef insisted we install. I swear I can smell gas. Can't you?"

"Dear me, I am getting a whiff of it," said Flora, wringing her hands. Brian put his arm around her shoulders.

Jude added, "I'm glad the celebrity chefs were already out of the building."

Sirens howled in the distance. We all huddled in a group on the sidewalk, staring as smoke billowed out the side of the building. The fire engine pulled up, followed by an EMT truck. Although we were only witnesses, I felt caught up in the drama of activity, noise, and urgency as firefighters unrolled the hose, hooked it up to a hydrant, and ran inside. Members of the emergency crew asked us all if we were okay.

Suddenly, a fireman came rushing out of the building and ran up to one of the paramedics, pulling him away from an ashen-faced waiter standing beside me. The fireman spoke in a quiet voice to the paramedic, but I was close enough to hear.

"I need a body bag," he said. "Someone was in the kitchen when the explosion went off and I don't want these folks to see what's left of the poor soul."

Chapter 4

THE NEWS THAT SOMEONE HAD DIED IN THE EXPLOSION struck me dumb. I looked around, wondering who was missing, but my brain was unable to process any useful information. I stared blankly from one face to another. All of a sudden, their names escaped me, drifting out of reach like the column of smoke blackening the night sky.

"Lila," Sean said, squeezing my arm. "Who didn't make it out?"

I turned to him and blinked. *Sean*. His touch freed me from my stupor. I swept my gaze over the clusters of shocked and terrified literary agents, chefs, and waiters and a pair of Arts Center janitors.

First, I located all of my coworkers. Flora's husband, Brian, had enfolded her in an embrace and her shoulders were shaking as she cried. Franklin and Vicky were standing absolutely still and I noticed that they were holding hands so tightly that their knuckles were white. Jude, Zach, and Bentley stood elbow-to-elbow, their eyes fixed on the building's front doors.

"Everyone from Novel Idea is here," I said, my voice betraying my relief. "I don't know all the folks from Voltaire's and have only met a few of the Arts Center staff, but let me take a head count of the chefs."

I noticed Klara and Ryan on the far side of the steps, flanked by Bryce St. John and Leslie Sterling. Charlene Jacques was clinging to Maurice Bruneau. No one spoke. From top chef to janitor, every individual stared with wide, glassy eyes at the Arts Center's façade.

"Oh, Lord," I breathed, realizing who was absent from the group. "I don't see Joel Lang."

Sean released my arm. "Okay. Let's not jump to any conclusions. Joel sat at our table. He was there during the coffee service because I remember him ordering green tea. And then he left in a bit of a huff, remember?"

I nodded, feeling a tiny spark of hope. "That's right. Hopefully, he's on his way back to the hotel."

"I'm going to ask around. Stay put." Sean moved off. He started with my coworkers, speaking so quietly that I couldn't hear what was being said. Truthfully, I didn't need to listen in. A cold dread had taken hold of me and I could guess what the agents, chefs, and ancillary people huddled on the steps would say. No one had seen Joel Lang leave the building and I thought I knew why. The expression of anger on his face after Klara had criticized his love story menu told me everything. Joel had probably gone to the test kitchen to practice. My guess is that he wanted to prove Klara wrong. I was also willing to bet that she'd touched a nerve and had heightened Joel's insecurities to the point where he wouldn't rest until he knew he was completely prepared for tomorrow's demonstration.

Maurice was the first to realize that his former partner was not outside with the rest of us. I watched him pivot this way and that, his brows furrowed in confusion. By the time Sean reached the spot where he and Charlene stood, the Frenchman's face had turned pallid. However, before Sean could talk to him, the paramedics emerged through the building's front doors and carefully maneuvered a gurney down the handicapped ramp.

We all watched in mute horror. Though the shape on the stretcher was entirely covered by a yellow blanket, it was clear that whoever had died in the explosion was concealed beneath the layer of bright cotton. The paramedics had strapped the corpse in tightly, but as the gurney bounced from the bottom of the ramp onto the sidewalk, the top of the blanket slipped a little, revealing a white body bag.

I sucked in a horrified breath. I didn't see anything gruesome because, thankfully, the bag hid the victim's features from view. But the shape of the dead person's head drove home the realization that a human being had just died a horrendous death. I closed my eyes and bowed my head, feeling a rush of sorrow and pity for the poor soul.

As if sensing that I needed comfort, Sean appeared by my side and drew me against him. "All of Voltaire's staff and the few Arts Center employees are accounted for. As of this point, no one saw Mr. Lang leave. That still doesn't mean he's the victim, but I'll have to ask the paramedics if they found any ID or clothing that could help us figure out who . . ." He trailed off, his eyes on the gurney. He didn't need to finish his sentence.

"Go," I told him. "I'll be all right. I'm going to stand with my coworkers."

I joined Franklin and Vicky. We put our arms around each other's waists and supported each other while the EMT truck drove off. Once it was out of sight, Bentley suggested we all relocate to the James Joyce Pub.

"I don't know about the rest of you, but I need a drink," she proclaimed. "We've all had a terrible shock and we need to . . . take a moment. Please." For the first time ever, I heard Bentley Burlington-Duke's voice waver. "It's on me. None of us should be alone right now."

The agents gathered the celebrity chefs, and together we silently trudged to the pub. Normally, the cheerful, wood-paneled bar and grill would have been cozy and relaxing, but tonight, I was too upset to focus on the charming framed illustrations of scenes from *Ulysses* and *Finnegans Wake* or to wave at the apple-cheeked bartender with the round belly and the hearty laugh.

Jude took charge of finding several tables close together, which he and Zach rearranged until they'd formed a long rectangle. Sinking into our chairs, we accepted shot glasses from a subdued waitress. Apparently, Bentley had made it clear that we were not here to celebrate the Taste of the Town, for the waitress placed a full bottle of Wild Turkey on the table and then returned with two pitchers of beer. She passed out chilled pint glasses with a solemn expression.

Once she was gone, Klara was the first one to break the silence. "Was it Joel on that stretcher?"

The question was directed at me. I stalled by pouring myself an inch of whiskey and drinking it down in one gulp. I wasn't fond of the bitter taste or the burning sensation in my mouth, but I was grateful for the feeling of warmth in my stomach and understood why people often reached for alcohol during times of shock and stress.

"Lila?" Leslie prompted gently. "We need to know."

"But that's just it," I said, surprised by how calm I sounded. "He's missing, but that doesn't prove he was killed during the explosion. Sean, I mean, Officer Griffiths, will find out everything he can and then he'll call me." I fished my cell phone from my purse and put it on the table. "As soon as I have new information, I'll share it with you."

Charlene passed her hands over her face. "This is like a waking nightmare. I didn't know Joel well, but he's one of us. If that was him back there . . . caught in that fire . . . And how did it start in the first place? Isn't that a brand-new building?"

Glancing toward the other side of the bar, where Bentley stood with her cell phone pressed to her ear, I wished that she'd complete her call and join us. I wasn't sure how to comfort the chefs, and Bentley, who was both unflappable and pragmatic, would undoubtedly restore a sense of normalcy to our gathering.

Jude filled my glass with amber ale. He passed the pitcher to Bryce and then touched my hand. "You okay?"

I nodded, though it was far from the truth. It wouldn't do for the person who'd invited all the chefs to Inspiration Valley to fall to pieces, but I was relieved when Bentley finished her conversation and joined us.

"I've called over to the Magnolia B&B. Joel hasn't come

back." While everyone absorbed this news, she turned to me and spoke sotto voce. "I also talked to Dominic about renting Voltaire's for tomorrow's demonstrations. He's charging me an exorbitant rate, especially considering the free publicity the event will give his restaurant, but I'm in no position to argue."

I couldn't think of anything to say. While I was still reeling from the explosion, Bentley was thinking ahead, ensuring that nothing would stop the chefs from creating their love story menus.

"Will they be up for it?" I whispered, jerking my head to indicate Leslie and Maurice, who were seated directly across from us.

Bentley frowned. "They're television personalities, Lila. They know the show must go on. Right now, they're shaken. We all are. But by tomorrow, their professionalism will take over. Unfortunately, you, Zach, and I don't have until then. I need to go over the details with Dominic, Zach has to contact the media and inform them of the new location, and you have three jobs. First, you need to figure out how to get the members of the public to Voltaire's in the morning. Second, arrange for Maurice to take Joel's place in tomorrow's demonstration in case he is unable to be there. Maurice will need to come up with a lovers' menu tonight. Lastly, find out from your boyfriend when we'll be allowed to resume our events in the Arts Center."

I almost reminded Bentley that Sean was a police officer, not a firefighter, but I kept my mouth shut. In a way, I was glad that she was doing what she did best: taking charge. I wanted to have tasks to complete—they'd help obscure the image of the figure on the gurney and the dreadful pictures

I'd created in my head of a man burned beyond recognition. Possibly a man I'd just shared a meal with.

"We should get the chefs back to the hotel after they've had a drink or two," I said. "They're going to need their rest."

Bentley nodded. "Have Franklin and Jude walk them to the Magnolia. The rest of us will figure out how to save Books and Cooks from being a total disaster."

I found that statement to be quite callous, considering someone had just died and an explosion had damaged our brand-new Arts Center, but there was too much to do to waste time or energy getting into an argument with my boss. Instead, I turned to Jude and, in a low whisper, shared Bentley's plans.

He nodded, and called Maurice's name. When Maurice looked up, I asked, "If the unfortunate soul killed in the explosion was Joel, do you think you could pull a famous lovers menu together in time for tomorrow's demonstration?"

"*Oui*, but of course." He stroked his chin and thought for a moment. "I will represent Napoleon and Josephine with a *pissaladière*, using a variety of peppers and olives to represent one and the other. And then a *tarte tatin* with plums." He rubbed his hands together. "Oh, it will be *magnifique*." Then, as if realizing that enthusiasm was out of place this evening, he whispered wistfully, "If only Joel . . ."

I pulled a pencil and notepad from my purse. "Write down the ingredients you'll need, and I'll make sure they're ready and waiting for you."

Jude waited until there was a break in the conversation before offering to walk the chefs to the inn. They looked to me before rising from their chairs and I held up my phone and shook my head, indicating that I'd received no new information. Exhausted, confused, and sad, the chefs allowed Jude and Franklin to lead them out of the pub.

Vicky produced a notepad and pen from her voluminous handbag and looked at Bentley expectantly. Bentley rattled off a list of assignments. Then, she stopped abruptly and told Brian to take Flora home. It was clear even to my tough-as-nails boss that Flora was too distraught to work.

Zach disappeared soon afterward to make calls from the quiet of his office at Novel Idea. Bentley and Vicky departed for Voltaire's, leaving me alone in the raucous pub. Sitting among the merry patrons, I knew that I'd have to walk home for I'd had too much to drink to operate my scooter. I was just rising to leave when my mother walked into the James Joyce, her face pinched with worry.

"Mama!" I waved at her and the moment she spotted me, she released such a deep breath that I could see her entire body sag in relief. Rushing over, she threw her arms around me.

"I saw fire!" she cried. "I was doing my usual tarot card reading before bed when flames started dancin' before my vision! It was awful, Lila. I sensed you were in danger." She pulled away, doubt entering her eyes. "Were you? In danger?"

I grabbed her hand. "Yes, but I'm okay. There was an explosion at the Arts Center. I think there was an accident involving the gas line we had brought into the kitchen." Hesitating, I smoothed the soft wrinkles on the back of my mother's hand with my thumb. "Someone was in the room when it happened. We don't know for sure, but it's looking like it was Joel Lang, one of the celebrity chefs."

"That's who I saw, then." She gazed, unfocused, at the flickering candle in the middle of the table. "Black smoke and a charred body. It was too awful, Lila. I couldn't rest 'til I laid eyes on you."

I told myself that the shivers running down my spine came from the cold beer. Most of the time, I doubted my mother's so-called gifts, but there were occasions such as this when I couldn't understand how she knew the things she knew. She'd recently bought a police scanner and loved listening to the calls relating to Inspiration Valley, though those were few and far between, and one of her clients was the chief of police's loose-tongued wife. But even Amazing Althea couldn't have known that a body had been found inside the Arts Center, could she?

"I'm sorry you had a scare," I told her. "And I'm so glad you found me. I'm in no condition to drive and I don't want to be alone right now."

She smiled and I knew I'd said what she wanted to hear. After all, there's nothing that makes a mother feel more valued than to be needed by her child. It doesn't matter how old the child is—toddler, college student, or middle-aged matron, none of us ever grow too old to be rescued, cared for, or comforted.

For me, that was the hardest thing about having Trey attending school at the other end of the state. Sure, he called and emailed, but it wasn't the same. I couldn't bake him a batch of chocolate chip cookies when he hadn't done well on an exam or make him hot tea with honey when he caught a cold. I could listen and sympathize and offer advice, but the distance was tough on me. Sometimes I ached to ruffle his hair or watch how his impish smile could transform him into a boy again. I even missed doing his laundry and straightening up his room. Those things served as a reminder that this wonderful young man was a part of my life. I sighed. I guess I'd yet to adjust to his absence.

"Don't worry, honey. He misses you, too," my mother said as if I'd spoken out loud. "Come on, let's get you home."

The moment we stepped outside and I saw her turquoise pickup truck parked at the curb, I knew I'd found the solution to the problem of how to get the public to Voltaire's to view the chefs' love story demonstrations.

"Are you busy tomorrow?" I asked as I hopped into the passenger seat.

"I have the feelin' I'm gonna be," my mother replied.

As she pulled out onto High Street, I thought about my idea and couldn't come up with a better solution. "When we get back to my place, can you call everyone you know who drives a pickup truck?"

My mother looked surprised. "Why, that's half the town!"

"Exactly," I said. "Ask them if they'd like to be a part of a very last-minute parade."

DESPITE THE TRAGEDY that rocked our little town, the atmosphere in Inspiration Valley on Friday morning was festive. My mother had convinced all her truck-driving friends to form the "Hillbilly Taxi Service," and they'd decorated their pickups with signs and streamers, balloons, and paper flowers. Many of them had lined the flatbeds of their vehicles with hay bales and quilts to accommodate the passengers who couldn't fit inside the cabs.

As Flora collected tickets and Jude and I diverted visitors from the entrance of the Arts Center to the motorcade that would take them to Voltaire's, I couldn't help but get caught up in the joviality of the event. People happily climbed into and onto trucks, eager to get to the demonstrations that would be presented by their favorite chefs. They greeted strangers as if they were friends, and seemed to be enjoying a marvelous time before the actual Taste of the Town events had even begun.

Scanning the scores of attendees who were lining up to board one of the trucks, I felt a pang of sadness for Joel. Sean had called me first thing this morning to give me the official news that Joel's was indeed the body taken away on the gurney last night. I couldn't stop thinking about him and how the chef would never know how successful this food festival was or that so many people had shown up for the demonstrations. Perhaps he might have sold more cookbooks than he ever anticipated as a result of the event. If not for the faulty equipment we had installed—

"C'mon, shug," my mother called from the driver's window of her truck. "Let's get this show on the road."

I shook off thoughts of Joel and last night's explosion and waved at her. Strapping on my helmet, I hopped onto my yellow scooter to lead the parade to Voltaire's. As I revved the engine, I called out, "Off we go!" and started down Redbud Road. A clatter behind me made me look back, and I realized that many of the trucks had strung tin cans on their bumpers. In this noisy and colorful way, we began our ride to the first scheduled event of Taste of the Town.

As I approached Center Park, it struck me that this hillbilly parade was a perfect way for the town's visitors to get a sense of Inspiration Valley. Sitting in the trucks, they would have a good view of our tree-lined streets, our wonderful Nine Muses fountain, and the charming shops and colorful gardens that gave the town its character. On a whim I rode right around the square of the park and the procession of trucks followed me. Shopkeepers and residents stepped outside and waved. I tooted my horn, as did several of the trucks.

On the corner of Dogwood and High Street, Nell, the owner of Sixpence Bakery, was placing a cake box on top of a stack that Big Ed balanced in his arms. At the sight of our entourage, he nearly dropped his load, but recovered quickly and hollered, "G'mornin' y'all!" I beeped and Nell blew us a kiss.

As I turned onto High Street, Makayla stepped out the door of Espresso Yourself. "Woo-hoo, girl!" she called. "We've got ourselves a parade."

I grinned at her and continued past Novel Idea, Sherlock Homes Realty, the Constant Reader, and the James Joyce Pub. On the sidewalk by the bookstore, Franklin was straightening a large sandwich sign that proclaimed: *BOOK SIGNING THIS MORNING! MEET AUTHOR DOUG CORBY OF* A FOODIE'S DIARY. As we paraded by, he stared at us, mouth agape, and then broke into a huge smile before giving me a thumbs-up.

Finally, we arrived at Voltaire's, where Vicky stood at the entrance waiting for us. She frowned at me and tapped her watch. I pulled my scooter around the back, quickly parking it and storing my helmet under its seat, and hurried to join Vicky in greeting the attendees.

"That was quite a spectacle," Vicky noted. "I can't believe you convinced all those people to ride in those trucks." She raised her eyebrows. "It's not safe on those hay bales, and it is most certainly illegal for them to ride without seatbelts."

"There was no harm done. Everyone was having fun. See?" I indicated the crowd with a sweep of my hand. "They're all smiling. And the Hillbilly Taxi Service got us here on time."

"Barely," she retorted. "Let's go inside. Chef Klara is due to begin in two minutes."

Dominic had set up his restaurant so that all the chairs faced the bar. I had only been in Voltaire's when the lights were dimmed to provide the proper dining atmosphere, and today, with the chandeliers blazing, I could see that the room was spacious and more than adequate for our needs. A few waiters were taking coffee orders and the celebrity chefs were gathered at one end of the bar. Bryce St. John was examining the two portable burners that had been set up alongside various cooking utensils and equipment. Behind the bar, Zach spoke to a technician who was testing the sound equipment. I admired the wisdom of Dominic in deciding to have the chefs do their demonstrations at the bar. Instead of the audience crowding into the kitchen, they were seated comfortably at tables and being served coffee and tea, for which they'd no doubt be charged handsomely. And the chefs would be presenting at a height from which everyone could see and hear them without obstruction.

"How are you all doing?" I asked the chefs.

"Hanging in there," replied Leslie Sterling, buttoning her chef's jacket.

Charlene Jacques finished tying a yellow floral apron around her waist. "I'm ready to cook. It always calms me."

"Me, too," said Bryce St. John. "When I'm in the kitchen, the whole world makes sense."

Klara smiled at him. "That's why your food is so amazing."

"Why, thank you, Klara. That means a lot coming from you." Bryce winked at her.

Klara's husband, Ryan, put his arms around Klara's shoulders. "Cooking soothes you, too, doesn't it, sweetheart."

A commotion at the door made us all turn, and Klara's assistants, Annie Schmidt and Dennis Chapman, came running toward us. Annie stopped short when she saw her boss.

"Klara," she said, her eyes wide. "You're all right!"

"Of course, why wouldn't I be?" Klara frowned. "Where have you two been? Ryan's had to do most of the prep."

Dennis looked petulant. "Our hotel is farther away from the Arts Center than your B&B. We had no idea the demonstrations had been relocated."

"When I heard about the explosion, I thought you—" Annie exhaled loudly. "I tried to reach you but the call went straight to voicemail. I was afraid . . ." She trailed off, surveying the group of chefs. "Was anyone hurt?"

"Yes, Joel Lang," I said. "The poor man died in the fire."

Dennis stared at me openmouthed. His eyes glinted. "I can't believe it." He glanced around and then seemed to come back to his senses. "But how is this going to work?"

"Don't worry, young man." Vicky indicated the bar with a wave of her hand. "Everything you need is here."

Maurice dragged the blade of a large knife across a honing steel. "I've cooked in many kinds of kitchens, but never one like this," he said as he pulled the knife across the metal rod again. To me, it sounded like the hiss of a serpent.

"It's ridiculous that we have to cook at a bar," Klara grumbled. "How like Joel to ruin my demonstration."

Her callous comment rendered me speechless, but not Vicky. "He died in an accident, Chef Klara," she said in a quiet but firm tone. "This was not his fault." Vicky leaned toward me. "I'll go find Bentley. She's going to do the welcome and introductions."

Klara sighed loudly. "I know the explosion wasn't Joel's fault. But we're here because of him."

Bryce St. John touched her arm. "Just be thankful that you weren't the one who got caught in the kitchen during the explosion. It could have been you this morning, if Joel hadn't tried to cook there last night."

"I suppose I should be grateful for that." Klara nodded. "His insecurities got him killed. He was probably trying to tweak those ridiculous dishes of his before presenting them to the public."

Leslie Sterling stared at Klara. "I bet you're also relieved that Joel no longer threatens your *New York Times* bestseller position, considering your cookbooks both release on the same day. He won't be around to promote it now."

"That hadn't even occurred to me," Klara protested. She pointed at Maurice Bruneau. "Joel's mishap is serendipitous for you though. You'll be taking his place in the demonstrations, correct? And you weren't scheduled to do anything before."

Maurice flushed. "That is true, Madame. Thanks to Joel's unfortunate demise, I have this opportunity to show the world that I am the better chef." He cleared his throat and added, "Not that I would have wished this misfortune on my former business partner. But it is my turn to shine."

I was having a difficult time listening to these people speak with so little compassion about the death of one of their colleagues. To think I had once admired them. Thankfully, at that moment Vicky and Bentley appeared.

"All right, chefs, let's get things under way." Bentley proceeded to walk behind the bar.

The chefs went to the seats reserved for them. There was only one empty chair left in the restaurant, and I indicated that Vicky should take it. I stood and leaned against the wall near the door, where I had a good view of the bar and the audience.

"Attention, everyone," Bentley said and waited until the chattering had stopped before continuing. "I'd like to welcome you to Inspiration Valley's first Taste of the Town festival. I am Bentley Burlington-Duke, CEO of Novel Idea Literary Agency, one of the major sponsors of the festival. Due to an unfortunate accident last night in the demonstration kitchen at our new Marlette Robbins Center for the Arts, we've had to relocate today's demonstrations here. We would like to thank you for your patience and understanding—"

"Psst, Lila." A loud whisper at the door caught my attention. I glanced over and saw Sean beckoning me outside.

"What is it?" I asked when I had joined him. "Chef Klara is about to start." The sun shone brightly, and the Hillbilly Taxi Service trucks were dropping off more people. Sean took my arm and we moved away from the door.

"I'm sorry to cut in on the demonstrations, but I thought you'd want to hear this."

My stomach clenched. "Do you have news about the explosion?"

"The fire inspector told us that the cause of the fire was indeed gas related—"

"The new gas line!" I interjected.

"He won't go into more detail at this point. Not until his report is finished." He shook his head. "We managed to notify Joel Lang's next of kin. That's the part of my job that I hate the most."

I hugged him. "It must be really difficult." Kissing his cheek I said, "And I didn't mean to interrupt you. What did you come to tell me?"

"The fire inspector has closed the kitchen wing while he completes his investigation, but he'll allow the other events of the festival to continue in the rest of the building."

"So other than the kitchen, it's safe?"

Sean nodded. "Yes. Apparently the explosion was specific to that wing and there is no risk to the other parts of the Arts Center."

"Well, that's a relief." I squeezed his arm. "I'd better get back inside. Thanks for coming by to tell me."

"How's it going in there? Is Chef Klara living up to your expectations?"

"She is a great chef, but on a personal level, she's a bit of a disappointment." I reflected back on her conversation with the other chefs. "It's when the chefs all get together. The mix doesn't quite result in an explosion, but sparks do fly."

Chapter 5

THE DEMONSTRATIONS WENT OFF WITHOUT A HITCH and the variety of succulent dishes created by our celebrity chefs captivated the audience. While the cameras were still rolling, Zach held out Klara's cookbook and announced that she'd be signing copies of *My Grandmother's Hearth* at the Constant Reader. He then produced a copy of Joel's cookbook and, with a solemn expression, explained that Chef Lang had passed away in a tragic accident the previous night.

"Sadly, *Fusing Asian* will be his last book, but I think it's his best work yet," Zach said. "It's available online and at a bookstore near you, so pick up a copy in his memory." The cameraman zoomed in on the cookbook's cover for a few seconds and then the show was over.

I cast a shocked glance at Bentley. Had Zach's last segment been scripted? Was he deliberately using Joel's death as a method for increasing the cookbook's sales? Bentley's face was unreadable, but I saw the immediate effect on the audience. Several of the women dabbed at their eyes with tissues while a few of the men declared that they wanted to hurry to the Constant Reader to check out the book for themselves.

Suddenly, people were scrambling to be first out the door of Voltaire's.

I rushed over to Klara, who had her hands folded across her chest and was glowering at the departing crowd. "We're going to have to hurry," I told her. "It looks like you're going to have quite a lineup of expectant readers."

"For me or Joel Lang?" she snapped. "I deserve the *New York Times* list. If that man lands a spot on it just because he died, then I'm going to be furious."

Stunned by her callousness, I looked to Ryan for help, but he merely shrugged and continued to pack his wife's cooking utensils, makeup kit, and soiled chef's coat into a box.

Annie came to the rescue. "You have a lifetime of book releases ahead of you," she told Klara softly. "This one will be a huge success and the next one will be, too. Poor Mr. Lang won't ever have another. And while you're filming new television shows, people can only see him on reruns. You're still the star."

Klara gave Annie a fond smile. "You're right. And I didn't mean to sound crass. You all know how much of myself I put into this cookbook—how much of my precious family memories are in each and every dish. I'm sure Joel's book was just as important to him and, truly, there's room for both of us on the bestseller list." She pointed at a garment bag draped over a nearby chair. "Dennis? Would you carry my black chef's coat to the bookstore?" Turning to me, she said, "I get so tired of wearing white. It shows every little stain."

I gestured for Klara and her entourage to follow me through the restaurant's rear exit. Leading them down back alleys and side streets, I tried to get Klara to the Constant Reader before the majority of the crowd arrived, but she insisted on walking at a leisurely pace.

"It's better if we make them wait," she explained. "Trust me, I have experience with this sort of thing. If there's a big line, it builds excitement. Besides, I need Annie to touch up my foundation and lipstick before I go inside. I'll have to pose for dozens of pictures during the signing."

"You're the boss," I told her breezily, but as we continued on I couldn't help but wonder if I could tolerate Klara's mercurial company all day long. I'd never met a woman who could behave with such warmth and sweetness one moment and then, in a flash, act completely selfish or cruel.

I glanced at Ryan out of the corner of my eye and considered what it was like for him, to be married to a successful, famous, and totally unpredictable person. I suppose there was never a dull moment for the spouse of Chef Klara, but I'd take my quiet, loving, and tender relationship with Sean over fame and theatrics any day.

Finally, we reached the bookstore's back door, where we paused while Klara donned her black coat and Annie fussed over her hair and makeup.

"I could use a cup of coffee," Klara said wistfully. "I didn't sleep well after what happened last night."

Ryan studied his wife sympathetically. "I knew it was bad when you left our hotel room in your pajamas and sneakers." He looked at me. "When she's upset or stressed, she'll take walks in the middle of the night. And then she'll get up the next morning and work a ten-hour day without breaking stride."

"That's show business," Dennis grumbled and shifted Klara's belongings from one arm to the other.

"Well, I'm sure we can find some coffee to perk you up. The Constant Reader is connected to the James Joyce Pub," I told Klara, unsure if she remembered seeing the bookstore the night before.

The scene inside the Constant Reader instantly buoyed my spirits. Scores of customers were in the shop, occupying every aisle and cozy nook of the rabbit warren–like store. Most of them already had Klara's cookbook in hand along with a few novels or how-to books on a host of subjects from making pottery to knitting to basket weaving. I also noticed that the section on regional gardening was nearly wiped out and I sensed that people were delighting in the temperate weather and, like me, dreamt of growing their own vegetable, herb, and flower gardens that could rival those in Monet's paintings.

"You made it!" Makayla exclaimed when I'd finally managed to wade through the crowd with Klara, Ryan, Annie, and Dennis. "I told Jay not to worry—that you'd be here any sec." She gestured at the man in the light gray sweater standing a few feet away from us.

Jay Coleman, owner of the Constant Reader, hastily finished assisting a customer and welcomed Klara to his bookshop.

"This is quite an honor," he said. He spoke in a low, reserved voice, but behind his Clark Kent glasses, his sky blue eyes sparkled with enthusiasm.

I'd only met Jay a few times since he'd purchased the store from the previous owner—a charming older gentleman who'd decided to retire and relocate to Arizona—but I could see that he'd made several changes over the past couple of months. The most noticeable was that he was no longer selling used books. He'd also replaced the well-worn recliners with leather club chairs and had added track lights to the ceiling. The walls had been painted a soothing moss green and a pair of wall speakers was piping out upbeat instrumental music. Before, the shop had been dimly lit, musty, and wonderfully cozy. Now, it felt clean and comfortable without losing any of its coziness, like a favorite blanket that had finally been washed.

"I didn't think the Constant Reader could possibly be improved," I admitted to Jay. "But that was before you made changes. Now, it's sheer perfection." I pivoted to take in the whole shop. "And I see you've expanded your romance and mystery sections. That's a wonderful thing for this literary agent to see."

He smiled shyly. "You represent mystery and romantic suspense authors, right?" He glanced over to where customers were eagerly browsing through the latest mystery releases. "They're my bestsellers. I read them all the time so that I can provide recommendations."

"Even the bodice-ripping kind?" Klara asked, clearly surprised to learn that a good-looking man in his early thirties spent his free time reading romantic suspense novels.

"That's a bit of a stereotype," Jay answered with the utmost respect, little spots of color blooming on his cheeks. He obviously didn't want to insult Klara, but I also guessed that he would champion any genre if he felt his beloved books were being slighted. "Personally, I like the historical romances. Those authors have conducted an incredible amount of research in order to transport their readers to another time and place and I'm always in awe of their talent."

Klara's eyes had glazed over. When Jay stopped talking, she made a big show of sniffing the air. "Is that the divine scent of coffee?"

"It is indeed. I'm Makayla, the proprietor of Espresso Yourself, a book-reading barista, and your angel of java for all the events scheduled at the Arts Center." Makayla held out a book to Klara. "Lila's told me so much about you that I just had to get you to autograph my brand-new copy of *My Grandmother's Hearth*." While Klara uncapped an expensive fountain pen, Makayla studied the celebrity chef's face, undoubtedly noticing the bags under Klara's eyes. "I'd love to treat you to the caffeinated beverage of your choice before you have to go up front and sign millions of copies of this fabulous cookbook. What'll you have?"

Preening, Klara gave Makayla her order and then headed to the sturdy wooden table where she would sit, regal as a queen, to greet fans, pose for pictures, and write her name in a flourish of black ink on the title page of *My Grandmother's Hearth*.

"You ordered so many of Joel's cookbook," she remarked to Jay ten minutes later. It didn't seem to matter that people were scooping up her book as fast as they could. Her eyes kept straying to the glossy cover of *Fusing Asian*. For a moment, I felt sorry for her. She was so obsessed with her competitor's possible success that she was unable to enjoy her own.

I chatted with a few of the bookstore patrons and then went behind the counter for a breather. Being near Makayla always improved my outlook and she didn't let me down. After pushing a caramel latte and a two-bite cinnamon streusel muffin in my direction, she handed a customer his change, and then beamed at him as he stuffed a dollar bill in her tip jar.

"Any new notes in there today?" I asked her.

"I got one yesterday and it's so gorgeous you'll want to cry!" She opened the portable cash box she used for off-site events and gingerly removed a crisp two-dollar bill from beneath a small pile of twenties. "Look how tiny the writing is."

The tidy print was too small for me to decipher without my reading glasses, so I slipped them on and murmured the lines of poetry aloud.

> *"A magic moment I remember:*
> *I raised my eyes and you were there.*
> *A fleeting vision, the quintessence*
> *Of all that's beautiful and rare."*

A small sigh escaped from between my lips and I looked up and smiled at Makayla. "Wow."

"I know," she replied. "The poem's 'A Magic Moment I Remember' by Alexander Pushkin. I've read it over and over again." She smoothed the paper currency with her fingertips, her eyes full of longing. "Whoever this guy is, he has exquisite taste."

"Obviously. He's in love with you, isn't he?"

Giving me a grateful smile, she stepped away to make a

café au lait for a woman who'd bought three copies of Klara's cookbook. Taking a sip of my sweet and deliciously creamy latte, I glanced to the front of the shop to see that Klara was still holding court and finally seemed to be enjoying herself. Jay's supply of *My Grandmother's Hearth* was rapidly disappearing. I decided I'd better see if he had more copies.

Jay was in the science-fiction and fantasy section, engaged in an animated conversation with a young man holding a copy of J. R. R. Tolkien's *The Return of the King*. Jay showed the enthusiastic reader a book called *The Dragonbone Chair* by Tad Williams and the young man nodded happily, grasped the book to his chest, and marched off in the direction of the checkout counter.

"It's nice to see that there are members of the next generation who don't spend all their waking time on Facebook," I said to Jay.

"Absolutely," he agreed. "And I don't believe the dire predictions about the future of the book. In whatever form it takes, the book will never disappear. Stories are too important to us. We can't live without them."

I nodded, admiring Jay's quiet passion. I felt exactly as he did. "Speaking of vanishing, do you have any more copies of Klara's book? I hate to use a cliché, but they're selling like hotcakes."

"Excellent. I've got another box tucked under the display table." He was just about to slide past me when I touched his arm. "I know this isn't the ideal time to ask, but do you recall anyone buying a book of love poetry recently?"

He paused to consider my question. "I sold a few back in February. A couple of guys bought them as Valentine's Day gifts, but I don't remember selling any lately. Are you look-ing for something in particular?"

I shook my head. "No, I was just wondering. Never mind me. I'm trying to help a friend solve a mystery." As Jay moved off, I stood there for a second. The mention of Valentine's Day made me smile and think of Sean, because he and I had already celebrated several holidays this year. I loved how we were slowly building memories together. And then, as if I had conjured him out of thin air, he was in the store, politely push-ing his way through a knot of book browsers.

His eyes locked on mine and all at once I felt like we were the only two people in that store. I could feel the inten-sity of his gaze, the pull of his body toward mine, and I wished we were alone so I could run to meet him. I wanted to throw my arms around his neck and tilt my face up to his so that he could kiss me. I wanted to forget about the chefs and last night's horror and get lost in his embrace, but I could see from his grim expression that he wasn't striding toward me out of desire, but out of concern. Or worse, out of fear.

"What's happened?" I asked the moment he drew along-side me.

He slid an arm around my waist and pulled me closer, wordlessly steering us to the back of the shop. His fingertips were pressing hard against my flesh and I could feel the ten-sion pulsing through them. Again, I whispered, "What's happened?"

Without answering, he led me into the storeroom and then closed the door behind us. In the cool, quiet space, populated only by stacks of cardboard boxes and wheeled carts loaded with books, he crushed me against him and then, just as abruptly, let me go.

"How is it that you always end up in the middle of my worst cases?" He tucked a strand of my hair behind my ear.

"Please, Sean." I couldn't take the suspense any longer. "You're obviously upset. Tell me why."

He released a heavy sigh. "I've just come from a meeting with the fire inspector. We've been over his findings a dozen times, but no matter how often we review the evidence, it doesn't change the fact that someone deliberately caused the explosion last night.

"What are you saying?" My question was a form of denial. I knew perfectly well what he meant. I just didn't want to believe it.

"Joel Lang's death was no accident," he said. "It was murder."

THE SHOCK OVER hearing the details about the explosion made for a restless night, causing me to arise later than I intended on Saturday morning. I was almost late for the "Food in Children's Literature" session at the Arts Center. I hurried through the crowded lobby toward the Ladybug Room. Attendees milled about looking at the displays, chatting, and showing one another books they'd purchased. Other than the yellow tape blocking the way to the kitchen wing, there was no indication that a tragedy had occurred in this building the night before. It seemed incongruous that the Books and Cooks festival continued and that people were enjoying themselves when a man had been brutally murdered just beyond that tape.

Quietly opening the door to the Ladybug Room, I let myself in, gratified to see groups of children immersed in the activities. In one corner sat author Caleb Herman, Flora's latest success story, reading to a captivated circle of kids from his current picture book, *Cookies for Critters*. Plush bugs littered the floor and each child was munching on a cookie.

"Oatmeal for the octopus," Caleb read, and a small, African-American boy held up a fuzzy purple octopus.

"Yum yum," the boy said as he put the cookie to the mouth of the toy octopus.

As I glanced over the titles of the books stacked on tables in the center of the room, Flora approached me. She wore a hat with long red woolen braids attached under the rim and was carrying a tray laden with plastic cups filled with red juice.

"Isn't this fun?" she said. "I just love all this youthful energy. It helps to keep my mind off poor Joel Lang." She shook her head, swinging the braids back and forth.

I wondered if I should brief Flora on what Sean had told me about Joel's murder. Somehow, it didn't seem right to weigh down the lighthearted atmosphere in the room by sharing my burden with Flora right now. The news could wait. I glanced at a table set up by the far wall, where a cluster of children was helping Big Ed make stone soup by throwing chopped vegetables into a pot while Ed stirred. "Soon, we'll heat this up and you'll taste the most delicious soup ever, you little munchkins," he announced with a boisterous laugh. His audience giggled along with him.

Turning back to Flora, I touched her arm. "The session certainly looks popular. What a great way to get the kids involved. Good job, Flora."

She nodded and held out the tray. "Would you like some of Anne Shirley's raspberry cordial?"

"Ah, so that's why you're wearing that hat. You're Anne of Green Gables," I suddenly realized. "I loved that book. But wait, didn't Anne get her friend Diana drunk on raspberry cordial? Should we be serving that to minors?"

"Oh no, dear," Flora tittered. "She got Diana drunk on Marilla's currant wine, which she *thought* was raspberry cordial. I would never give anything so potent to these children."

"I guess I should reread the book. I had forgotten that," I said as I took one of the cups. "Although I do remember how Anne nearly lost her best friend because of her mistake. Anne was always so theatrical, but I used to quote her lines all the time." I placed my hand on my heart. "'My heart is broken. The stars in their courses fight against me, Marilla. Diana and I are parted forever.'" I sighed. "My teenage heart broke for Anne in that passage, even if she was given to dramatics."

Flora nodded. "When I was twelve, I emulated Anne as well."

Sipping the tart beverage, I followed the aroma of pancakes and frying eggs to the back of the room, where two food preparers from How Green Was My Valley, our local grocery store, were cooking up treats on large griddles on a counter. The counter was on a platform well above the tables at which their audience of kids and their parents were seated, ensuring that no little fingers could get burnt. A large mirror hung overhead so everyone could see what was happening on the counter.

"I *like* green eggs and ham," declared one of the cooks, a thin, tall man dressed in a raggedy yellow shift and a red top hat. Except for his face and hair, he was a perfect mimic of Sam-I-Am from the famous Dr. Seuss book. As he spoke, he carefully separated egg yolks from their whites and placed them in a bowl.

"I do, too, but my pancakes are even better," the other cook said as she removed several crepe-like pancakes from a special skillet and placed them on a plate. A petite young woman, she wore a red and white striped sweater, a blue jean jumper, and red and white striped stockings. Her long red hair, shaped into two braided pigtails, stuck out at wonky angles from the sides of her head. She looked as if she had stepped out of the pages of a Pippi Longstocking book. I wondered how she made her braids stick out like that. Wire, maybe? Or gel? She handed the plate of pancakes to Nell from Sixpence Bakery, who was dressed in her baker's coat and chef's hat.

"Who wants to try some?" Nell asked, holding up the plate.

"Me! Me!" came the reply in a chorus from the audience, and Nell distributed pancakes to the eager children.

Pippi turned back to Sam-I-Am. "So how do you make the eggs green?" she asked.

"Yeah, how?" echoed a little blond girl at a table in the front.

Sam-I-Am held up the bowl of egg yolks. "You see how I separated the egg yolks from the whites? Now I'll add this basil pesto to the whites and mix it in and then we'll pour these little suns back into the whites, being careful not to break them." He proceeded to do as he described, and then slowly poured the concoction onto the griddle. I looked at the surface of the griddle in the mirror. A sea of green egg whites with bright yellow circles spread and sizzled. Sam-I-Am sprinkled what appeared to be dried parsley onto the yolks, speckling them with green. "And now we wait for them to cook and then we can cut them apart with this round cookie cutter. And let's paint a bit of pesto onto these ham slices, too."

I leaned against the wall and watched him create his version of green eggs and ham. As interesting as this was, my mind inadvertently left the culinary world of Dr. Seuss and began to process my conversation with Sean.

Joel had been murdered! The details Sean had divulged from the fire inspector's report made it a certainty. The inspector concluded that the wall oven had exploded and killed him. The oven was installed at Joel's height and the force of the eruption threw the oven door into his sternum. It flung him, no doubt in terrible agony, ten feet away.

"So there was something wrong with the oven?" I had asked, clinging to the distorted hope that it was the fault of the equipment and not the maliciousness of another human being.

Sean shook his head. "No. Someone had placed several cans of nonstick cooking spray inside the oven, which provided more than adequate combustion. Nobody would store them in an oven unless they were trying to cause an explosion. Apparently, Mr. Lang had turned the oven to broil, and in a matter of minutes, it got hot enough to detonate the cans."

"So if he had checked inside the oven before turning it on, he would have noticed them and still be alive?" In the back of my mind, I recalled my mother once drying a pair of damp hiking socks in her oven, using the heat of the pilot light, and forgetting she'd put them in there. The next day she preheated the oven to bake banana bread and burned her socks. Ever since that incident, I have always checked my oven before turning it on.

Sean shrugged. "It's possible, but the saboteur also tampered with the gas connection inside the oven. Therefore, for a period of time, gas was flowing into the oven, and it would have exploded anyway once it got hot enough. Between the aerosol cans and the gas, the killer was taking no chances at failure."

"But gas has such a noticeable odor. Wouldn't Joel have smelled it when he walked into the kitchen?"

Sean shrugged. "The oven door was closed. And these newer models seal quite efficiently. Maybe Mr. Lang was so focused on what he was doing that he didn't notice."

We stared at each other for a few minutes without saying anything. I envisioned Joel's last moments—his anxiety about his dishes following Klara's criticism and his determination to prove himself with his food. He could easily have been distracted enough to simply turn the knob on the oven before rubbing his tuna with Szechuan pepper. And then, while he prepared his food, the oven exploded, ripping off the door, throwing fire at Joel and hurling him to the floor in excruciating pain.

I flinched, as if the flames had been surrounding us.

Sean had put his arms around me and hugged tight. "Just be careful," he whispered in my ear. "Someone in this group of egotistical chefs bore enough of a grudge against Joel Lang to want him dead and had the boldness to carry it out. Someone at this festival is a murderer."

A tugging on my sweater pulled me away from Sean and back into the Ladybug Room. The little boy with the plush octopus held his toy up to me. "Thee my otoputh?" he lisped. His large brown eyes were wide with innocent delight. "My mama bought him for me."

"Come on, Matty. Don't bother the lady." His mother, standing behind him, held out her hand.

"Oh, he's no bother," I said as I crouched down to his level, glad of the distraction from my distressing recollections. "Does he have a name?"

"Uh-huh. It'th Thilly Otoputh." He giggled and ran to the door, waving his eight-armed toy in the air. His mother followed, and as I watched them head into the hall I felt an overwhelming urge to hug Trey, who'd had the same adorable lisp when he was young. Unable to do so, I'd have to settle for a phone call.

As I pulled my cell phone out of my purse, Franklin appeared at the door, stepping aside to let Matty and his mother through, and then entered, scanning the occupants until his gaze rested on me. I waved.

"Did you hear?" he asked as he approached. "Joel's death was intentional. Someone deliberately caused the explosion."

"Sean told me. But I'm having a hard time coping with the news. Who would want him dead? Who hated him enough to blow him up? And why?" As I asked the questions, the faces of the chefs and their assistants crowded my head. I slipped the phone back into my bag, no longer wanting to call Trey. He would only worry and become distracted from his studies.

"I don't know. I find it difficult to imagine that anyone could be so vindictive and inhuman." Franklin squeezed his temples, as if to push away a headache. "The police are going to question everyone, including all the agents."

Sean had told me that, too. It was ludicrous, of course. He knew that none of us had any motive to kill Joel. "I guess the authorities can't afford to overlook anything or anyone who's been in contact with Joel since the festival started."

"True. I just hope they catch whoever did it quickly."

"Me, too. Joel's killer not only took the life of another human being," I said, suddenly feeling angry. "They also affected the festival, damaged the Arts Center, and cast a shadow of evil over Inspiration Valley."

Chapter 6

AS SOON AS THE CHILDREN'S PROGRAM WAS FINISHED, I planned to retreat to the peace and quiet of my office at Novel Idea. Flora told me that she also intended to head over to the agency after grabbing something for lunch. She kindly offered to pick up a sandwich for me and I accepted, though in truth I wasn't very hungry. I'd been surrounded by food most of the morning, but my appetite had been quelled by the news about Joel Lang.

I had two hours until I needed to return to the Arts Center and moderate a panel called "Killer Tales From the Kitchen." Two of my clients, a pair of gregarious cozy mystery authors, would be joining three of the celebrity chefs (Klara Patrick, Leslie Sterling, and Bryce St. John) and a renowned food critic to address the joys and challenges of writing about food. This would be followed by a lengthy question and answer session in which the members of the audience could query the panelists about their professional experiences.

It would take a great deal of energy to moderate this panel, and even though I'd be sharing the responsibility with Jude, I was grateful to have a brief respite before it started. I stayed to help Flora clean up after the kids program, waved good-bye to the guest author, and then headed for the front door.

A swarm of laughing children burst past me, racing toward the main entrance of the Arts Center while their parents shouted for them to wait. Watching them made me smile and when I stepped into the spring sunshine, I felt lighter and more hopeful. Yes, Joel Lang had been murdered and there was a killer on the loose, but I had to decide how to handle myself in the face of these dire truths. Was I going to spend the future glancing over my shoulder in fear, or was I going to do my best to ensure that the rest of the festival was a resounding success?

"I have to be tough for my town and my agency," I said, addressing the Taste of the Town banner hanging from the nearest streetlamp.

Strong and determined, I walked briskly to where I'd parked my scooter. Just the sight of its bright yellow paint gave me a zap of positive energy, and yet, even from a distance, I could see that something was hanging from the Vespa's handlebars. Something that hadn't been there before.

"What the—?" I murmured to myself, feeling slightly anxious.

Drawing alongside the scooter, I could see that the mystery object was a paper gift bag—the kind sold in any stationery or grocery store. This one, however, was covered in what looked to be hand-drawn stencils of an old-fashioned quill pen.

Inside, I found a tissue paper-wrapped bundle. I carefully unfolded the small package, revealing a necklace with a purple crystal pendant. The crystal, which winked in the midday sunlight, was held in place by delicate silver wire. Attached to the wire was a dainty stainless steel chain that felt cool in the palm of my hand. Intrigued, I peeked inside the bag again and noticed a sheet of paper tucked into a corner. It was rolled up into a tight cylinder and tied with an indigo ribbon.

Sliding the ribbon free, I unfurled the letter and began to read.

Dear Ms. Wilkins,

This is my own unique way of delivering my query to you. Everyone in town knows that you drive a yellow scooter and so I thought that instead of sending this with a boring stamp and plain envelope, I'd tell you about my novel in a more creative way. The whole process will work better if you wear the crystal. It's an amethyst and the regal purple crystal represents creativity, imagination, and intuition. I know that your intuition is amazing because of all the wonderful authors you represent, but everyone could use a special boost now and then. So now that you've got your energizing necklace on (you have it on, right?) you're properly centered and energized and ready to hear about my book.

My novel is called The Crystal Color Wheel Witch *and it's about a woman named Jade who's studied the*

powers of crystals but decides to use them to make her-
self beautiful, younger looking, and richer instead of
helping other people develop their spiritual selves. Jade
is a yoga teacher and she's tired of making a crummy
salary and spending all of her free time sanitizing other
people's dirty yoga mats. One day, she decides to kill
another instructor by making a hot yoga class really
hot. Deathly hot.

I stopped reading and tucked the paper back into the gift bag. I then eyed the necklace on my palm with slight revulsion. There was something creepy about having an aspiring writer leave a token and a query letter attached to my scooter. Not only was it unprofessional, but it also felt incredibly invasive. I'd heard other agents tell stories of being stalked, but those cases usually occurred in the streets of Manhattan and ended up with the hopeful author being permanently blackballed in the writing community. The literary agent network was closely knit and all of us kept an *Agent Beware* file. There was no doubt that this query was going straight into that folder.

Shoving the entire bag into my purse, I put my helmet on and eased the Vespa into the slow-moving traffic. At the first red light, I glanced around and saw that most of the drivers had their windows down and their radios turned way up. The country twang being piped out of a battered truck competed with the rhythmic bass of hip-hop from an SUV while the occupant of a Lexus sedan swayed in time to Vivaldi, his expression one of dreamy contentment.

Following his gaze, I took in the sunny faces of the daffodils crowded in the oversized terracotta pots lining the sidewalks and inhaled the scents of freshly cut grass and peonies. The pear trees were dressed in silky white petals, and bluebirds and robins darted among their branches. Pedestrians strolled down the sidewalks with a light, easy gait, and laughter floated in the soft currents of air.

No one was in a hurry. No one wore a frown. The people of Inspiration Valley had been infected by spring fever, and everyone I saw seemed to be enjoying a carefree Saturday.

"'The peace and beauty of a spring day had descended upon the earth like a benediction,'" I proclaimed to my fellow motorists, quoting a line from Kate Chopin's short story "The Locket." However, my voice was drowned out by the sounds of their own crooning, steering wheel drumming, or beat boxing.

I tried to hold on to the feeling of benediction as I climbed the stairs to Novel Idea's offices, but the moment I reached the top, the warmth of the spring sun vanished with the suddenness of a spent match. For there was Sean, dressed in uniform, notepad in hand, standing over Vicky's desk in a rigid posture that told me this was no friendly visit. My boyfriend was questioning my coworker and though I'd been anticipating a police presence in the agency, I was hoping to first eat a quiet lunch at my desk while reading through emails.

"Hello," I said, including both Sean and Vicky in my greeting. "What's going on?"

"We're interviewing everyone at Novel Idea," Sean answered. His tone was strictly professional and served as a reminder that he was here in an official capacity, not to visit with me. And with a murderer on the loose in Inspiration Valley, Sean clearly had little time for pleasantries. "I'd like you and Vicky to join us in the conference room. My team is trying to gather all the information we can on the people who knew Joel Lang and had access to the kitchen at the Arts Center. The members of this agency have had the most contact with Mr. Lang's fellow chefs. Franklin in particular. He's the agent to most of the guest chefs, correct?"

"That is correct," Vicky said, sitting as erect in her chair as a soldier at attention.

"Then he should prove very useful," Sean continued. "But we'd like to hear everything there is to know about the chefs—every impression, piece of gossip, or detail, no matter how small."

I nodded solemnly and followed Sean and Vicky into the conference room. A cop about fifteen years Sean's junior had pulled a chair into the corner of the room and sat with a notebook open on his lap. He had obviously positioned himself so that he could observe all that happened in the room. Meanwhile, a pretty female officer in her mid twenties whom I recognized from a previous investigation finished drawing a series of lines on our whiteboard. The names of all the guest chefs had already been printed in neat block letters on each line. Officer Burke replaced the cap of the dry-erase marker and looked at Sean expectantly.

"I see neither Mrs. Meriweather nor Mr. Cohen have arrived yet," Sean said, casting his gaze around the room.

"Flora's grabbing some lunch," I explained. "I don't know where Zach is."

"He's needed elsewhere," Bentley stated tersely. "If he doesn't spin this to our advantage with our media contacts, they're certain to ruin this festival. And we've worked far too hard to have that happen."

Sean stared at her, incredulous. "With all due respect, Ms. Burlington-Duke, a man has been murdered. I believe my request was to gather your employees here without delay. No exceptions." He lowered his voice to a dangerous growl. "I could have insisted on having everyone come to the police station in Dunston, but I was trying to make things easier on all of us. The best way to protect the people who are attending the festival is to apprehend Mr. Lang's killer. For that, I need the cooperation of this agency. That sounds reasonable, doesn't it?"

Bentley was unfazed by Sean's icy tone. "It does, yes. However, Zach will be of little help, as he doesn't know these chefs from Adam. Franklin, Lila, and Vicky are the only agents who can aid you on that score. I'm simply sitting in on this meeting because they are in my employ and the chefs listed on that whiteboard are the clients of my agency. I want to make sure that none of them are subjected to frontier-style justice."

Sean's brow darkened with anger and I felt indignant on his behalf.

"Officer Griffiths has investigated a homicide involving this agency before," I reminded Bentley, doing my best to sound calm and impartial. "He's always treated everyone fairly and with the utmost courtesy and professionalism."

Bentley peered at me over the rim of her lilac reading glasses and was silent for a long moment. Finally, she removed her glasses and rubbed her temples. "You're right, Lila," she said and then turned to Sean. "I apologize, Officer Griffiths. I must admit that I'm feeling rather unsettled in light of the news that the gas explosion at the Arts Center was deliberate and that its purpose was to murder a man we invited to Inspiration Valley as an honored guest. I feel . . . responsible."

"We all do," I told her softly. "But what we need to focus on now is catching the person who truly *is* responsible."

Sean shot me a fleeting look of gratitude before taking a seat between Bentley and Vicky. "Let's start by discussing Maurice Bruneau. Mr. Bruneau told us that he and Mr. Lang were once business partners, and that they had a falling out over how their restaurant should be run and went their separate ways. Mr. Bruneau feels that he's the superior cook, though he admitted to being envious of Mr. Lang's cookbook successes and his forthcoming cookbook release." He gestured at the whiteboard. "The question is, was Mr. Bruneau's jealousy consuming him? Was it powerful enough to convince him to commit murder?" He locked eyes with Franklin.

Franklin wrung his hands together and I realized what a difficult position he was in. The names on the board belonged to his clients, to men and women he'd known for years. He was invested in their futures and he was a part of their pasts. He'd listened to their hopes and dreams, had negotiated their contracts, critiqued their proposals, and had counseled them on their careers. I also suspected that he'd been a friend to each and every one of them.

"Every author wants his or her work to do better than everyone else's," Franklin finally said. "But no, I don't think Maurice or anyone else on that board would have killed Joel because they felt threatened by his possible success. They've all been in this business long enough to know how capricious a mistress Success is. One day she's in your corner and the next she's in someone else's. She's as slippery as an eel, if you'll forgive the cliché."

"I'm sure that's true, but I'd like to concentrate on Mr. Bruneau for the moment," Sean said. He searched Franklin's face and was clearly poised to push the subject of Maurice further.

Sensing the weight of Sean's gaze, Franklin straightened his bow tie and murmured, "There are some things I'd rather remain confidential. Not everything about the private lives of my clients should be laid bare for all to see and judge."

After a brief pause, Sean nodded. "All right, we can discuss Mr. Bruneau in greater length later. You and I can meet in your office after we're done here." Franklin relaxed a fraction and nodded gratefully. "And what of Ms. Patrick?" Sean continued. "Was her competition with Mr. Lang as superficial as Mr. Bruneau's would appear?"

Franklin released a pent-up breath and I wondered why he was so eager to move away from the topic of Maurice. As Franklin spoke of Klara's obsession with the *New York Times* bestseller list, I thought back on the few times I'd seen Maurice and Joel in close contact. I realized that the two men interacted with a great deal more emotion than was warranted by a broken business partnership. There was something deeper between them, a lingering wound that I believed to be the result of one thing and one thing only: a broken heart.

Suddenly, their strained behavior and pained expressions made sense. The mentor relationship that had brought the two men together must have grown into a more intimate relationship. A romantic one, most likely. And when Joel struck out on his own, Maurice had lost more than a friend and associate. If my assumptions were correct, he'd lost a lover as well.

I wondered how to raise the subject without putting Franklin on the spot. I sensed that he didn't want to talk about a romantic partnership between the two male chefs because he was involved in a secret relationship of his own. Franklin never spoke of his partner to anyone. In fact, he didn't talk about his private life at all if he could help it and made a concerted effort to hide his homosexuality. I only knew about the good-looking music teacher he was dating because I'd blatantly spied on my unsuspecting coworker a few months ago. I told myself then that I'd had to pry because I was investigating a crime. Now here I was again, involved in a new investigation, and I couldn't remain silent.

"Excuse me," I said after Vicky had finished describing her impressions of Klara Patrick. "But can we go back to Maurice for a moment? I have to say that when I saw him with Joel, I got the feeling that they'd been much more than business associates at one point and that their partnership hadn't ended well." I kept my eyes on Sean, hoping to spare Franklin any discomfort. "And I'm not referring to their restaurant."

Sean looked intently at me first and then turned to Franklin. I followed his gaze. My coworker reached inside his suit jacket and withdrew a silk handkerchief. He delicately dabbed his brow and then stared at the embroidered initials on the cream-colored material. Hurriedly, he wadded the handkerchief into a ball. "Yes," he said stiffly. "They were a couple until Joel decided to spread his wings. He wanted to try new dishes and create an ever-evolving menu and visit food markets around the world. He was determined to take chances, to experiment. Maurice didn't want that. He was happy with the status quo."

Sean rubbed his chin thoughtfully. "It must have been difficult for Mr. Bruneau to have his former lover and protégé flourishing on his own. The question is, was he angry enough to take a life? To ensure that Mr. Lang would never outshine him again?"

"No," Franklin insisted. "Maurice is passionate. He's a Frenchman and a chef. But he's no killer. He loved Joel. Still does, or did, if you ask me. And he's grieving over Joel's death, though he's doing his best not to show it. He told me that he only wanted to take Joel's place in today's cooking demonstrations to honor him." Franklin held out his hands, palms up. "And consider, Officer Griffiths, that Maurice has little to gain by killing Joel. Their partnership had already been dissolved. I can't see anyone rigging a gas explosion to earn a ten-minute television slot and that's all Maurice gained from Joel's passing."

Sean considered Franklin's argument in silence and then nodded. "Then who does benefit? I've been told that the kitchen remained unlocked after Ms. Wilkins had finished her tour of the Arts Center. Anyone who went on the tour could have studied the layout and then returned later that afternoon to place the cans of cooking spray inside the oven. The building's staff had access, too, but my team has already interviewed these individuals and none of them have raised our suspicions, so let's focus on our visiting chefs for now."

We all looked at the names on the board.

Again, I had to speak up. "Klara seemed pretty obsessed with her cookbook outselling Joel's. She made a few nasty remarks about him and though I don't think that makes her a suspect, I have to admit that several of the chefs seem to be a bit duplicitous."

"Oh, please." Bentley groaned in exasperation. "They're TV personalities! So you saw Klara's mask slip a little," she said to me. "You saw a crack in Maurice's façade. These people have artistic temperaments, just like many of our authors. They can be petty and jealous and insecure, but they're not villains. They're *artists.*"

"And yet one of them probably murdered Joel," murmured Jude as he doodled on a notepad. He seemed very removed from the discussion.

"Do you have anything to add, Mr. Hudson?" Sean gazed inquiringly at Jude.

Jude shook his head. "Not really. I haven't had specific dealings with the chefs since none of them are my clients. My main experience with them has been on the periphery, and my observations are on par with everyone else's. They may be artists." He glanced at Bentley. "But most of them struck me as egotistical and self-centered, and while murdering one of their own is extreme, I could well imagine them having it in for one another."

The room was struck silent by the sudden slam of the door downstairs, followed by echoing footsteps slowly climbing the steps. We all turned toward the doorway to see who had arrived, and Flora appeared, panting in exertion. She carried a carton in one hand containing bottles of Cheerwine, her favorite cherry-flavored soda. In her other hand she held a paper sack from which emanated tantalizing aromas of mozzarella, tomatoes, and basil, the ingredients of my sandwich order, Pinocchio's Panini. The aromas aroused my dormant appetite.

"Oh, you're all here!" Flora exclaimed. "I brought lunch for Lila, but not for anyone else. I'll share my Cheerwine with you though." Then she noticed Sean and the other two police officers. "Hello, Officer Griffiths. What are we doing?" She glanced around the room.

Sean pulled out a chair. "Ms. Meriweather, please have a seat. We're interviewing everyone who has had contact with the chefs, and I'd like to hear what you might have to contribute."

"Contribute?" She placed the take-out bag in front of me and sat down. Clearing her throat, Flora said, "I do have something to tell you about Klara."

"Anything you've noticed might be helpful," prompted Sean.

"Well, I'm not one to spread stories." Flora stared at her hands. "But after the Arts Center tour, I witnessed Klara and Bryce St. John engaged in an . . . activity . . . that makes it unlikely that either of them could have rigged the explosion before dinner."

Sean's brow furrowed. "What kind of activity?"

Flora fidgeted with the cuff of her sleeve. "When I was walking home to get ready for the dinner, I passed Bertram's Hotel and saw them go in together. I went after them because I thought that maybe they had mistakenly gone to the wrong hotel. But when I entered the lobby . . ." Her cheeks flushed bright pink. "They were kissing. And Bryce was squeezing Klara in places where a person would never touch a colleague. I snuck back out before they saw me."

Shocked, I sat back in my seat. Were Klara and Bryce having an affair? Klara had given me the impression that she was completely devoted to her husband. Was that all an act? Could she be that duplicitous? The woman I was getting to know over the last few days did not mesh with the chef I had admired on the television screen. My mother's warning about her rang in my ears. How had she known?

"When exactly was this? Do you know the time?" Sean inquired. "And did you see them leave the hotel?"

Flora's hands went to her cheeks, as if to cool them. "Like I said, it was right after our tour. Four-thirtyish perhaps? I was one of the first ones to leave the Arts Center, and they had gone before me. And I didn't linger at the hotel after I'd followed them inside either. I went home to change." She shifted in her seat. "I don't want to tell tales when I don't have all the facts, but they were headed up the stairs when they were behaving so . . . so amorously. The stairs lead to the guest rooms. The hotel doesn't have an elevator, you know."

Vicky frowned. "Do you mean to say that they checked into the hotel together? Klara, who is supposedly happily married, and that handsome chef?"

Flora shrugged. "I don't know for sure, but that's what it looked like to me."

Sean glanced up at the whiteboard where Officer Burke was writing beside Klara's name, *Alibi—Bertram's Hotel?* He said, "If they were otherwise occupied at the hotel, then that would certainly provide an alibi for the two of them." He turned to the officer in the corner. "Rick, when we're finished here, go to the inn and check out their registration records."

The policeman nodded and wrote on his notepad.

Sean checked his watch. "Does anyone care to add anything?" He gazed intently at each of us in turn, his blue eyes staying on mine just a tad longer than the rest. We all shook our heads.

"I believe we've told you all we know," Bentley said. "If

there's nothing else . . ." She scraped back her chair and stood.

Sean and the other two police officers got to their feet as well and went to the door. "Thank you all for your time," Sean said, pulling it open. "I'll keep you informed as our investigation develops. And I'll be back to speak with Mr. Cohen."

When they had gone, we let out a collective sigh, as if a tension release button had been pushed.

"Flora, I can't believe that Klara and Bryce would be so blatant about their affair," I said. "You'd think they'd be afraid of getting caught."

"It is quite a revelation," Franklin said sadly. "I must admit that Bryce's actions don't surprise me, as he can be a bit of a ladies' man. But Klara's involvement has me stunned."

"And what about Ryan?" I asked no one in particular. "I wonder what he'll do when he finds out, because I don't think Klara's affair can stay a secret now that it's part of the investigation." My heart went out to the man who was working hard to prepare for his wife's next event while she was in the arms of another man. Would his world be shattered?

"Perhaps he knows about it," suggested Bentley. "Maybe they have an open marriage."

Franklin shook his head. "No, I don't think that's the case. I have spent many hours with the two of them, and I am convinced that Ryan believes wholeheartedly in his monogamous marriage to Klara." He rubbed his forehead. "How can people betray one another like that?"

Jude leaned forward on his elbows. "I realize Klara couldn't have sabotaged the oven, but even from what little time I've spent in her presence, I'd say she's more than capable of hurting another person."

"What makes you think so?" I asked. Jude's statement irritated me and I felt the need to defend Klara, even though her behavior distressed me as well. The image that I had built in my mind of the talented, gregarious, and friendly chef was shattering. I was dismayed to discover that she was both arrogant and deceitful. However, Jude was making an assumption that went beyond those characteristics.

"I had coffee with her assistant yesterday. Annie is sweet and quite cute." Jude grinned. Of course he would have tried to cozy up to Klara's attractive assistant. I rolled my eyes. "Anyway," he continued. "She told me stories about Klara. The way she treats her staff, and even her peers, makes me think that Chef Klara cares about only one person. Herself. And she's so ambitious, I don't think she'd let anybody get in her way to the top."

"But she was busy with Bryce St. John," Vicky countered. "So she couldn't have caused the explosion."

Flora sighed. "Well, if it wasn't Klara, and Franklin is convinced that it wasn't Maurice—an opinion I agree with, by the way—then who murdered Joel?"

Who indeed. Suddenly, everyone began talking at once. Voices got louder as my colleagues became more and more animated. I looked from one to the other. This was not the peace and quiet I'd sought when I returned to Novel Idea for a respite. Eager to escape the fray, I grabbed my lunch and headed for the calm of my own office.

Chapter 7

I MANAGED TO READ A DOZEN EMAILS AND WOLF DOWN half of the panini sandwich Flora had brought me before Sean poked his head into my office.

"I'm meeting with Franklin in private and he requested that you be there, too. He said that, unlike the rest of his coworkers, you tend to reserve judgment until you have the facts, and he'd like a friend present when he tells me more of Mr. Bruneau's story. Would you join us now?"

Moved by Franklin's faith in me, I took a final swig of Cheerwine to wash away the taste of basil, tomato, and mozzarella and stood up. "Of course."

Franklin was pacing between the window and the file cabinet when we stepped into his office. He paused when Sean and I entered, but after indicating that we should sit in the two chairs facing his desk, he clasped his hands behind his back and continued to walk a straight path from one end of the room to the other.

"Maurice has always had a flair for the dramatic," he began, his gaze fixed on the carpet as if he were fascinated by its diamond pattern. "He makes over-the-top, passionate, and theatrical declarations all the time. Later, he'll recant each and every one, claiming that he was caught up in the heat of the moment. I've learned not to take them seriously."

Sean nodded to show that he was listening, but didn't speak. I'd been present for interviews before and knew that this was intentional. Sean believed that silence was often a useful catalyst. Silence could weigh heavily on a person with a secret to share. It could fill the air with a powerful presence, coaxing an individual into speech. I could see that Franklin was responding to the quiet. It clearly made him uncomfortable for he quickly straightened his bow tie, continued his pacing, and began to talk again.

"I believe this weekend has proved to be quite a challenge for Maurice." He stopped and turned to Sean. "I'm not making excuses for him because he's my client, Officer Griffiths. I just wanted you to know that one cannot always take his statements as gospel."

This time Sean chose not to remain mute. "Could you give an example of something Mr. Bruneau said that pertains to my investigation of Mr. Lang's murder?"

There it was. He hadn't danced around his purpose in order to make things easier for Franklin. There was a killer in Inspiration Valley, and Sean needed Franklin to share what he knew without further equivocation.

Franklin cleared his throat. "Yesterday, I heard Maurice

tell a few of the other chefs that Joel was nothing without him. But to me, he confessed that he missed Joel terribly—that no one had such a profound understanding of food, love, and beauty as his former partner did. That he'd do anything to win him back."

"What a sweet thing to say," I blurted.

"So it would seem," Franklin answered solemnly. "However, no sooner had those words crossed his lips, then Maurice transformed from the remorseful ex-lover to an angry and envious rival. He declared that if Joel didn't return to him, begging for forgiveness, that he would see his ex ruined. He'd make sure Joel's life was reduced to . . ." He couldn't seem to complete the sentence. Touching his throat, as if the rest of the thought had gotten lodged there, he looked to Sean for help.

Sean leaned forward in his chair and said, "It's all right, Mr. Stafford. I'm not going to rush out and slap handcuffs on Mr. Bruneau because of what you say. I just need to gather all the information I can to have a clear view of this case. Please. Go on."

"Maurice said that Joel's career would go up in flames and his life would be reduced to a pile of ashes," Franklin said rapidly, as if he couldn't hold on to the words a second longer.

"When was this comment made?" Sean asked.

"A few minutes before we went into dinner at the Arts Center," Franklin muttered unhappily. "Bryce and Joel were discussing Joel's upcoming cookbook release and I think it was too much for Maurice. He just issued those threats in a fit of temper and envy. They were empty threats, I'm sure of it. And he only uttered them to me."

Considering how Joel had died, I couldn't share Franklin's faith in his client, but Sean approached my coworker and put a hand on his arm. "Thank you for being forthright. I promise to question Mr. Bruneau without prejudice."

Franklin was obviously relieved by Sean's gentleness. Thanking him, he locked eyes with me. "I meant what I said earlier about Klara Patrick. I know you've long been a fan of hers, Lila, but she's more likely to act on her insecurities and jealousy than Maurice. Have you noticed the cracks in her façade? Most unsettling."

"I have to admit that she isn't exactly the person I thought she was," I admitted with genuine regret. "It was naïve of me to assume that she'd be as warm and charming as she is on television. As Bentley said, these folks are TV personalities. The key word is 'personalities.' Klara can be delightful, but I've also seen her being cruel, petty, and envious. Does that make her a murder suspect? I don't know. After all, she has an alibi. You heard what Flora said about Klara and Bryce St. John."

Franklin drew his brows together in thought. "I did, yes, but Officer Griffiths mentioned a rather significant window of time in which a determined person could easily slip into the Arts Center kitchen and place a few cans of cooking spray in the oven." He held out his hands in an expression of helplessness. "Believe me, I don't want to point the finger at any of our clients, but Klara did goad Joel during our group dinner. It was as if she deliberately planted seeds of doubt regarding his menu. Those seeds grew with such swiftness that Joel felt compelled to practice his dishes before heading back to his hotel."

"We're just exchanging theories," I complained to Sean.

"There's no evidence against either chef, right? All we have is proof that neither Maurice nor Klara were saints."

"I need to speak with both chefs," Sean said. "In my experience, envy and anger are two emotions that can slowly consume a person, overpowering their goodness and their ability to think clearly until eventually, they do something rash. I'm hoping to peek behind both Mr. Bruneau's and Ms. Patrick's masks, and the sooner the better. Thank you, Mr. Stafford." Sean shook Franklin's hand and then gestured for me to follow him out of my coworker's office. I took a moment to give Franklin's arm a comforting squeeze before leaving, and he managed a small smile of gratitude.

In the corridor, Sean stopped and, after glancing up and down the hall to make sure we were alone, tucked a strand of hair behind my ear. "What are you thinking?"

"Of a John Updike quote, actually. He said, 'Celebrity is a mask that eats into the face.'"

Sean grimaced. "Sounds like *Phantom of the Opera*."

I nodded. "Franklin was right. There's something ugly inside Klara. When Flora revealed that Klara is conducting an affair right under her husband's nose, I realized that she might be one of those people who believe that they don't have to play by societal rules. Klara might consider herself above such conventions. Or the law."

"That's what I'm afraid of," Sean said. "And I would like you to be present when I question her. Act like you're on her side. Give her the impression you're there to defend her sterling reputation, and if you can, convince her to speak freely to me. I want her to feel comfortable and confident. No matter what she says, her body language will give her away if she's lying." His hand dropped from my hair to my shoulder.

"Should I remind you that Klara Patrick is a client of this agency? Your boss may not approve of your helping me."

"That's too bad for her," I declared firmly. "A man's been killed. If Klara or any of our other clients is guilty, then I don't care how much money they've made the agency or how famous they are. Joel deserves justice, and I intend to see that he gets it."

Sean gazed at me, pride shining from his blue eyes. There was a trace of amusement there, too. "You are so beautiful when you're on a case, Detective Wilkins."

My cheeks grew warm. "Sorry, I didn't mean to sound like some kind of B-movie action hero. Are we going to talk to Klara at the station or someplace more relaxed?"

"According to the itinerary Vicky gave me, Ms. Patrick was scheduled to have a late lunch with her staff before this afternoon's panel. If we're lucky, she'll be lingering at a patio table at the James Joyce."

Pausing to grab my purse from my office, I glanced at him in surprise. "How do you know she's dining alfresco?"

Sean smiled. "Because Vicky has been receiving updates on Klara's whereabouts from Annie all day and has been passing those on to me per my request. Your office manager is a marvel. I could use her at the station."

"Don't even think of trying to steal Vicky away from us," I warned. "If it weren't for her, I'd be spending all my evenings here reading query letters instead of curling up on the sofa with you."

As we passed Vicky on the way to the stairs, Sean saluted her. "Novel Idea has a real treasure in you, Ms. Crump."

Her face radiating pleasure, Vicky tugged on her cardigan and sat up straighter in her chair. Her posture was already so perfect that I couldn't imagine she could improve it, but she raised her chin and squared her shoulders. "Might I quote you the next time I ask Ms. Burlington-Duke for a raise, Officer Griffiths?"

The sound of Sean's laughter echoed in the stairwell.

Once we'd reached the first floor and crossed through the lobby, I whispered, "That might be the first joke I've heard her make since she started working at the agency."

Opening the front door for me, Sean winked. "I'm not sure it was meant to be a joke. I do believe Ms. Burlington-Duke has met her match."

WE RUSHED FROM Novel Idea to the James Joyce, but we needn't have worried for we found Klara and her entourage settled at a table in the far corner of the patio. They were talking and sipping glasses of iced tea flavored with sprigs of mint and clearly enjoying their surroundings. How could they not? There were spring flowers everywhere. Clusters of regal irises towered over red and yellow tulips, and pink phlox spread across every inch of the garden beds bordering the flagstone patio. Hyacinths perfumed the air while songbirds hopped between the branches of a dogwood tree and the breeze rippled the tree's white flower petals until they resembled the sails of tiny boats. The scene was so peaceful that I was sorry we had to spoil it.

"Good afternoon," Sean said casually and waved his arm around the patio. "It's such a nice day that Ms. Wilkins and I thought we'd have a cup of coffee before the chef and author panel. Ms. Patrick, we'd like for you to join us."

Klara was too self-absorbed to recognize that while Sean

was being cordial, his invitation was not a request. "Thank you, but no, I've had too much caffeine already." She gave him a dismissive smile and dabbed her lips with her napkin.

I put my hand on Sean's arm for a fraction of a second, signaling that I'd find a way to get Klara alone. "I really have to talk with you, Klara. We need to review a few things before the panel, and I'd like to ask you a particular favor regarding Bryce St. John."

Her composure never faltering, Klara gave me a measuring look. She must have seen the message I was trying to convey with my eyes, for she leaned over and whispered in Ryan's ear. He grinned, kissed her on the cheek, and scraped his chair back. "Dennis, Annie, let's take a stroll. Klara tells me there's a wonderful ice cream parlor called the Snow Queen a few blocks away. I know we just ate, but I'd love to finish off our meal with two scoops of rocky road."

"So not subtle," Dennis grumbled to Klara. "If you wanted us to leave, you could just tell us to go."

Annie looped her arm through his and tugged him out of his seat. "Come on, Dennis. It's too beautiful outside to be grumpy," she said, her face shining with anticipation. "Besides, I never say no to cookie dough in a waffle cone."

I smiled at her gratefully, thinking how pretty she looked in a floral blouse and rose-colored skirt. Yesterday, she'd been so quiet and unobtrusive that it was almost possible to forget she was there, but now I could see how she constantly worked to keep everyone happy. Being Klara's assistant couldn't be easy. As I watched her walk away, I wondered if Annie was aware of her employer's extramarital activities.

The waitress appeared shortly after Ryan, Annie, and Dennis left. Sean ordered two iced coffees and then inhaled deeply, as if he had all the time in the world to sit back and enjoy a lazy Saturday afternoon. "Did you have a nice lunch?" he asked Klara.

"It was fair," Klara said with a shrug. "I had a lackluster corned beef sandwich, but what can I expect of an Irish pub in a small town in the middle of North Carolina?"

I bristled. This was a far cry from the praises Klara had rained down on Inspiration Valley when I'd first met her at Big Ed's.

"Yes, it must be difficult to have to travel all the time, to meet with fans, and to stay in hotels." Sean's tone was sympathetic. "Exhausting, I'd imagine. But you make it look easy."

I could see Klara instantly warm to Sean. "This life can be a challenge, but if you don't take advantage of every opportunity, someone else is waiting in the wings to replace you."

The waitress returned with our iced coffees, and Sean became very preoccupied with stirring sugar into his. "That's a lot of pressure—a subject I'm all too familiar with. In your opinion, how did Mr. Lang handle the demands of such an intense career?"

"Not well, obviously," Klara answered, her voice smug. "I only mentioned a few problem areas with his famous-lovers menu and the next second, he rushes off to the kitchen to practice it. People critique my food on a daily basis, but I don't let the criticism affect my behavior. I'm a professional."

"And how would you describe your relationship with Mr. Lang?" Sean continued and Klara shot a brief, quizzical glance at me. I knew that I'd better join the conversation soon or she was likely to become tight-lipped and peevish.

However, Klara needed to answer the question so I just gave her an encouraging nod.

Klara took a sip of tea. "I thought he was a creative chef, but wasn't cut out for television or public appearances. Far too sensitive, if you ask me." She held out a finger. "And before you ask, I'll tell you that Joel and I didn't know each other on a deep, intimate level. True, I was irritated that his cookbook was releasing on the same day as mine, but he had no control over that. I'd hardly blow him to smithereens over a publication date."

"Would you be upset if he planned to go public regarding your affair with Bryce St. John?" Sean let the question hang in the air and then he gave me a nearly imperceptible nod. It was my turn to intervene.

I put my hand over Klara's. "You were seen with Bryce at Bertram's Hotel," I told her softly, my eyes full of concern. "Did Joel know? Did he try to blackmail you perhaps?"

Recovering quickly from her shock, Klara pulled away from my touch and wadded her napkin into a tight ball. "No, and even if he had, I wouldn't have paid him. Frankly, I don't care who saw me with Bryce. I'm sick of sneaking around." She seemed pleased to admit this aloud. "Besides, Joel was too honorable to mention my affair. He might have been a talentless, insecure pansy, but he wasn't a gossip."

I don't know what shocked me more: Klara's derogatory comments about Joel or her absence of shame about cheating on her husband. I couldn't help but look at Sean to see his response to Klara's statement, but his gaze was fixed on the duplicitous chef.

"Wait a minute," Klara said, and I turned back to her. She frowned at me and then her eyes narrowed. "You're trying to trap me into saying something incriminating, aren't you?" I opened my mouth to protest but she held up her hand, palm out. "Please, I've seen enough cop shows to know how it goes. I had nothing—*nothing*—to do with Joel's death." Scraping back her chair, she grabbed her purse and stood up.

"Ms. Patrick," Sean interjected in a calm but commanding voice. "Please." He gestured toward her, indicating that she remain at the table. "We are not accusing you. Or anyone, for that matter. I am merely gathering information so I can get to the bottom of Mr. Lang's murder. I am sure you want that as much as I do."

She slowly lowered herself to her seat. I didn't know what I could say that would undo the damage I'd done during the conversation, but felt I should try to make amends.

"I'm sorry if I gave you the wrong impression, Klara. I didn't mean anything. I was just trying to be sensitive to your . . . relationship with Bryce." I held out my hand in an offer to shake. "Will you accept my apology?"

She stared at me for less than a second, but it was long enough for me to understand that she was reassessing my motives. Then she nodded and clasped my fingers, almost immediately letting go again. "It's ridiculous to think that I would have set that explosion," she said. "If I were ever going to murder someone, I certainly wouldn't do it by blowing up a kitchen." Placing her hands over her heart in a dramatic gesture, she cried, "All that beautiful equipment!" She shook her head vigorously. "If you want my opinion, you should look more closely at Maurice. He had some serious issues with Joel, although I wouldn't think he'd have the guts to do something as drastic as murder him. Or maybe Leslie Sterling. That woman is extremely competitive and vindictive. I could tell you stories about how she's denigrated other chefs—including Joel—that would make your toes curl. Have you interviewed her yet?"

"Why don't you enlighten us?" Sean encouraged her.

Klara sat back in her chair, tapping her nails on the table while she considered. As she was about to speak, Ryan reappeared behind her chair. His shadow fell across the table, blocking the sun. "Here she is," Ryan said, putting his hands on her shoulders and kissing the top of her head. "Sweetheart, look who I bumped into at the Arts Center."

As Sean and I got to our feet, a young man and woman stepped out from behind Ryan. They were clearly twins, and obviously Ryan's children, as they both had his tall physique, dark hair, and square chin.

"Darling." Klara rose to peck Ryan on the cheek. Her transformation was astonishing. She was once again the loving wife, as if she hadn't declared to us a few minutes ago that she was glad her affair with Bryce was in the open. She reached out her arms to embrace the twins. "Carter. Carrie. How was the train ride?"

They stepped back, obviously trying to avoid contact with her, and neither of them responded to her question. Ryan directed his attention to Sean and me. "Ms. Wilkins, Officer Griffiths, these are my kids, Carter and Carrie."

The young man stepped forward. "Pleased to meet you, sir." He shook hands with Sean and nodded his head at me. "Ma'am."

Carrie just raised her hand in a little wave hello.

"Wow, you guys look just like your dad," I said. Ryan beamed, and Carrie rolled her eyes. I had to smile. Her reaction was so much like Trey's would have been. "I bet people tell you that all the time, don't they?" I added. "I have a son close to your age. Are you in college?"

Carrie nodded. "I'm a senior at NYU."

"And Carter has just been accepted into law school," Ryan boasted. "My kids have done me proud."

"Yes, aren't they wonderful!" Klara gushed.

"You must be proud of your parents, too," I said to Carrie and Carter. "Considering all they've accomplished in the culinary world. I'm Lila Wilkins, the coordinator for the Books and Cooks festival. Your mother's been taking the town by storm."

"She's not our mother," Carrie corrected indignantly.

Ryan leaned toward his daughter. "Carrie, watch your manners," he whispered.

"Dad married Klara after we were already grown," Carter explained in a gentler tone. And though he gave me a little smile, I didn't miss the fleeting glance of disgust he directed toward his stepmother.

"You were only thirteen!" Klara exclaimed. "That's hardly grown."

Carrie's face flushed. "And you were *hardly* a mother. All you cared about was your precious career. We might as well have been invisible."

"Invisible?" Klara seemed unfazed by Carrie's insults. "You were impossible little hooligans who'd been allowed to run wild for far too long. I could have been a whole lot worse."

"Klara, let's not get into that here. Those times are in the past." Ryan was making an obvious attempt to keep his voice even. "And this is not the place."

Carrie pointed her finger at her stepmother. "The famous

chef Klara. You only married my father because you needed his culinary skills."

Carter snorted. "Guess that's better than marrying him for his money."

"Kids, knock it off." Ryan's tone had a dangerous edge to it that I hadn't heard before.

"Sorry, Dad." Carter spoke the words, but his eyes didn't reflect an ounce of genuine regret. "I'm going inside to use the restroom."

Carrie grabbed Carter's sleeve. "Wait up. I'll come with you."

When the twins had gone into the pub, Ryan turned to Sean and me and shrugged. "Families," he said, shaking his head. "Sorry about that, but kids will be kids, no matter how old they get. You'd think since mine are in their twenties, they'd act more mature . . ." He trailed off and entwined his fingers with Klara's. "You okay, hon?"

"Of course." She pulled her hand back. "I'm fine."

I glanced at Sean. The Patrick family dynamics had added another element of disquiet to this relaxed setting.

Sean clapped Ryan on the back in a show of solidarity. "Consider the incident forgotten. Children can be difficult at any age." He nudged me. "Can't they, Ms. Wilkins?"

I nodded, remembering the challenging time I'd had with Trey at the end of his senior year in high school. "Even when their parents would like to believe they're perfect." I smiled.

"Ms. Patrick." Sean indicated the chairs. "Let's continue our conversation. You were about to enlighten me about Ms. Sterling."

Ryan put his hand on Klara's arm. "I apologize, Officer

Griffiths, but Klara has a panel to get to. Can she do this later?"

I checked my watch. "Ryan's right. Klara and I both need to go, but we can meet again after the panel."

Sean didn't have a chance to respond for Carter and Carrie reappeared at the entrance to the patio section, arguing heatedly. I couldn't hear what they were saying, but I could see by their furrowed brows, abrupt gestures, and hostile glares that they weren't having a friendly conversation.

"What now?" Ryan ran a hand through his hair.

"Do something with them," Klara demanded, putting on her sunglasses. "They're going to make a scene. What if members of the press are here?"

Ryan hurried forward and Klara, Sean, and I followed. After all, there was only one exit through the pub and I was in a rush to get to the panel on time, too.

"I'm not moving until I tell the cop what I have to say," Carrie told her brother as she crossed her arms over her chest. I could tell by the defiant jut of her chin that she meant what she said.

Carter threw out his hands in a show of defeat and Ryan glanced at his children in confusion. "What are you talking about, Carrie?"

"We heard about what happened to Joel Lang. There was a reporter on our train and he told us everything. Even how the poor guy died." Her eyes flashing with anger, she gave Klara a withering stare. "I bet you did it. I bet you'd do *anything* to keep the truth from getting out."

I turned to see Klara's reaction to this incriminating statement and noticed that Sean was studying her intently as well. The skin of her face had gone pale, but I couldn't see her eyes beneath her sunglasses. She was gripping her cell phone so tightly that her knuckles were white and her chest seemed to be rising and falling more rapidly. But most of these physical tells only lasted a few seconds. Klara quickly recovered her poise and laughed derisively. "What drama are you stirring up now, Carrie?" she asked in a cool, haughty voice. "You're always searching for your father's attention in such juvenile ways."

I couldn't tear my gaze away from Klara's hand. She'd yet to release her iron clasp on her cell phone. No matter what she said, Klara Patrick was furious. Or scared. Or both.

Carrie smiled smugly while Carter stood behind her, looking pained. "I'm talking about your affair with Bryce St. John. Carter and I know all about it, and we came to tell Daddy so he could get rid of you once and for all."

Klara began to protest but Carrie cut her off. Addressing Sean, she said, "Klara was always badmouthing this Joel Lang guy. You should find out if he was about to spill the beans like I just did. My precious stepmother would have had to shut him up. She's nothing without my dad and she knows it. And he doesn't know about her fling. Not until now." She pointed at Klara, her expression one of raw hatred. "Take her in for questioning, Officer Griffiths. Hopefully, there's a reporter nearby who can snap a picture of the famous Chef Klara being led away in shame." She shifted her focus back to her stepmother. "There's no such thing as bad press, right, Klara? You'll probably sell out of cookbooks. People love it when a celebrity takes a fall."

Ryan looked from Carrie to Klara, clearly too stunned to speak. When he finally found his tongue, his words came out as a sorrowful rasp. "Is it true, Klara? Is this true?"

The pain in his voice was terrible to hear. He had spoken softly, almost tenderly, and I wished he could be spared from the hurtful truth, but it wasn't my place to intervene. This was between Ryan and his wife.

But Klara ignored him completely. With a little toss of her head she said, "I have a panel to attend," and pushed past Carrie and Carter. She disappeared into the pub, leaving the rest of us standing in shocked silence. And in that moment, the flower-scented patio lost its charm. No amount of birdsong or sunlight could erase the shadow that had just fallen over us.

Chapter 8

STILL IN SHOCK, I RAN ALL THE WAY TO THE ARTS CENTER and only paused on the steps for a minute to catch my breath. As I entered the lobby, Jude grabbed my arm. "It's about time you arrived. All the panelists are here except Klara. Do you know where she is?"

"Right behind me," I said. "But I suspect she'll be a little late." I hurriedly told him what had happened at the pub.

"Such drama," Jude remarked when I was finished. "Klara's life is straight out of a novel. Perhaps she'll pen a tell-all instead of a cookbook."

I wasn't as amused as he was by this notion and I was certain that Ryan wouldn't be either. However, there was no time to brood over the Patricks' marriage, so I followed Jude to the panel room. Right before we entered, I ran my fingers through my hair and straightened my skirt. "Do I look all right?"

"You look fabulous, as always." He reached forward to reposition a lock of my hair.

I stepped back. "Don't, Jude." As charming as he could be, there were times when I didn't welcome his invading my personal space.

"What? It was sticking up." His smile was all innocence. "Let's go."

The room was buzzing with conversation, and it seemed that every chair had been taken. Jude and I made our way to the front where the panelists sat behind a long table, their books on stands in front of them. As I greeted my two cozy author clients, the food critic, and the other chefs, Klara came rushing up to the table and took her place beside Bryce St. John. I retrieved my index cards from my purse and settled into my seat.

Taking a moment to scan the audience, I saw Klara's assistants, Annie and Dennis, in the front row. Beside them, Charlene Jacques was talking to Franklin. I was delighted to see my mother sitting near the back with Makayla. My mother was waving frantically and grinning from ear to ear. I wiggled my fingers at her and my friend, wishing I had arrived earlier so I could have chatted with them.

"May we have your attention, please?" Jude tapped his microphone. The hubbub quieted. "Welcome to our panel, 'Killer Tales From the Kitchen,' where we will explore the joys and challenges of writing about food," he began. "Our illustrious panelists have a range of expertise and I'm sure you'll come away from this event having been entertained and educated. I'm Jude Hudson, an agent at Novel Idea, the company sponsoring this event. And at the other end of the table is my lovely co-moderator and fellow agent, Lila Wilkins."

I smiled at the audience and raised the microphone. "Good afternoon. Can you all hear me okay?" At the many nods and yeses, I carried on. "We are going to have so much fun this afternoon. Sitting before you are mystery authors, celebrated chefs, and a renowned food critic. Every one of these individuals writes about food from a different perspective. Let me introduce them. Directly beside me is Lizzie Abbot, author of the Vegetarian Murders mystery series. Her latest book, *Tofu Terror*, was just released. Lizzie, when I read your books and come upon a passage containing food, I almost want to become a vegetarian. How do you do that?"

Lizzie straightened and held her book in front of her. She was tall and thin, with long, strawberry blond hair. "Thank you, Lila. Well, when my protagonist, Andrea, makes a dish, it is always something I've prepared and enjoyed myself. I'll often go through much trial and error to come up with a satisfying flavor, so I know the dishes intimately. When I describe them in my writing, I use my personal experience to express the joy I felt when I feasted on the dish."

"That's certainly reflected in your writing, Lizzie. Continuing on—"

"Sorry to interrupt." Lizzie leaned forward toward the audience. "I just want to say that, contrary to the title of my latest book, tofu is a wonderful food. So versatile."

"Thank you, Lizzie. I've never actually made anything with tofu before, but I will definitely consider trying it now." As the audience chuckled, I smiled and indicated the woman sitting beside Lizzie. "Our next panelist is Judith Alain. She's a cozy mystery author whose first book in the Delectable Desserts mystery series, *Killer Sweets*, was just released. Judith, your main character, Karen, seems to be an expert when it comes to desserts. Does that come from research or experience?"

Judith grinned widely. Slightly overweight, she wore a stylish multicolored sweater that brightened her face and emphasized her sea blue eyes. "A bit of both, I guess," she replied. "But mostly experience. My mother was a *Cordon Bleu*–certified pastry chef, and even from a young age, I would be at her side as she created exquisite dishes. I learned a great deal from her, especially when it comes to appreciating quality ingredients and pure, rich flavors." She smiled sadly. "My mom died a couple of years ago, and I think I wrote the Delectable Desserts series to honor her. My character Karen is a lot like her."

"What a wonderful way to pay homage to your mother, Judith," I said. A few members of the audience clapped. Looking over at them, I noticed Sean at the back of the room, standing beside Ryan Patrick.

Ryan looked like a specter. His face was gray with shock, and his eyes were dark and haunted. He stood with his arms pinned to his side, his shoulders slumped and his expression one of absolute dejection. I felt a rush of sympathy for Klara's husband, but all I could do was offer him a compassionate smile before turning my attention back to the panel.

"Next to Judith is renowned food critic Doug Corby, whose book *A Foodie's Diary* was on the *New York Times* bestseller list for several weeks. Doug, you have very high standards when it comes to food and those standards are reflected in your reviews. Do you find it difficult to criticize a chef's work, knowing that they've put their heart and soul into their craft?"

I couldn't help but feel that Doug's pointy, ferret-like

features reflected the personality that came through in his writing. He twirled his pencil-thin mustache. "Not at all. I write truthfully about what I taste, and I have no trouble whatsoever with being honest."

"But you have a lot of trouble understanding good taste," Klara sputtered as she rose from her chair. Both Bryce and Jude took an arm and persuaded her to sit back down. Bryce whispered something to her, and I couldn't help but watch Ryan as his wife immediately responded to her lover. His face was a mask of anger and humiliation, and his hands had coiled into tight fists. Sean gave him a friendly pat on the shoulder, as if to say, "I feel your pain. Hang in there, man."

Gazing around, I knew I needed to return the focus to Doug. "I believe you ruffled some feathers in the culinary world with your book, and you've probably made some enemies over the course of your career. Does that bother you?"

Doug grinned. "I love it when chefs hate what I write. Listen up people: Food is ambrosia and should be treated with respect. If I see that it's not, I will call the erring chef to task." He leaned his head toward the other end of the table. "Even you, Klara."

Klara glowered at him, but Jude had a firm hand on her arm. The audience tittered animatedly.

"This should generate some interesting discussion," I said. "But first, let's introduce the rest of the panel. Next to Doug, we have the lovely television chef and author Leslie Sterling. Her latest cookbook is called *Over the Top*. Leslie, you've received criticism that your food is too rich and too expensive for the average cook. What is your response to that?"

She sighed. "People love to dream," she said. "My recipes are delicious. So what if they use expensive and rare ingredients? I'm sure I'm not alone when I say that one of my favorite kinds of books to read is a cookbook. Am I right?" She waved her hands at the audience. A brief burst of applause ensued, and she held up her palm to quell it. "But that doesn't mean I try every recipe in the book. I just love reveling in the food descriptions, imagining the flavor combinations, and drooling over the photographs. My books are filled with culinary dreams. And sometimes, it's good to step out of the box and try something new, even if it is a little more expensive than a plain bean soup or bland semolina. Decadent food makes life more exciting."

I glanced at Klara. Leslie's comments were an obvious reference to our conversation at the chefs' dinner and Klara's famous-lovers dish. But Klara stayed quiet and merely glared at her peer. I hoped she'd be able to put on a positive face when it came time for her introduction.

"Thank you, Leslie," I continued. "Next we have Bryce St. John, owner of the famous St. John's Bistro, with locations in both New York and Washington, D.C. His cookbook, *Samplings From St. John's*, came out several years ago and continues to delight readers and cooks. Bryce, owning a restaurant provides its own challenges I'm sure, but I would imagine that it would also give you a unique perspective on food, as is evidenced in your cookbook. How do you balance a writing career with the demands of a restaurateur?"

Bryce held up a copy of his book. His handsome face graced the cover, which was probably why it continued to sell. In my opinion, the book itself was like any other restaurant cookbook. "It is difficult, to be sure." He grinned. "As you can see, my output as a writer has only culminated in one book so far. But I love food, and I love sharing it with others. How lucky I am to be able to do that with my restaurants and with my cookbook."

A few women in the audience hooted. One of them called out, "And you're darn handsome to boot."

Bryce dipped his chin. "Why, thank you, ma'am."

"That is a sentiment I would agree with," I said, glancing quickly at Sean before continuing. He smiled, understanding that I was putting on a show, and secure in the knowledge that I thought him the handsomest man around. "Last, but certainly not least, we have the gregarious Klara Patrick. Her newest cookbook, *My Grandmother's Hearth*, has just been released to exemplary reviews. Klara, the influence of your Dutch grandmother is very prevalent in your book. Yet some critics have remarked that the recipes are simplistic and rustic. Would you like to comment on that?"

Klara stroked the cover of her book. "My *oma* meant the world to me, and everything I know about cooking I learned from her." She looked up at the audience, her television personality coming to the forefront. She clasped her hands over her heart and described her grandmother's kitchen, recalling how large and strong her *oma*'s hands had been and how magical it had been to watch her crush herbs and knead bread with her soft, deft fingers. The audience was captivated and I saw several women dab at their eyes with tissues. If Klara had been at all affected by her husband's discovery of her affair with Bryce, she didn't let it show. She was as entrancing as always and I was amazed by her ability to cast a spell over the crowd. "If the recipes seem simple," she concluded, "it's only because that's the Dutch way. Or at least it was in Oma's time. And believe me, I work very, very hard to perfect the recipes in order to create dishes that satisfy even the most particular palate."

"Oh, give me a break!" A chair scraped loudly in the audience, and everyone turned to look. Dennis Chapman, Klara's sous chef, stood. His face was red and the armpits of his shirt were wet with sweat. "*You* work hard?" he shouted, the crimson in his face becoming a darker shade. "*You?* Give me a break. Your *staff* works hard and you just lap up all the accolades. I've never worked like a dog for such an unappreciative boss in my life!" He made his way to the aisle, not caring about the people he stomped past. He jabbed his finger at Klara. "You continuously refuse to give me any kind of recommendation no matter how many times I ask. I know I didn't get that head chef job at Austin's because you badmouthed me to the owner. You and the other celebrity chefs have it in for me. You're afraid of my talent, afraid I'll be better than you. So to hold me back, you make me chop, chop, chop, without ever giving me a chance at the stove. You pay me peanuts, spit in my face, and have now ruined my life. Well, I quit. Chop your own vegetables from now on, you lazy, scheming bitch!" Breathing heavily, he marched his oversized frame down the aisle and out of the room. We were all struck silent as the door slammed behind him.

BY THE TIME the question-and-answer segment was over, I felt more like a circus ringleader than a panel moderator. After Dennis Chapman's outburst and theatrical exit, I'd tried my best to cajole the audience into quieting down. Finally, Jude had taken over, charming the crowd into submission long enough to allow the stunned panelists to respond to a few queries. Luckily, no one asked Klara about

Dennis's allegations. Even so, I was wound as tight as a spring until Jude thanked everyone for coming and invited the attendees to proceed to the lobby in order to buy books and have them signed by the esteemed panelists.

As people streamed out of the room, tittering like a flock of high-strung hens, I saw Sean lingering in the back row. Ryan was close by and had taken a seat in one of the vacant chairs. He was bent over, his face hidden in his hands.

Making my way over to Sean, I gestured for him to move a few feet away from Ryan. "The awful truth is sinking in, isn't it?" I whispered.

He nodded. "I think so. I can only imagine what he's feeling right now, but I also can't let him confront his wife about the affair at this time. I need to question her about Mr. Lang. Ryan's kids might be accusing her of killing Mr. Lang purely out of spite, but they may very well be onto something and I need to discover the truth. One of my team has already taken Mr. Bruneau to the station for questioning."

I shot a glance at Klara. "She's supposed to join the other authors in the lobby now. If she comes with you, she'll look guilty."

Sean's jaw hardened. "I'm not interested in how this affects her career, Lila. I'm interested in catching a killer."

"I'm sorry." I was instantly contrite. "I've got this whole Books and Cooks agenda stuck in my head and I'm fixating on it as a way of feeling in control. But the more this weekend progresses, the more I realize how ridiculous that notion is. A man has been murdered, Klara and Bryce are having an affair, our new Arts Center's been damaged, and members of the press are everywhere, waiting to dig up all the dirt they can." From the corner of my eye, I saw Klara stand up and collect her purse. "You'd better move in. I'd rather she make a scene in a relatively empty room than in a packed lobby."

Sean brushed my cheek with his fingertips. "I'm on it. And Lila, if Ms. Patrick has nothing to hide, I'll return her to you as soon as I can."

I smiled at him. "I'd rather have *you* back by my side, Officer."

"Keep your ears open," he counseled. "People won't edit their own conversations in front of you like they would around a policeman. Who knows what you might overhear as you continue to spend time with the chefs?"

As my mother made a beeline for us, I quipped, "I can also ask Amazing Althea if she has any insights."

"Go for it," he replied seriously, even though I'd been teasing. "She's a skilled listener. A rare and useful talent."

I watched Sean approach Klara, touch her on the elbow, and gesture toward the exit. Her brows knit together in anger and she shook her head in defiance, but when Sean pointed at the handcuffs dangling from his utility belt, she quickly conceded to his request.

"I don't think she did it," my mother said as Sean escorted Klara from the room.

"Really? Do you know something I don't?"

My mother shrugged. "I know women. Most of my clients are female. For more years than I'd care to name, I've been hearin' about their triumphs and complaints, their hopes and dreams, their joys and trials. And this is what life boils down to for most of them: Women want to be loved for who they are. And when that doesn't happen, they'll change themselves on the outside over and over again to get folks to adore them. But it's not real."

"What does that have to do with Klara?" I jerked my head to where Ryan was seated. "I believe her husband loved her for who she was, but that clearly wasn't enough considering she's been cheating on him with Bryce St. John."

"No surprise there," my mother snorted. "Remember when we ran into that beefcake chef on the street? He was wearin' those clingy runnin' shorts and that tight, tight . . . oh, that's neither here nor there. Anyway, there was enough electricity between him and Klara to fuel a power station. They tried to hide it, but I knew they'd swapped more than just recipes."

"Let's sit outside for a spell," I suggested before my mother could elaborate on her metaphor. "I'd like to know what else you've observed." Steering her through the lobby, I paused a moment to be certain that Jude had the signings well under control. He did, so I caught his eye and indicated that I was leaving by pointing at the exit. He gave me a thumbs-up before turning his attention back to a pretty young woman wearing high heels and a very short skirt.

My mother and I sat on a bench situated between a pair of maple trees and listened as a blue jay scolded a squirrel for creeping too close to its nest.

"It starts before the little one is even born," my mother began. "A mama's urge to protect her young." She put her hand over mine. "Wish I could flap my wings and send the wicked creature who's come sneakin' into our town away, but I can't. All I know is that when I touch the cards, I feel the presence of the person who killed that Joel Lang fellow. He or she is still hangin' around and I don't think they're goin' anywhere." She sighed. "Wish I could tell you more, but all of my senses are tellin' me that they're not done yet. This is an angry person, Lila."

I studied her, hating to see the lines of worry tugging at the corners of her mouth. "What card reveals that kind of information?"

"More than one, shug. I've turned over the devil, the tower, the four of cups. But I've also gotten the hanged man a bunch. That combo says that this person feels persecuted. They see themselves as a victim who needs to make things right for themselves. They're burnin' to exact their own brand of justice."

"So Joel was killed as an act of revenge?" I asked.

My mother lifted her gaze to the maple leaves. The sun had painted them a golden green and they rustled gently in the breeze. It was perfect reading weather and I'd have liked nothing better than to throw a towel over a lounge chair and spend the rest of the day in my garden, absorbed in a novel. Alas, I had other things to do.

"Things aren't as clear as I'd like them to be, hon," my mother said in answer to my question. "I'm seeing the star card in reverse, too. That tells me that this person's goals in life are as warped as a fun-house mirror. No matter how they act, this man or woman is deeply dissatisfied with their lot." She squeezed my hand. "They can't stop, Lila. They're empty inside and they wanna make someone pay for that emptiness. They think these acts will heal them, but they won't."

"Everyone's been hurt at one point or another," I murmured to myself. "But which of the chefs has been truly wronged? Who could be viewed as a victim? Maurice probably could. And now Ryan could."

Faces flashed before my eyes. Klara's, Ryan's, Maurice's, Bryce's, Leslie's, and so on until the features of the celebrity chefs, their assistants, and today's panelists all morphed together to form a single, grotesque mask. "It's all muddled, Mom. The people we've invited to this event seem decent on the surface, but I can't tell what's going on in their minds. I know they all want to be successful and I believe they're fiercely competitive, but they're so accustomed to putting on a show that I have no idea when they're being sincere. How am I supposed to help Sean find a killer when I can't trust any of the chefs that my own agency invited to Inspiration Valley?"

"Keep hangin' around them," she advised. "I heard that Leslie woman say that she and Klara's lover boy were gonna grab a coffee at Espresso Yourself after they put their pretty signatures in people's books. Maybe you and Makayla can learn a thing or two while these high-falutin chefs whisper secrets to each other over lattes and scones."

I smiled at her. "That's a wonderful idea, Mom. If nothing else, I can always work on solving the mystery of Makayla's secret admirer. It's a much more pleasant task than trying to discover the identity of Joel's killer."

"She showed me one of the little notes in her tip jar. I know diddly-squat about poetry, but I know words of passion when I hear them." My mother fanned her face. "Lordy, lordy. If Makayla doesn't fall madly in love with this fellow after you finally track him down, send him on over to me. I could think of a few things to do with a man with that kind of fire in his soul."

"I'll keep that in mind."

She winked at me. "Until he shows up at my door, I suppose I'd better mosey on home and work on my new banana bread recipe. At my age, trying a different recipe is as wild as some women can hope to be."

"What a relief that you're not one of those women," I said with a grin. Suddenly, I remembered the necklace I'd been given by the aspiring author. "You want to hear something weird?"

"Naturally," my mother answered.

I told her about finding the gift bag on my scooter and produced the necklace with the purple crystal pendant. Taking it out of my purse, I handed it to my mother. She frowned and studied the piece of jewelry as it lay curled in her palm like a silver and plum snake. Surprisingly, she then asked for the query letter. Seeing no harm in having her read it, I passed it to her.

Her fingers closed around the necklace as she read. "What do you think of this?"

"Nothing about her query had me hooked," I replied. "Vicky will mail her a form rejection letter on Monday. Why?"

"This silly woman thinks she can influence you with her crystal. When she gets that letter, she'll see it as you rejectin' not only her book, but her powers, too. She could spell trouble for you, hon."

I reclaimed the piece of jewelry and shoved it into a dark corner at the bottom of my purse. "Just what I need. More trouble."

MAKAYLA HAD HUSTLED back to Espresso Yourself as soon as the panel had ended, but the traffic at the coffee shop was fairly slow, so she was restocking her display shelves with muffins, scones, and biscotti when I arrived.

"Grab a seat!" she instructed. "I'll fix you something."

I didn't argue. Makayla had a special gift when it came to knowing what her customers needed, even if they had no clue themselves.

"I got another poem," she whispered in excitement and placed a cup of hot tea and a white plate bearing two biscotti in front of me. "In honor of my secret admirer's Japanese haiku, I've given you black tea and almond biscotti."

Thanking her, I asked to see the latest poem.

"You'll need two hands for this one." Her face was radiant as she placed an origami butterfly in my palm. The delicate insect had been made out of a five-dollar bill.

"How pretty!" I exclaimed. "And the poem's inside?"

"Look under its wings," she told me.

Complying, I spotted two tiny lines of poetry written beneath each wing in thick black marker and read them aloud:

"Lady butterfly
Perfumes her wings
By floating
Over the orchid."

Makayla pointed at a bud vase containing an orchid with bright pink petals and streaks of white leading from the center to its fragrant tips. "That gorgeous bloom was attached to the butterfly's body. It smells like heaven."

"So he gave you the poem as well as the butterfly and the flower described in its lines. You know, this might be our first tangible lead," I mused and blew on my tea before taking a sip of the strong, soothing brew. "Someone at the

Secret Garden must remember who bought this orchid. It's not exactly a common plant."

"I will march right on down there after I close," she assured me. I dipped my biscotti into the tea to soften it and took a bite, relishing the subtle almond flavor. As I ate, we discussed the panel and Dennis Chapman's dramatic outburst. I told Makayla that both Maurice and Klara were at the police station in Dunston being questioned about Joel Lang's murder.

She listened as I recounted the scene from the James Joyce Pub and how Klara had broken her husband's heart and then sat on the panel as if nothing extraordinary had happened.

"Lord have mercy, that poor man." Makayla made a *tsk-tsk* sound. "But is Klara so cold that she'd put cooking spray in an oven in hopes that another chef would get blown up? Is she a killer?"

"I don't know," I admitted. "But I'm hoping that Sean will have someone behind bars before the day is out."

A gust of wind wafted in as the door opened and Jude entered the café. When he saw Makayla and me sitting together he grinned. "Sorry to interrupt you ladies, but could I get a skinny latte, please?"

Makayla jumped up. "What size would you like?"

I picked up the paper butterfly while Jude bantered with Makayla as she prepared his order. Absently fingering the wings of the paper insect, I pondered the concept of love. It could make someone glow, like Makayla with her secret admirer or me with Sean, but it could also shatter a person, as it had done with Ryan Patrick.

"I figured you'd be here, Lila." Jude interrupted my thoughts and placed a file folder on the table as he took the chair that Makayla had vacated. "Bentley and I have finally read through the twenty-seven entries for the short story contest, and we've narrowed the possible second- and third-place winners down to two writers of equal mediocrity."

"Jude!" I cut in. "Those writers have put a lot of themselves into their stories. They deserve some respect."

"You know what I mean," he protested. "You come across queries like that all the time—acceptable writing but not outstanding." He tapped the file folder. "They're decent stories, and better than the majority, but comparable in writing and quality. Bentley and I gave these two equivalent ratings, so you can decide on the second and third placements for them." He pulled a printed document from the folder and handed it to me. "However, for first place we have a clear winner. It's a story about a chef in a bistro. The author hooks you in right away with a description of an osso buco that the chef is preparing. The opening paragraph makes your mouth water. But the plot becomes more and more intricate as the author weaves in tension, humor, and suspense. The chef is not who he seems." He took a sip of coffee. "But I don't want to give anything away. I need you to read this story without any spoilers."

I leafed through the pages of the typed document, feeling the rush of anticipation. "Do you think this author has the potential for more than winning a few cookbooks?" I asked. "Do you think he or she might be a prospective client for other works?"

Jude beamed. "Better than that. The spellbinding voice in the story is remarkably similar to that of Marlette's novel." He grabbed my wrist. "Lila, I think we've found our ghost writer for the *Alexandria Society* sequel."

Pulling my hand away from his, I smiled. "Do you really think so? It would be fantastic if this person could solve that problem for us. We haven't had much luck with the project, not that we've been spending a lot of time on it."

"There have been a few distractions," he said sardonically.

"But writing a short story is very different from writing a novel. Not everyone has the stamina to produce a work of that length. I suppose we could coach them if they need it." I envisioned meeting with the author. "Can you imagine how excited this person will be if we tell them that they have not only won the short story contest, but that we're considering offering them a chance at a major book deal?" The thrill I always experienced about a prospective client coursed through me, and I suddenly wanted to be at my desk. "The contestant list is in my office, so I'll find out who the author is and we'll proceed from there."

"Sounds good," said Jude as he picked up his coffee "Oh, by the way, Doug Corby left Inspiration Valley right after the signing, so we need to cancel his hotel room and his seat for the banquet. He said there was too much drama with the murder and the presence of so many chefs in one place."

"Just as well," I remarked. "The fewer fireworks the better."

"I'm with you there. See you upstairs." Jude pushed back his chair and left the coffee shop.

"Back to work for you two?" asked Makayla, who had tactfully occupied herself while Jude and I discussed business. She gathered the trash from the table.

I nodded and stood. "I need to go upstairs and read a story about a chef who is not who he seems. Be sure to let me know what you find out at Secret Garden," I said, handing her the origami butterfly. Our fingers touched and an unsettling thought entered my mind. What if Makayla's poetic admirer was not who he seemed? What if, instead of a love-struck admirer, he was something far less romantic? Something darker? Something to be feared?

Chapter 9

I NEVER MADE IT UPSTAIRS. WHEN I OPENED THE DOOR leading from Espresso Yourself to the lobby of our building, I nearly collided with Ryan Patrick.

"I'm sorry," he said, looking so forlorn that I immediately assured him the fault was mine.

He managed a smile of gratitude and I stepped backward, all thoughts of the short stories waiting for my perusal forgotten. I couldn't leave Ryan here alone. He was wounded and confused and needed a dose of kindness.

"Can I buy you a drink?" I asked him, indicating the menu board. "You might feel better with a warm cup of comfort. I'll sit with you if you'd like."

"That would be really nice," he said. "What do you recommend?"

"I'll let Makayla make that decision," I said. "She always knows exactly what her customers need."

Ryan made himself comfortable at the café table at the far side of the room. Nestled between a pair of bookcases stuffed with Makayla's lending library and walls covered by watercolor paintings of the seaside, the table was a small corner of heaven.

"I thought you were dashing upstairs to send some aspiring writer to cloud nine," Makayla said when I appeared at the counter. She told a customer who'd come in from the street entrance that his order would be up in a moment and then gestured for me to follow her to the other end of the counter where the espresso machine sat.

I subtly pointed at Ryan. "He needs special treatment."

I held out a ten-dollar bill but Makayla waved it away. "If I can do anything to ease his heartache, I will. I'll fix him a shot of compassion mixed with some froth of hope. Just give me a second to serve Mr. Littleman."

By the time Makayla came to our table carrying a mug of café Americano, a tall glass of ice water garnished with a cheerful lemon wedge, and a warm strawberry cream scone, Ryan had sent a text to his children inviting them to join him at Espresso Yourself.

I sat with him as he sipped his coffee and took small bites of his scone, noting his mechanical movements and how he seemed to take no pleasure in his food. Finally, he put his fork down and sighed mournfully. "Everything's delicious," he assured me. "I just don't have much of an appetite."

"Of course you don't," I sympathized.

"I can't believe I've been such a fool." His expression morphed from sorrow to anger. "She's been cheating on me right under my nose. Sneaking out for her so-called walks every night. All this time. Her and Bryce. *Bryce*." He spoke the name of his wife's lover as if it were a foul and dirty thing. "What he knows about cooking could fit in a thimble. What a vain, arrogant, shallow . . ." He trailed off and then let loose a bitter laugh. "What am I saying? He and Klara are perfect for each other!"

I laid a hand over his, covering his trembling fingers with my own. "It's her loss. I haven't known you long, but I can tell that you're a fine man."

"I used to believe that, too," he said ruefully. "But I guess I wasn't good enough for Klara. She probably thought she'd settled for less right from the start. And yet, what would she be without me? She's forgetting who put her on that pedestal from which she likes to stand and look down upon the rest of humanity."

Having no idea what he meant by that statement, I searched for words of comfort. Luckily, I was saved from having to speak by the arrival of Ryan's kids. Carter and Carrie immediately spotted their dad and rushed over to him.

"I'm so sorry, Dad." Carrie's eyes were swimming with unshed tears. "I should never have told you the way I did. It was totally selfish of me. It's just that I was *so* mad, but I shouldn't have blurted it out in front of everyone. Do you forgive me?"

Ryan slid his hand out from under mine and opened his arms for his daughter. They embraced and he whispered, "There's nothing to forgive, sweetheart. There is no good way to tell me that kind of news. In fact, I'm glad Ms. Wilkins was nearby when you did. She's been kind enough to sit here and listen to me gripe and groan about my situation."

"Thank you," Carter said to me. He was clearly the

politer twin. "Can I get you anything, Ms. Wilkins? I'm going to grab vanilla lattes for me and my sister."

"I've already had my daily supply of caffeine. Go ahead and take my seat." I stood up, but Ryan seized my hand before I could move away.

"Don't go. Carter can pull up an extra chair." His eyes pleaded with me. "Really. I could use a woman's advice."

Giving him a reassuring smile, I settled back into my chair again. What choice did I have? If I could help Ryan Patrick in any way, I would, regardless of the fact that Jude was undoubtedly waiting for me in my office at this very moment, drumming his fingers on my desk and glancing impatiently at his watch.

Carter and Carrie exchanged a quick, meaningful look and walked to the counter to place their order with Makayla.

"I don't want to lose her," Ryan murmured sotto voce when they had gone. "Bryce can't have her, and after all we've achieved together, I won't let him. What should I do?"

This was the last thing I'd expected him to say. Did he truly love Klara that much? Did he want to work on their marriage or was the idea of giving her freedom to be with her lover too much for him to stomach?

A moment ago, he'd been angry and sour. Now he was desperate and determined. I wondered about him being so mercurial that he could move from bitterness to blind loyalty toward his cheating wife in the space of a few heartbeats. "Are you still in love with her?" I asked. "Even now? Knowing what you know?"

Staring down at the table, he rubbed his temples and sighed wearily. "God help me, but she's all I have. Bryce can't take her away from me." He lowered his hands and balled them into tight fists. "He won't, I tell you."

Carrie and Carter returned to the table and Ryan did his best to put on a brave face. By this time, I was more than ready to leave, but just when I was mulling over how to make a graceful exit, Leslie Sterling and Charlene Jacques entered the coffee shop, chattering and laughing until they spied Ryan.

Instantly, they fell silent. They both gave him awkward, little waves before focusing their attention on the menu board.

"Why don't you catch a flight back to New York, Dad?" Carter asked. "You don't need to stay here for the whole weekend."

"Exactly," Carrie said, instantly warming to her brother's idea. "Go home and pack up the tramp's things. Toss them onto the sidewalk and have the locks changed."

Ryan shook his head. "Klara and I are partners. Beyond being husband and wife, we're also business partners. Things are more complicated than you realize."

Carter shot a sidelong glance at Carrie. "Tell him," she prompted.

"Dad," Carter began. His voice quavered and I could see that he was nervous. "I think Klara's been deceiving you in more than one way."

"Oh?" was all Ryan could manage.

"Remember how you gave us a copy of your safety deposit key? Just in case something happened to you?" Carter said.

Ryan nodded, obviously befuddled.

"Well, I know you didn't expect us to use it if it wasn't an emergency, but I lost my birth certificate and I couldn't apply for a passport without it, so I went to the bank and opened up the box."

Ryan's mouth hung open in surprise. "Why were you applying for a passport?"

Carter squirmed in his chair. "A bunch of my buddies are going on a dive trip to Mexico next month and I wanted to go, too. It's super cheap and I knew I could get my passport order rushed, so I went to your bank. I didn't think I needed to tell you about it. Well, until . . . um . . ."

"Until he got worried enough to talk to me," Carrie continued. "We know you've always kept cash in your safety deposit box. You told us last summer that you've been stockpiling money away—that after the bottom fell out of the market a few years ago, you only trusted cash and certified bonds and wouldn't invest in stocks ever again."

Ryan's face was unreadable. "That's true."

Leaning closer to his father, Carter said, "How much of it did you keep in the safety deposit box, Dad?"

Rubbing his chin, Ryan hesitated. I couldn't blame him. After all, I didn't discuss my finances with Trey. What I did with my money was no one's business. All my son had to do was study hard and graduate in four years from the college I worked so hard to pay for. I was available to him if he needed financial advice, but he'd never asked what my portfolio looked like and I'd find it odd if he did.

"Dad, you need to tell us," Carrie urged.

"All of it," Ryan finally mumbled.

"It's gone," Carter croaked. "There was no money in there."

"What?" Ryan was aghast. "There was over a hundred thousand dollars in there!"

Stunned, I looked from one face to another. Carrie's eyes, which had been wide with shock, suddenly narrowed and she uttered a low, hissing growl. She sounded like a tomcat backed into a corner. "Ask *her* where the money went."

Klara breezed into Espresso Yourself as if she hadn't a care in the world. Bryce St. John and Maurice Bruneau were right on her heels.

"How did we all end up at the same place?" Bryce declared to the room at large. His glance passed right over Ryan as if he didn't even exist.

Klara, on the other hand, gave her husband a dazzling smile and wriggled her fingers in greeting before joining Leslie and Charlene at the counter. I didn't know whose behavior angered me more, Bryce's or Klara's, but I didn't have time to reflect on the question because Annie was half dragging a reluctant Dennis Chapman through the door. Her purse was slipping off her shoulder, and because it was partially unzipped, I feared it would fall and spill its contents all over the floor, so I jumped up to grab it for her.

The moment she felt my hand on her bag, she whirled around, startled by my touch. "Oh! Thanks." She took the bag from me, smiled, and turned outside to Dennis. "You have to apologize," she said in a gentle, coaxing tone. "She'll ruin you if you don't."

"She already has," Dennis protested sullenly.

Annie propped the door open with her hip and tried to wave Dennis through. "You don't know that for sure. You need to confront her in person."

Dennis folded his arms across his chest and refused to budge. "Why? She'll just lie. She lies to everyone. Look at her marriage! A total sham. Your salary raise? Never materialized. And the excellent references she promised me? The worst lie of them all. She dissed me instead. Why do you always defend her? She treats you like crap, Annie. I'll come in there if you agree to quit. Then you and I can go back to New York and start searching the classifieds for a decent job."

"She'll blackball us," Annie said pointedly. "I don't know about you, but I can't afford to be out of work. I'm living paycheck to paycheck."

That last comment got to Dennis. "Damn it," he muttered and stepped into the café.

If I'd had any sense, I would have brushed right past him and left the potential powder keg that was my best friend's coffee shop. Two things stopped me. First, I felt responsible for this assembly. My agency had invited these chefs and their associates to Inspiration Valley, and I had to do what I could to broker truces, no matter how temporary, and to keep our schedule moving forward. Second, I couldn't leave Makayla alone with Dennis, Ryan, Klara, or Carrie. There was a high probability one of them could explode without warning. I'd seen the result of uncontrollable rage before and didn't want to chance having violence erupt in Espresso Yourself.

Another thought struck me. Klara and Maurice were both here. Obviously, the Dunston police had released them, which meant the chefs were innocent of killing Joel. Either that, or one of them was guilty but Sean and his team hadn't been able to exact a confession or gather enough evidence to take the murderer into custody. I glanced at them. Klara looked completely at ease and Maurice, who was pouring sugar into his coffee at the condiment bar, seemed to be enjoying having Leslie and Charlene hang on his every word as he described his interrogation. Catching a few phrases, I couldn't help but scowl. Maurice was dramatizing what I was sure had been a very calm and civil interview. Sean insisted on courtesy and respect at all times, especially during interviews.

"Annie!" Klara shouted over Maurice's monologue. "Where on earth have you been? There's too much foam on my latte and it's not strong enough for my tastes. Order me another one, please. And Bryce would like an iced chai tea."

Nodding, Annie hurried to see to Klara's needs while Dennis circled around behind Klara and slid into a chair near the tall counter Makayla had dubbed the "Fixin' Station." He poured himself a glass of water from the tall pitcher and stood to the side to give Carrie room to add a sprinkle of nutmeg to her drink. Maurice and Leslie were there, too, and it seemed like half of Makayla's customers were sharing two square feet of floor space.

Maurice wound up his tale and made to add a splash of milk to his black coffee. Giving the stainless steel jug a shake, he frowned and said, "There's no more."

I crossed the room and took the jug from him. Makayla was too busy at the espresso machine to deal with this task and I knew my way around her walk-in refrigerator. Grabbing the depleted jugs of half-and-half, I asked everyone to be patient while I refilled the containers. Out of the corner of my eye, I saw Ryan get to his feet, his gaze fixed on Bryce. Praying that he wouldn't do anything stupid, I hurried toward the back of the café. Makayla gave me a grateful smile as I passed by.

When I came back, people were packed in a tight cluster around the fixing station. The moment I put the jugs down, hands grabbed at them from several different directions. Sugar packets went flying, the cinnamon shaker was knocked into the trashcan, and a coffee cup was overturned. Hot, brown liquid seeped across the countertop and over the edge, pooling onto the floor.

Simultaneously, everyone around the counter jumped back. Agitated comments ricocheted around the fixing station, intensifying the confusion.

"Oh, you clumsy—"

"Look out, that's hot!"

"Watch it!"

I hurried to the sink to grab a towel and returned almost immediately. By then, Annie was crouched on the floor, mopping the spill with wads of napkins, while the others hovered close by. Sponging up the mess on the counter, I wiped around three cups filled with steaming beverages and no lids. The names of their owners were written on the sides: Klara, Bryce, and Carrie.

"Annie, Carrie, are these drinks ready?" I called out.

Dumping her soggy papers in the trash, Annie reached for Klara's and Bryce's cups and proceeded to put lids on them. "Yes, thanks."

I stepped out of the way as Carrie grabbed her beverage and people moved in to continue doctoring their own beverages. Annie held the two cups above her head as if to avoid spilling them. "Thank you for helping me clean up," I said.

"My mother taught me to take care of messes right away," she said, and went to deliver the coffees.

"One of you fools spilled my latte," Leslie declared. "I had just added the perfect amount of nutmeg and cinnamon, too. Somebody owes me a coffee."

Attempting to diffuse another tense situation, I touched her shoulder. "I'll get you one, Leslie. Have a seat and I'll bring it to you."

I waited for people to clear away from the fixing station and then went to the order counter, where Makayla held out a cup. "Here's another latte for Leslie, on the house. I'd put a shot of vodka in there if I had any. These folks need to learn to relax a bit. Thank goodness you stayed after Jude left. I'm not used to such prickly customers."

I leaned in close and whispered, "I'll be very glad to have this Books and Cooks thing over and all these temperamental people out of Inspiration Valley."

"I hear you. This group is as friendly as a nest of wasps," she said quietly.

"You son of a bitch!" Ryan's angry voice filled the café, striking everyone silent. All eyes turned toward Klara's table, where Ryan and Bryce stood facing each other like two rams preparing to butt horns. Fury emanated from Ryan as he stepped in almost nose-to-nose with Bryce, whose hands clenched into fists at his side. He retreated a pace.

I moved to intervene, but Makayla grabbed my wrist. "Don't get in the middle. Let it play out or you might end up with a shiner," she cautioned.

Together, we stood watching the drama unfold. Bryce and Ryan continued to glare at one another, while Klara sat at the table with her coffee, seemingly oblivious to the tension in the room. Dennis smirked from his stool, and Annie stood behind her boss with a stricken look on her face. At their table in the corner, Leslie and Charlene sat mute while Maurice had his mouth open as if he'd been rendered speechless midsentence.

Standing beside her brother, Carrie darted a hateful glance in her stepmother's direction and tugged at her father's arm. "Daddy, don't fight with him. *She's* the one you should be mad at." She pointed at Klara.

He shook her off. "Don't interfere, Carrie," he said sharply. "I will deal with Klara in my own way." He darted his finger at Bryce. "How dare you? You had dinner at our house, you bastard."

Mirroring his sister's movements, Carter pulled Carrie away from the two men. "Come on, Carrie. This isn't the way to get back at her."

Klara appeared unmoved that her family was in the midst of a turmoil precipitated by her actions. Calmly she held her cup to her lips; the only indication that the events affected her was how quickly she guzzled down her coffee.

Leslie and Charlene got to their feet, directing looks of disdain at Klara. "Honestly, Klara," Leslie hissed, sidling past her on her way to the ladies' room. "Could you air your dirty linen in a less public place?" The others in the room stayed frozen where they were, as if they didn't know how to respond to what was happening. I felt the same way. There I stood, clutching Leslie's latte, with no idea of how to diffuse the situation.

However, Leslie's comment induced Klara to rise. She scrunched her cup and flicked it to the floor by Annie. "That coffee had an odd taste, Annie. Dispose of this and get me a glass of water. We need to get out of here."

As Annie hastened away to do Klara's bidding, Klara turned to her husband and her lover. "Boys, please." Her chest heaved. Obviously she was more affected by the events than she had let on. She certainly seemed more distressed than she had a minute ago. Her face was flushed and she was breathing rapidly. "This isn't the place to discuss our issues," she continued, placing her hand on Ryan's arm. "Darling, you know you're—ooh!" Her hands went to her belly and she dropped back into her chair.

Bryce looked from Ryan to Klara, and back to Ryan again. "Listen, man, I don't need this crap. I'm outta here. Talk to you later, Klara."

Ryan bent over his wife. "Darling, what's wrong?"

"I'm a little dizzy . . . I feel sick." Using Ryan to pull herself up, she reached out toward the door, which Bryce was just opening. "Bryce!" she called in a weak voice, almost gasping. "Don't go."

Ryan yanked his arm out of her grasp. He glared at her. "Klara, how can you—" His voice changed to one of concern when she stared at him wide-eyed, clutching her abdomen and groaning. He grabbed her shoulders. "What's the matter?"

She wrenched free. "I'm going to be—" Her hand went to her mouth and abruptly she bent double and vomited on the floor. Ryan leaped back. A look of disgust crossed Carrie's face and she opened her mouth to say something when suddenly Klara sank to the ground, shuddering. Immediately, the atmosphere in the café was charged with alarm and concern. I set down the cup I was holding and ran over, Makayla hastening right behind me. Bryce dashed back inside. The other patrons circled the prostrate chef, carefully avoiding the puddle of vomit on the floor. Klara shook violently, convulsing as if she were having a seizure, and then went still. Ryan dropped down beside her and gripped her hand. "Sweetheart," he pleaded, patting her cheek. "Klara, wake up."

"Is she breathing?" I asked, kneeling as well. Pressing my fingers to her wrist, I put my ear to her mouth, recoiling slightly from the garlicky odor on her breath. Her pulse was racing. "She is," I announced. "But very weakly. Someone call 911."

"I already did," said Carter, holding up his phone with a shaking hand.

Beside him, Carrie stood frozen in place, her face drained of color.

Bryce touched my shoulder. "Let me."

I stood aside as he knelt and took her wrist. Ryan sent a dark look in Bryce's direction as he touched his wife.

Turning to Ryan, I asked, "Could this be some kind of allergic reaction? To something in her coffee, perhaps?"

Ryan's eyes were wild. He shook his head. "She doesn't have any allergies." He watched in anguish as his wife's lover stroked her forehead. Carrie leaned against her dad and he put his arm around her.

I began to be fearful, too, as I was starting to suspect that Klara had been poisoned. She'd become ill so rapidly. Not only had she vomited, but she started convulsing almost immediately after she'd drunk her coffee. Had she not complained that it tasted odd? Had she not groaned in pain? I'd read enough murder mysteries to know what poisoning symptoms looked like.

Quickly, I scanned the faces of the people in the room. Did one of them put something in her coffee in the earlier confusion? A cold dread washed over me as I recalled Klara's lidless cup sitting on the counter with so many people crowding around it. If she really were poisoned, the remnants of her drink would have to be analyzed.

"Annie," I said urgently. "Where's the coffee cup Klara gave you to throw out?"

Still holding her boss's requested glass of water, her face a mask of fright, she pointed to the fixing station. "I put it in the trash like she told me to."

I ran over to the bin and took off the lid. There, in the plastic trash bag, were dozens of empty coffee cups. Many of them were scrunched just like Klara's had been. I sighed in frustration.

Makayla tiptoed up beside me and whispered in my ear, "Why are you rooting through the garbage?"

"I think somebody might have poisoned Klara's coffee," I whispered back. "Don't you think the way she got so sick so quickly is strange?"

With a horrified look on her face, Makayla glanced around at the people in her café. She tied the ends of the bag together and pulled it out of the bin. "The police techs will figure it out. But don't you worry; I won't let this garbage out of my sight until they come for it."

I squeezed her shoulder and returned to Klara. Ryan and Bryce were still hovering over her, their faces drawn and worried. Spotting my bag on a table alongside the forgotten file folder of short stories, I ran to it and retrieved my phone. With trembling fingers, I dialed Sean's number. As it rang, sirens pealed in the distance, getting louder and louder with each passing second. Soon the paramedics would arrive.

Please let Sean be with them, I thought. And please don't let Klara become another murder victim.

Chapter 10

THE PARAMEDICS ARRIVED ON THE SCENE WITHIN minutes and we all watched in silent dread as they listened to Klara's heart, took her blood pressure, and peeled back her eyelids to shine a light on her tiny, black pupils, which seemed to float, unmoving, in a sea of too much white. Throughout the rushed examination, Klara remained completely unresponsive.

The EMTs loaded her onto a stretcher and then wheeled her outside where the ambulance was double-parked, its rear doors open and waiting to receive her. I expected Ryan to dash after his wife, but he was anchored to the ground, his stunned children on either side. Carrie had her arm looped through her father's, and Carter was supporting him around the waist. I couldn't tell if they were holding him up or holding him back.

In the end, it wasn't Klara's husband who rushed forward

to accompany her in the ambulance. Nor was it her lover. Bryce seemed completely paralyzed by what had happened. We all were. Except for Annie.

"I'm going with her!" she cried to the room at large. No one replied, but there was a collective sense of relief that Annie was shouldering the responsibility.

She'd barely made it outside before a policeman strode into Espresso Yourself through the lobby entrance.

"Folks! Your attention, please!" He raised his hands in the air as if demanding quiet, even though the coffee shop was eerily still. "I've been asked to have you wait until Officer Griffiths arrives. He'll be here shortly, so take a seat and don't touch anything."

If he was hoping for mute cooperation, he was to be disappointed. Charlene shouted that she refused to be retained against her will while Leslie threatened to call her attorney. Bryce demanded to know why anyone had to stay, while Carrie repeated a string of four-letter words that had me gaping in shock. All of them fought to be heard, their voices rising until Makayla stepped from behind the counter and bellowed, "SHUSH IT!"

Her voice was deep and strong and cut through theirs like a sharp blade. She held out her hands in surrender. "Please, friends. I know you're all reeling. I am, too. I feel like I just got off a roller coaster and the ground doesn't seem very solid beneath my feet either. But hooting and hollering won't get us anywhere. Let's grab a chair, have a glass of water, and give ourselves a minute to calm down." She walked over to join Charlene and Leslie at their table. "Lord, I'm shaking like a wet kitten," she said softly, showing them her trembling hands.

Her honesty had an instant effect on the two women.

"Me, too," Charlene murmured with a wobbly smile and sank into a chair. Leslie did the same.

The police officer nodded at Makayla in gratitude and then looked up as Sean walked into the shop via the street entrance. The ambulance was still parked outside but I could see one paramedic signal to the other and slam the rear doors shut. The sound allowed me to breathe a little more freely. In a matter of seconds, Klara would be on her way to the hospital in Dunston. Trained professionals would take care of her. And we now had Sean to handle the mess here. Knowing he'd soon make order out of the chaos created by Klara's sudden collapse was an incredible relief.

Sean spoke a few words to his fellow officer and then headed straight for me, his face implacable, and took me by the elbow. Steering me into a private corner, he gazed at me with such intensity that I nearly flinched. "What happened?"

"I think Klara was poisoned," I said and quickly described her symptoms.

Without saying a word, Sean turned and beckoned to Makayla. She hurried right over.

"I need your keys, please," he said. "No one can leave and I don't want any customers coming inside and compromising the scene. *If* this is a scene."

Makayla was obviously unhappy about hanging her closed sign and locking both doors, but she did as he asked. No sooner had Sean started to explain to the room at large that we'd all have to be patient when someone began pounding on one of the locked doors.

Believing Annie to be already gone, I was surprised to

see her standing outside. When Sean let her in, she glanced mournfully around and then burst into tears. "They wouldn't let me go with her. They said that I . . . that I wasn't immediate family." She pointed at Ryan. "You should be with her. She shouldn't be alone!"

But it was too late. The ambulance had already pulled away from the curb and was racing down the street, siren wailing.

Ryan was about to respond to Annie when Bryce pushed in front of him and glared at Sean. "By what right are you keeping us here? Klara got sick and we're all upset, but it's out of our hands now. So why do we have to stay?"

Sean nodded calmly and said, "I'm faced with a difficult problem, Mr. St. John. One of your colleagues was murdered Thursday night and now another celebrity chef has become seriously ill without warning. In my experience, when someone is perfectly healthy one moment and is being rushed to the hospital the next, that individual either has a preexisting medical condition or has fallen victim to violence." He shifted his gaze to Ryan. "Mr. Patrick, did your wife have any preexisting medical conditions?"

Ryan shook his head. "She's mildly allergic to wool, but that's it. Klara has an iron constitution. She never missed a day of filming because of illness. Every now and then she'll come down with a cold, but she's one of the healthiest people I've ever met."

Carter frowned in confusion and looked at Sean. "So you're suggesting that someone in this room deliberately made Klara sick? As in poison?"

"I'm open to all possibilities at this juncture," was Sean's cryptic reply.

Carter was on the verge of saying more, but his sister laid a hand on his arm and he closed his mouth. The twins exchanged a quick look and seemed to withdraw into themselves. For a moment, I envied their closeness. At a time like this, it must be such comfort for them to have each other.

"I need to conduct individual interviews," Sean murmured softly and then gestured at Makayla, who was wiping down her espresso machine even though it looked perfectly clean. She scrubbed the stainless steel furiously, completely absorbed in her task. "Does she have an office in the back?"

"No. There's only a restroom and a closet, but I'm sure you could borrow our conference room. You'll need people out of the way while your team checks this place out, right?"

He lowered his voice to a whisper. "I know you think Klara was poisoned, Lila, but that isn't enough for me to call in a forensic team just yet. The whole station is aware of our relationship so I need to go by the book on this one. In short, I'll have to wait for word from the hospital before I launch a full investigation."

"Then bring all these folks up to Novel Idea," I suggested, waving at the agitated ensemble. "I'd hate for Makayla to lose customers because the doors are locked and two policemen are guarding a bunch of out-of-towners inside. It's not good for business and the ambulance will be enough to set tongues wagging."

"Makayla will have to be interviewed as well," Sean said. "And it's not my job to worry about whether or not her customers can get their soy lattes." He shook his head, immediately contrite. "That came out wrong, Lila. This is a difficult situation and my actions are limited until I have more information. That frustrates me, but I don't mean to take it out on you. Let's get Bentley's permission to use the conference room. Everyone can gather there and then I'll take people into your office for individual interviews. Hopefully, I'll have word from the hospital by the time we're ready to begin."

"You'd better let these people know what's going on," I said and steeled myself for their response. It wasn't pretty. The second Sean announced his intentions, the coffee shop once again echoed with shouts and indignant protests. The shock and fear I'd seen on people's faces after Klara had lost consciousness was replaced by a different kind of terror. Before, the concern had been for her welfare, but now, every person in the room realized that he or she was about to be interrogated. I could see them already guarding their emotions, as if they could wall off their private thoughts, actions, and secrets. I'd been questioned enough to know that this was nearly impossible, and I completely understood their feelings of panic.

When we got upstairs, Vicky informed us that Bentley was in the middle of an important phone call and didn't want to be disturbed. Sean outlined his plan, and Vicky gave her cardigan a firm tug, assuring him that Novel Idea was completely at his disposal.

"I think she has a crush on you," I whispered to Sean as we headed to my office. I wanted to tidy my desk before turning my space over to him.

Sean's radio crackled and he paused to listen to the exchange. When it was obvious that the codes were unrelated to Klara's condition, he turned down the volume slightly and moved to catch up to me.

I opened the door to my office and was surprised to find

Jude reclined in my desk chair, his feet stacked on top of my desk. For some reason, he'd kicked off his shoes, loosened his tie, and unbuttoned the top button of his dress shirt. I glanced from his argyle dress socks to his face and back again, failing to comprehend why he'd decided to make himself so comfortable. He wiggled his toes and grinned.

"Where've you been, sweetheart? I've been waiting and waiting." His voice was deliberately husky. I knew he was only teasing by the impish glint in his eyes and the way the corners of his mouth had turned upward.

A low growl rumbled from behind me. Sean couldn't see Jude's expression and therefore didn't realize that my coworker was just fooling around. I knew I had to respond quickly before Sean got the wrong idea.

"Get your feet off my desk!" I made a shooing gesture at Jude. "This is so unprofessional. Look at you!" Frowning, I gestured at his shirt. "I don't care what state of dress you're in when you're in your office, but this is *my* office. And don't call me sweetheart."

Jude raised his hands in surrender and eased his legs down. "Sorry, Lila. I didn't mean any harm. It's just that I've been patiently waiting for . . ." Sean must have appeared behind me, for Jude's words died away and his playful expression instantly vanished.

"I'm sorry to interrupt your work," Sean said without a trace of emotion. "But I need to commandeer this space. Perhaps you and Lila could relocate to your office."

"Absolutely. Sorry, Lila." Slipping his feet into his shoes, Jude pushed the knot of his tie back into place and hustled out like a chastened schoolboy.

At that moment, Sean's cell phone rang. "It's dispatch,"

he said, bringing the receiver to his ear. "There must be an update on Klara." And then he spoke to the operator. "Griffiths here."

I knotted my fingers together. Part of me wanted to know how Klara was doing, but the other part of me wanted to be anywhere but here. Having to stand inert and wait for news while the seconds moved with molasses slowness was torture.

Sean grunted once and then nodded. "They're sure? Yes, tell the team to get over here ASAP. Thanks, Trudy."

Ending the call, he exhaled heavily and said, "You were right about Klara. She was poisoned. Most likely by arsenic, though it'll take time for the lab results to come in. My team's on the way and I have to get started on those interviews now. We've got another murder case on our hands." He put his arms on my shoulders and squeezed gently. "Are you up to giving a statement after I get the others settled in the conference room?"

I looked at him, unable to process his question. "She's really dead?"

"I'm afraid so." He spoke in a hushed tone. "Are you okay?"

"No," I whispered, my throat dry. "I need to sit down."

Dropping into one of the chairs facing my desk, I put my face in my hands. I wanted to block out the light, to block out the truth. I wanted a long minute of darkness and silence, but it didn't bring me any peace. Someone had poisoned Klara Patrick. She was gone.

"It doesn't seem possible," I said to myself. "She was full of life an hour ago. Walking and talking and griping about her coffee. I just can't . . ."

Sean rubbed my back, but I knew he had more important things to do than comfort me, so I told him I'd be fine. "I'll be ready to give my statement in a little bit. I need to collect myself first."

"Of course." He gave my shoulder another squeeze and left.

I sat there, thinking back on all the times I'd watched Klara on television. I remembered seeing her in person for the first time at Catcher in the Rye. She'd been so gregarious, so utterly charming and engaging. And though I'd come to learn that the woman I'd liked and admired as a TV personality could be petty, egocentric, and cruel in real life, I was deeply troubled by her passing.

The fact that someone had murdered her undoubtedly explained my clammy palms and the roiling in the pit of my stomach. After all, there were only a few of us in Espresso Yourself. One of the people I'd come to know by name—Bryce, Ryan, Leslie, Charlene, Dennis, Annie, Carter, or Carrie—was a killer. One of them had dumped arsenic into Klara's coffee and then sat back to watch her suffer.

"Who could stay so calm when another human being was dying?" I wondered aloud, horror-struck by the notion.

I'd barely begun to consider everyone's motives when Bentley stormed into my office.

"What on earth is going on here, Lila?" she demanded. "Is this three-ring circus your doing?"

Confounded, I stared at her. "Haven't you heard what happened to Klara Patrick?"

"What has that woman done now?"

"Bentley, she . . ." I swallowed. "She's dead. Someone poisoned her at Espresso Yourself."

"What?" Bentley paled and slowly lowered herself into the chair beside mine.

"It happened about an hour ago. Sean—Officer Griffiths—needs to interview everyone who was in the café when she collapsed. I gave him permission to use our conference room. Didn't Vicky tell you?"

She shook her head. "She was too busy directing all those people around the agency so I didn't bother to ask. When I heard the noise in the hall I came right to your office, knowing it's likely that you had something to do with the commotion." Her brow furrowed. "We'd better cancel the literary banquet tonight before another crisis strikes, and have a short closing to the event tomorrow to award the contest prize. I'll have Vicky see to the details immediately. All the ticket holders will have to be reimbursed." Rubbing her temples, she said, "This is a disaster. First Joel Lang, now Klara Patrick. Our public image will be sullied."

I was about to respond when she abruptly stood. "I can't let that happen," she declared and strode out of my office.

Bentley's attitude reminded me that even in the midst of this crisis, I had work to do. Although it would be difficult to focus, Jude and I needed to go over those short stories. Checking my bag to make sure I still had the folder, I headed for the door, only to have my path blocked by Sean and another police officer.

Sean was all business. "Lila, could you go over your statement with Officer Davis so he can record it? Then you'll be free to go."

"All right," I said. "We can do mine in the kitchen so you can start the interviews in my office."

Officer Davis placed a recorder on the table, announced

the date, time, and my name, and then gestured for me to begin. I recounted all that had happened from the moment that Ryan had entered Espresso Yourself. He took notes continuously while I spoke.

"When I get this typed up, you'll have to sign it," he instructed.

I nodded, having gone through this before. He packed up his recorder and went to join Sean. I headed for Jude's office, wondering how I'd be able to concentrate on the short stories.

Jude wasn't there. Propped on his desk was a note. *Lila*, it read, *I had to run an errand. Let's meet first thing tomorrow.*

I was relieved that our meeting was postponed. The trauma of witnessing Klara's collapse and then having to go over the events again for Officer Davis had drained me. I wanted to go home.

No, not home. What I wanted was to see my mother. Over the past year, I'd come to realize that in times of crisis, my mother could comfort me like no one else. Somehow, with her unique homegrown wisdom and well-intended advice, she helped me find the resilience to carry on.

I glanced down the hall. The other agents' doors were closed. From the conference room, unintelligible snippets of conversation spilled out. As I walked past my office, I heard the murmuring of voices through the closed door, and wondered whom Sean was interviewing. Had he narrowed down the suspects yet?

In the lobby, Vicky's desk was unmanned. Most likely she was in the conference room supervising the witnesses. She wouldn't leave while there were still people in the office.

I scribbled on her notepad to let her know I'd gone for the day and headed downstairs.

As I passed Espresso Yourself, I couldn't help but peer through the door. The forensic team was hard at work. A woman was taking photographs while another officer was dusting the fixing station for fingerprints. Their presence seemed like an unwelcome infestation of Makayla's peaceful, happy place. I wanted to erase what had happened here, to return Espresso Yourself to the cozy café it had been this morning. A quote from Joseph Conrad came to mind. "There is a taint of death, a flavour of mortality in lies—which is exactly what I hate and detest in the world—what I want to forget." Sadly, I turned away and went out to my Vespa.

It was a beautiful evening for a scooter ride. The cerulean sky was cloudless and the sun was beginning its descent. But my pleasure was eclipsed by thoughts of Klara's murder. Her death, and Joel's, dogged me like shadows. I was determined to find out who had so casually taken their lives and in the process tainted the character of Inspiration Valley and the agency's festival.

Preoccupied by the day's sad and disturbing events, I barely noticed the meadows of tall grass and wildflowers passing by. Before I knew it, I had arrived at my mother's house. She was sitting in her rocker on the front porch, and as I pulled up, she stood.

"I had a notion you'd show up here," she said, shielding her eyes from the setting sun. "I heard some of what happened to that chef lady on my police scanner, so I knew you'd wanna hash things out with me over a nice, cold drink."

Placing my helmet in the basket on the back of my scooter, I climbed the steps. "Oh, mama." I sighed, kissing her cheek. "You do know what I need."

" 'Course I do. A glass of sweet tea and a slice of chocolate banana bread still warm from the oven." She held open the screen door. "Come in, shug, and tell me all about it."

Aromas of chocolate and baked banana wafted through the hall as I followed her to the kitchen. Sitting at her table, I fortified myself with her amazing homemade bread and a tumbler of sweet iced tea. My mother had flavored the tea with lemon zest and mint. It was both refreshing and energizing.

When she had cleared away my empty plate, my mother sat across from me and put her hands over mine. "Now, why don't you tell me what happened down at Makayla's café," she said. "I know just from lookin' at you that it was an ugly thing."

I took a deep breath. Having just related it all to Officer Davis, I was reluctant to go over it again. But the warmth from my mother's hands and the concern emanating from her eyes unlocked something inside me and I found myself recounting my conversation with Ryan and the discovery his children had made about Klara. I described the undercurrent of tension that entered the coffee shop along with Klara, and how both she and Bryce seemed oblivious to the hurt they had caused Ryan. When I came to the part about Klara getting sick and then collapsing, my mother squeezed my hand.

"The thing is, I might have prevented it if I had been paying more attention to all the people around the fixing station." I concluded with a sigh. "Maybe the coffee was spilled on purpose to create even more confusion than was already there and to take the focus off Klara's beverage. When I came back with the towel, her cup was just sitting there with no lid. Any one of those people could have slipped the arsenic, or whatever it was, into her drink."

"Lila, you couldn't have stopped that wickedness any more than you could keep a bull that's been bit on the rump by a horsefly from chargin'. Stop blamin' yourself. Whoever killed that woman would have done it no matter what."

"But who killed her? Almost everyone there had some reason to want to get back at Klara." I took a sip from my glass while I sifted through the names of the people who were at Espresso Yourself. "Even though Ryan was playing the wounded husband, he certainly had a strong motive. Klara betrayed him and flaunted her affair openly."

"Humiliation can make folks do things they wouldn't regularly do," my mother concurred.

"And Ryan's twins, Carrie and Carter, hated Klara. Not only because of the kind of stepmother she was to them, but also because of the way she treated their father." I stared at my mother. "Do you think a person as young as Carrie or Carter could poison someone?" I couldn't help but remember how they'd reminded me of Trey when I first met them.

"People can surprise you, no matter how old they are." She downed her drink and got up for a refill.

I gazed into my glass. "Dennis Chapman also had it in for Klara. You heard his outburst at the panel. And there was certainly no love lost between Klara and Leslie Sterling. Klara was very critical of her—so much so that Leslie's popularity diminished and there were rumors of her show being canceled." I shook my head. "That's just what I know.

I'm sure there are all kinds of secrets and resentments that I'm not even aware of."

My mother folded her hands on the table. "I sensed right from the start that Klara was the type to make enemies. And it seems that her worst one finally got to her."

"Right after Joel got killed, too. Their deaths must be related."

"One thing's for certain, Lila," my mother declared. "The person who killed those two chefs wanted them to suffer. Because they suffered, sure enough."

I PASSED A quiet evening at home. I had hoped that Sean would have joined me for supper, but he'd called to say he wouldn't be able to come over until later. So I cooked myself an omelet with tomatoes, green onions and goat cheese, and watched some TV before putting on my pajamas and climbing into bed. I tried to occupy my mind by reading the short story entries for the agency's contest, but my mind kept wandering. When I heard Sean's key in the lock, I jumped out of bed to greet him.

"You're so late, I thought you wouldn't be coming." I hugged him tightly.

"I did consider calling to cancel, but after the day I've had I just needed to see you." He kissed me. "I figured you could use a bit of company, too."

"Boy, could I." I hoped my smile conveyed how glad I was that he was here. "How did the interviews go?"

He shrugged. "We're still sorting through all the information, but no suspect jumps out immediately." He gave a half smile. "If you don't mind too much, could we not talk about it tonight? I know you want to hear everything, but I'd rather not think about Klara Patrick or Joel Lang for the rest of the evening. Okay?"

"Of course." Now that I really looked at him I could see how exhausted he was. "Why don't we go to the bedroom and I'll give you a massage?"

"Now that's an offer I can't refuse."

I started out by rubbing his shoulders and he fell asleep almost immediately. Only slightly disappointed, I snuggled up beside him and began to drift off myself. For the first time since Klara's collapse, my thoughts traveled away from her to dreams of a future with the warm, sweet man lying next to me.

The ringing of the doorbell startled us both awake. Heart pounding, I sat up as the chimes echoed through the quiet house. "Who could that be?" I squinted at the clock. It was after midnight.

"Stay here," Sean said. "There's a murderer in town, so let me see who's there." He climbed out of bed and went to the dresser to take his gun from its holster. Holding it down by his side, he ventured into the hall.

I ignored his instructions and followed, finding it unlikely that a murderer would ring the doorbell. Light from the streetlamps cast an eerie glow through the transom above the door, turning Sean into a shadowy figure. In this half dark, his pale blue boxers glowed.

The doorbell rang again. With his hand on the knob, Sean called out, "Who's there?"

"Mom? Is that you?"

Sean pulled open the door and Trey stood on the welcome mat, his mouth agape in surprise.

"Sean? Uh, hey. Uh . . ." Trey tried to peer behind Sean, who stepped behind the open door in order to conceal himself. I think he was embarrassed to have my son see him in his underwear.

At that moment I didn't care that Sean was feeling self-conscious. Having Trey on my doorstep at this hour sent my imagination in a hundred different directions. "What's wrong?" I demanded and pulled him inside. "I don't know what you're doing here in the middle of the night, but I hope you're not in any trouble. I've had about all the trouble I can handle for today."

Chapter 11

"I'M HERE BECAUSE I WAS WORRIED ABOUT YOU, MOM,"
Trey said, keeping his gaze averted from where Sean hid
behind the door.

I hadn't expected this answer and gave him a quick hug
in response. Deciding it would be prudent to move the conversation out of the front hall, I said, "Come on into the
kitchen. I know it's spring, but I'll make us some hot chocolate. If nothing else, it'll soothe my nerves."

"Sounds great." Trey's voice was full of relief. Without
looking at Sean, he hurried down the hallway.

Covering a smile with my hand, I turned to Sean. "Go
on, cover up that manly bod of yours."

Sean wore an expression of dismay. "I thought he knew
about us . . ."

"He does," I assured him. "But it's one thing to be aware
that your mother is involved with someone and quite another

to show up at her place to find the man she's dating in his boxer shorts. This isn't how kids care to picture their mothers. To Trey, I'm the woman who cooks and gardens and nags him to turn down his music or clean up his room. He doesn't see me as a single woman with an active love life."

"It'd be even more active if people didn't keep dying in this town," Sean grumbled and then jerked his thumb toward the bedroom. "I'm going to make myself decent. Should I give you two some privacy?"

I shook my head. "That's sweet, but if Trey drove home in the middle of the night because of me, then he's really worried. I could use your help convincing him that I'm not in any danger."

"You got it." Sean stepped out from behind the door and tiptoed down the hall, trying to move lightly on his feet. Holding the gun by his side, his movements were a bit ungainly and I couldn't help but chuckle.

In the kitchen, I took a bar of semisweet chocolate from the cupboard and began to chop it into pieces. As I worked, I asked Trey to tell me what had spurred him into coming home.

"Inspiration Valley is all over the news, Mom," he said. "Two celebrity chefs dead in a single weekend. Murdered. Chefs involved in a festival you helped arrange. I was just finishing my last big project due before spring break when this reporter appeared on the TV screen in the common room. She was doing interviews right in front of Espresso Yourself. I took one look at that yellow police tape and I thought about you working away in your office right upstairs and . . ." He trailed off but not before I heard the catch in his voice.

I put the knife down and went to him. Squeezing his wide shoulders, I whispered, "You were scared for me. Oh, sweetheart, I'm sorry you had to go through that. And when you were working on a project, too. I should have called to tell you that I was okay, but I had no idea the news of Klara's murder had become public already."

"The media got wind of the case late this evening," Sean said upon entering the kitchen. He held out his hand to Trey. "Sorry about how I answered the door. How are you, Trey?"

Trey took Sean's hand and smiled. "I'm glad to see you, actually. Knowing you're here means that my mom is safe."

Sean sat down at the table and I poured several cups of milk into a saucepan and set it on the burner over low heat. While Sean recapped all that had happened, I whisked the milk, added a tablespoon of pure vanilla extract and a sprinkle of cinnamon, and then let the mixture simmer for a minute. Trey interrupted Sean's narrative every now and again with a question and though I wasn't listening closely to the words, I enjoyed hearing the voices of my two men entwining.

Picking up the cutting board, I pushed the chocolate into the pot and added a few tablespoons of confectioners' sugar. I watched the chocolate turn the milk a luscious golden brown and inhaled deeply. With my eyes closed, I imagined the scene in *Charlie and the Chocolate Factory* in which Willy Wonka's guests catch a glimpse of the chocolate waterfall.

His whole factory must have smelled just like this kitchen, I thought, pouring the steaming liquid into three large mugs and garnishing each drink with a squirt of Reddiwip. After serving Sean and Trey, I joined them at the table.

As they both blew on their hot chocolate, pushing curls of steam into the air, I felt a rush of contentment. Here, in this warm room filled with conversation and the scents of cinnamon and chocolate, I was truly at ease. The outside world and its groundless displays of violence were held at bay within this cozy space and I wished we could remain here forever, in my little haven of food and light and love.

"This is really good," Sean said after he'd taken a sip of his drink. "Sure beats the powdered stuff."

"My mom would never use that." Trey informed him proudly. "I remember coming inside on a winter's day feeling like I was frozen from head to toe and she'd have hot chocolate waiting. Plus, she'd give me a whole bowl of marshmallows to go with it. That was awesome, Mom." He toasted me with his cup. "You always did special things for me. Thanks."

I stared at him in astonishment and tried not to tear up. Instead, I smiled gratefully and ruffled his hair. "I have to admit that I've missed not being able to look after you. But you're a man now, Trey. Look at this role reversal. You were so worried that you left school to check on me." The realization of what he'd done suddenly hit me. "Wait. What about your midterm exams? Your projects?"

"Relax, Mom. I took my last test Friday and emailed my paper to my prof before I left. Trust me, it's cool." He shrugged. "Guess I'm just starting my break a little early. It's a good thing. I mean, Sean can't be with you all the time, right? He's got a bad guy to catch." He eyed Sean seriously. "Are you close to doing that?"

Sean sighed. "I wish we were. We have too many suspects in this case and not enough hard evidence with which to convict any one person." He shifted his gaze to meet mine.

"You should be forewarned that none of the chefs will be free to leave Inspiration Valley until the murderer has been apprehended."

The idea of having to listen to an endless stream of complaints from the inconvenienced celebrities made me groan. And then I considered the other people who'd been present when Klara collapsed. Would I have to try to reassure Carter, Carrie, Dennis, and Annie, too? Any one of these people could be a murderer.

"Was arsenic the poison used on Klara?" I asked.

"Yes," Sean said. "Because this is a high-profile case, the lab results were fast-tracked and the report was very clear that a significant amount of arsenic was stirred into Ms. Patrick's coffee." He studied the wisp of whipped cream floating on the surface of his chocolate and frowned. "She ingested enough poison to put her body into a state of crisis. Arsenic attacks multiple systems at once and that's why you saw such a range of symptoms, Lila."

I recalled how Klara had rapidly progressed from feeling dizzy and feverish to being too weak to stay seated in her chair. I thought of how she became confused and then nauseated, how she'd developed an accelerated heart rate, and lastly, how her body had jerked and convulsed on the floor as she was wracked by seizures. "It was awful," I told Trey and he covered my hand with his.

Sean pushed his mug away, folded his arms, and leaned heavily on the table. "Our best guess is that the killer poured arsenic into Ms. Patrick's coffee at the fixing bar. Apparently, there was a knot of people gathered there at the same time, giving our culprit the perfect cover."

"Yes," I agreed. "And there wasn't a person in that space

who didn't have some sort of grievance against Klara. I suppose they all spent their interviews pointing fingers and declaring their innocence."

As I expected, Sean didn't respond. There was a limit to what he'd discuss with me, particularly in front of Trey. Deciding on a different tack, I asked, "What about Makayla? Surely you don't think she's responsible for an iota of this villainy?"

"No, I don't. Our forensic team has finished gathering all the available evidence and she's free to open for business in the morning."

"Then it's only a matter of time until you find the killer. After all, his or her fingerprints will be on Klara's coffee cup." I felt a surge of hope. "You'll probably know by the end of tomorrow, right?" I glanced at the digital clock on the microwave. "Or today."

Sean wore a troubled expression. "At this point, we haven't found a single trace of arsenic in the trash bags my team removed from Espresso Yourself. Not on a cup, a napkin, a wooden stirrer, nothing. And no cup with Klara's name on it, either."

"How can that be?" I asked in dismay.

"I don't know," Sean admitted and then gave me a faint smile. "But don't be discouraged. We'll find something somewhere. Anyway, Makayla's done all she can to help us. You won't have to worry about her losing business. I expect she'll have a line out both doors minutes after she hangs up her open sign, especially with tonight's media coverage. By first light, every network will be sending a team and they'll all park right in front of your building, Lila."

I didn't like the sound of that and neither did Trey. "Are you going to work tomorrow, Mom, even though it's Sunday?"

I nodded. "All the agents are working this weekend."

Trey frowned. "I'd better come to work with you, Mom. Reporters can get pretty pushy and I don't want any of them messing with you."

He sat back and puffed out his chest, trying so hard to look tough that I nearly smiled, but I managed to keep a straight face. "That would be nice, Trey. Maybe you could lend Makayla a hand, too. She hasn't had much time to rest and recover after what happened and I bet she could use a strong, hardworking young man by her side."

Trey stood up, collected our empty mugs, and put them in the sink. "Well, this strong, hardworking dude is beat. Goodnight, Mom." He leaned over and kissed my cheek and then gave Sean an awkward little wave. "Goodnight, ah . . ."

"Call me Sean. You're the man of the house, after all. We should be on a first-name basis."

Clearly pleased by the suggestion, Trey picked up his backpack from the hall and jogged upstairs.

"We'd better try to get some sleep, too," I said. "In a few hours, you'll be doing your best to solve two murder cases and I'll be trying to mollify our celebrity chefs as well as their assistants and family members while silently wondering which of them is a killer."

"Keep your eyes and ears open," Sean said as I turned off the lights.

I let him go on ahead and stood for a moment in the dark kitchen. Visions of what the day would bring had driven the warmth from the room and I rubbed my arms, feeling a sudden chill. How quickly the shadows had filled in the voids left by our voices. Unbidden, I thought of Klara and of the speed with which life had been stolen from her.

After checking to see that the front door was locked, I joined Sean beneath the covers. I drew as much comfort as I could from his body heat and the steady rhythm of his breathing, but it seemed like a long time before I was able to let go of the day's images and surrender to a series of fractured and disquieting dreams.

SEAN HAD BEEN right in his prediction that every television network would have a van parked outside my office building the next morning. In some places, they'd double-parked. Trey and I passed an angry cameraman arguing with a stony-faced policeman over the ticket placed beneath the blade of his windshield wiper.

"Should we go straight upstairs?" Trey asked.

I cast my gaze over the throng of people on the sidewalk blocking the entrance to Espresso Yourself and shook my head. "We'd better check on Makayla. The café must be mobbed and I want to make sure she's all right."

We decided to push our way through the crowd lined up at the lobby entrance, and even though we received a few indignant cries of "No cutting!" or "Can't you see the line?" no one tried to bar our path.

Inside the café, all was orderly. Every seat was occupied and people were standing almost shoulder-to-shoulder around the tables. I noticed that almost everyone held a beverage or an Espresso Yourself take-out bag and that Makayla was amazingly composed. She moved with her customary grace, listened to the orders as they were relayed to her by the cashier, fixed the drinks, and smiled at every customer. She didn't seem the slightest bit perturbed by the masses of people gathered outside, all of whom were desperately eager to gain entry.

Edging around a man holding a cappuccino in one hand and a microphone in the other, I stepped up to the counter.

"How are you this calm?" I asked Makayla. "And more important, how are you keeping this lot in line?"

She gave me one of her dazzling smiles. "I have an occupancy limit, so the only folks I'll let in are bona fide customers. These folks can stay for fifteen minutes and then they have to make room for those waiting outside. Anyone who argues isn't served." She shot a warning look at a man in a trench coat and then lowered her voice. "As for the radio and television folks, I told them that I'd be happy to talk during my next break. Can I help it that I don't have time for a break for at least another hour or two?" She winked at me and then spotted Trey. "Trey! Lord, are you a sight for sore eyes! Have you grown two feet since Christmas or am I shrinking?"

Trey's cheeks reddened. "I was wondering if you could use some help. I'm on spring break so I'll be in town for the next ten days." He waved his hand around the café. "But it looks like you've got everything under control."

"Trey Wilkins, you are the answer to my prayers," Makayla said and pointed down the hall. "Open that closet and get yourself an apron. You're hired. And your first job is to act as my bouncer." She turned to me. "You okay with that, Mama?"

"I am," I said, knowing Trey would watch over Makayla while treating her customers with courtesy. "Just don't encourage him to punch any reporters. Inspiration Valley has enough bad press at the moment."

Makayla grunted and placed a cup on the counter. "Your caramel latte."

I grabbed her hand and whispered, "Are you really okay?"

"Really and truly," she assured me. "Tossed and turned all night like I was a fairy tale princess with a pea the size of a boulder under my mattress, but I wasn't worried about this place. Folks know I didn't hurt Klara. Besides, they need me. They've got to see my face, hear my hello, and let me put a cup of the best coffee in the world in their hands before they can do the things they've got to do. Their day won't be the same without me." She grinned. "Just like mine wouldn't be the same if I didn't see you. Or Mr. Matthews. Or Mrs. Crosby. Do you get what I'm saying? We're all connected."

I squeezed her hand. "You're the heart and soul of this town, Makayla."

"Then you're its poetry," she said. "I know you're broken up over these terrible deaths, Lila, but don't let one wicked person undermine how important it is for all of us to celebrate words and food and fellowship. Don't let them steal that from the readers and writers and fans who came to be a part of Books and Cooks."

Squaring my shoulders, I promised her that I wouldn't. After wishing Trey good luck, I took my latte and headed up to my office, vowing to pour all of my energy into the short stories I should have read yesterday.

I thought of one of my favorite quotes from Margaret Atwood and spoke it aloud as I mounted the stairs. It filled me with strength and renewed my commitment to my job. "'A word after a word after a word is power.'"

The killer's power was significant, but it wouldn't last. Words would. And that's what I meant to focus on now.

DESPITE BEING DISTRACTED by my conversation with Makayla, I was able to sit quietly at my desk and read through the contest entries Jude had given me. The one he and Bentley had chosen as the best was definitely a cut above the others. And Jude was right. This writer had the same spellbinding voice as Marlette had had in his novel. If the short story author were willing to make the commitment, we'd found our ghostwriter for Marlette's sequel.

Eagerly, I pulled up the contestant list to see the writer's identity and was thrilled to discover that it was Jay Coleman, the owner of the Constant Reader. I knew that Jay was an avid reader and book lover, but I had no idea that he was a talented writer as well. I was delighted by the thought of informing him that he'd won. After all, he was a friend and neighbor and one of the kindest people I'd ever met. Smiling, I gathered all the papers into a folder and headed to Jude's office.

"You aren't going to believe this," I said after rapping on his door and walking in. Jude looked up from his computer monitor. Unlike yesterday, his appearance was completely professional. His tie was in a perfect knot at his collar, which was buttoned to the neck, and his shoes were still on his feet. I placed the file folder on his desk and took a seat in his guest chair. "The winner of our short story contest is Jay Coleman."

"The bookstore owner? That's great." He leaned back, stretching his arms behind his head. "One of our own, and a bibliophile at that." He grinned. "Do you agree that his writing style is similar to Marlette's and that we should submit his name to pen the sequel to *The Alexandria Society*?"

"Definitely. I'll go over and tell him at lunchtime. The news should make his day."

Jude sobered. "I guess our final Books and Cooks event won't be the happy celebration we'd intended, with two of the chefs murdered and the other participants under suspicion."

"I know. Bentley will give a small speech and then we'll announce the winners of the writing contest and the reader-voted best cookbook award and that'll be it." I gave a rueful shrug. "Our festival didn't quite turn out the way we expected, did it?"

"No, but there's no way we could have foreseen what transpired. I only hope things can return to normal soon." He ran his fingers through his hair. "Shall we get back to work? Let's figure out the other placements for the contest and put together some kind of proposal for Jay."

Our mood had altered with the talk of the past days' tragedies, and without further discussion we got on with our tasks. We worked diligently for a while, and were wrapping things up when Franklin tapped on the door.

"Sorry to interrupt," he said, stepping into Jude's office. "But I have a favor to ask of you, Lila."

"It's okay, we're almost done. What can I do for you?" I shuffled papers together.

"I just received a phone call from Charlene Jacques. She is most distressed. Apparently, the police have obtained warrants and are searching all the rooms. Leslie Sterling was with her when she called, and I think they are frightened by the goings-on. They asked if I'd keep them company during the search. Of course, I said yes, but . . ." His cheeks flushed pink. "I'm not very good at dealing with semi-hysterical women and I wondered if you'd come along to help with the handholding."

"Absolutely." I welcomed the opportunity to be at the Magnolia Bed and Breakfast while the police were present. If they found something, I'd be one of the first to know it, giving me the opportunity to put everyone at ease during the festival's final event.

CHARLENE AND LESLIE were sitting side by side on the bed when we arrived. They looked like two nervous schoolgirls, clinging to each other, their eyes wide as marbles.

"Oh, Franklin. Lila. We're so glad you're here," said Leslie, letting go of Charlene and standing. "The police have rifled through all of my things. The audacity. It's given me a terrible headache." She massaged her temples.

Charlene twined her fingers together. "They don't really believe that Leslie or I had anything to do with Klara's death, do they? That we brought arsenic to the festival?"

Leslie glared at her and then turned back to us. "We just want to go home. Can you help us do that, Franklin? After all, you were the one who invited us to this place."

I touched her arm. "I'm sorry, Leslie, but no one can leave until the police say so. They have to find out who murdered Joel and Klara, and until they can identify the culprit, everyone is a suspect."

Charlene snorted. "Not everyone. I'm sure they don't think you or Franklin did it."

Franklin cleared his throat. "That's because we have no reason to want them dead."

"But neither do I," sputtered Leslie. "What would I have to gain by—"

A disturbance in the hall stopped her and we all hurried to the door. Bryce St. John was being escorted toward the lobby by a police officer. He held Bryce's arm, and Bryce's hands appeared to have been secured behind his back. Another officer followed, carrying a large navy duffel bag.

"But Klara gave me that money to hold!" Bryce protested, resisting the pull on his arm. "I didn't *take* it. And I certainly didn't poison her to get it."

"Sir," the cop said sternly. "You're under suspicion for murder and are being charged with assaulting a police officer." He touched his free hand to his lower lip, which was split. A line of dried blood clung to his chin. "Don't make things worse. Just move it."

Bryce glowered at him, but he stopped struggling and walked quietly from then on. When he passed us by, he saw Franklin and his face instantly brightened. "Franklin. Tell them. I wouldn't steal money from Klara. Tell them our quarrels were just friendly competition. I wouldn't have hurt her. I loved her."

I exchanged a troubled glance with Franklin, who obviously didn't know how to respond. The cop jerked Bryce's arm. "Sir. Now."

Bryce reluctantly acquiesced. We watched in solemn silence as they left the hotel. My mind was racing. I couldn't believe that they'd taken Bryce St. John. Was the money they found in his hotel room the same money that was missing from Ryan's safety deposit box? If not, why would he bring all that cash to the festival? Was he telling the truth when he said that Klara had given it to him for safekeeping? Had Klara planned to use Ryan's nest egg to run away with Bryce? But then, why would Bryce poison his lover? Or murder Joel? Surely he wasn't the killer.

None of it made sense.

I HAD THOUGHT about having lunch at Espresso Yourself. It would give me the chance to see how Trey was doing and to share the news about Bryce with Makayla, but I was too worked up to stop. Not only that, but I certainly didn't want to put myself in the middle of a pack of reporters. So instead of the coffee shop, I picked up a Thai chicken noodle salad and lemonade from How Green Was My Valley and sat on the edge of the fountain to eat. I didn't really have much of an appetite at first, but the spicy peanut dressing kindled my taste buds, and in the peaceful calm of the park, I finished the salad with gusto.

While I ate, I thought solely about Bryce St. John. *Was* he the murderer? He seemed too affable to have such an evil streak in him. Dipping my hand into the fountain I stared up at the Nine Muses. "'The devil's agents may be of flesh and blood, may they not?'" I asked them, quoting Sir Arthur Conan Doyle.

Of course they didn't answer. Water spilled from their hands, splashing into the pool. Just being in the park centered me and I felt better. I could not help that Bryce might be guilty of murdering his colleagues. I could not help that Ryan's heart was broken. And I could not help that our festival had been sabotaged by events beyond my control.

But I could help an aspiring author realize his dream. It was time to do something positive. Throwing my trash away, I walked briskly to the Constant Reader.

To me, there is a special atmosphere in every bookstore, as if all the stories within the books are just waiting to come alive. The Constant Reader was no exception, and I found myself smiling as I meandered between the shelves looking for Jay. He was busy assisting a customer, so I checked out the cookbook display while I waited.

It seemed almost indecent to see Klara's smiling face on the large poster display near where she'd had her book signing. Still, this was a better image to have in my memory than the one from Espresso Yourself. My jaw dropped when I saw the empty table beside the poster. At her signing the day before, there had been stacks of her cookbook, *My Grandmother's Hearth*. Now there were none.

"It's amazing how death sells, isn't it?" Jay came up behind me. His voice was solemn and I sensed that he'd prefer Klara alive and writing, to a cash register stuffed with bills. "There was a run on her cookbooks this morning, and I've completely run out of everything she's published. It's been so crazy here that I haven't had a chance to change the display." He folded his arms across his chest and looked at Klara's picture. "That poor woman."

"Yes," was all I could think of to say.

"You were there when she collapsed, weren't you? It must have been horrible."

"It was," I said without elaborating. I didn't want to linger

Lucy Arlington

on the subject a second longer. "But Jay, I didn't come here to talk about Klara. I have some news for you."

He glanced at a customer leafing through a book and signaled to his assistant. "I'll be in the back," he told her. Then he turned to me. "Let's talk in private."

The room at the rear of the store was just the way I imagined a bookshop's office to be. Stacks of books of all sizes on the floor, shelves overflowing with books, papers on the desk. It looked like something out of Dickens, except for the computer.

"Sorry for the mess," he said as he took a mound of paperbacks off his guest chair. "I never have enough room for everything."

"It's perfect," I said. "Very bookish." I picked up the slim blue volume on his desk and saw that it was a collection of poetry. I opened it to a random page. "*I carry your heart with me,*" I read aloud. "*(I carry it in my heart) I am never without it.*"

"E. E. Cummings," he said.

"Are you a big fan of poetry?"

He shrugged. "I love all genres of writing. That book was from the display celebrating National Poetry Month and I've been reading it during my breaks. It's amazing how much emotion a poet can convey in a few lines." Sitting down, he indicated the chair he'd emptied. "Have a seat. What did you come to tell me?"

I returned the poetry book to the desk. "Two pieces of good news, actually. First, your short story, 'Diner in the Rough,' has won first place in our short story contest. You'll be awarded your prize at the final festival event this afternoon. Congratulations."

He broke into a huge grin. "Really? That's awesome." He raised his hands and punched the air above him.

I laughed. "It was well deserved, Jay."

"Thank you."

"You're welcome," I said, still smiling. "But there's more."

"More?" He held on to the armrests of his chair as if to keep himself from floating away.

"You remember *The Alexandria Society* by Marlette Robbins?" I asked.

He nodded vigorously. "I loved that book. It's too bad Mr. Robbins isn't around to write a sequel. I can envision so many plots stemming from those he introduced in that amazing first novel."

"That's what I want to talk to you about. The book's publisher wants a sequel, and Jude and I have been looking for a writer who's up to the challenge of serving as ghostwriter. It's been difficult, because Marlette's voice is so unique and spellbinding that we haven't found anyone who could write in the same vein." Pausing, I could see that Jay was hanging on my every word, as if he could anticipate what I was about to say but afraid to hope for it. I continued. "Until now, that is. Jay, we believe we've found the person to author Marlette's sequel. You."

"Are you saying what I think you're saying?" he asked in a tremulous voice.

I nodded. "We're confident that if you submit a good proposal, the publisher will agree with our opinion and offer you a contract. Do you want to write the sequel? It's a huge commitment."

"Are you kidding me? Of course I want to write it! It's

been my dream. I have half a dozen manuscripts tucked into drawers, but I never imagined . . ." He leapt out of his chair and grabbed my hand, shaking it. "Thank you, thank you, thank you!"

His enthusiasm was contagious and I found myself grinning. "It's not definite yet, you understand."

"I know, I know. But I have *so* many ideas. I bet I can write a bang-up proposal."

"Tell you what," I said, standing. "Call Vicky and set up a meeting with Jude and me. Bring your ideas, and we'll get a proposal ready for the publisher by the end of the week."

"I will. Thank you, Lila. You've made me a very happy man."

I left Jay's office feeling more content than I had in days. My world was in balance once more. I was doing what I loved—changing the life of an aspiring author. And in the process, we were continuing Marlette's legacy.

Considering the two heinous murders this weekend, I hoped that balance had been restored to Inspiration Valley as well. Perhaps having Bryce St. John in custody meant that the person who had tainted our town was off the streets.

If the police had the right man, that is.

Chapter 12

IT WAS TEMPTING TO LINGER IN THE CONSTANT READER. The bookshop was a haven and I could easily picture myself settling into one of the leather-upholstered chairs and whiling away the rest of the day reading about imaginary people and places. It was an attractive thought, and as I headed for the exit, my fingertips touched the colorful spines of the books in the fiction section. Since I'd met with Jay, the gilt lettering imprinted into the cloth and leather covers seemed to shine a little brighter and I was filled with happiness at the thought that his novel would one day find a place on these shelves.

As my favorite Vivaldi concerto danced through the speakers, the late afternoon sunshine bathed the coffee-table books displayed by the front door in a soft glow. I thought of a quote by Gilbert Highet, a literary critic, who'd once said that books were not lumps of paper, but minds alive on the shelf. That's exactly what I was feeling at the moment—I was among friends as real and vibrant as my mother or Makayla, and I was reluctant to leave them.

Still, there was work waiting for me at the office and, hopefully, exciting new writers waiting to be discovered. Possibly, there were more unique and powerful voices like Jay Coleman's in the queries piled on my desk. I might have given Jay the news of his lifetime, but his jubilant reaction to it had reignited my own passion for the written word. Determined to catch up on my stack of unread letters and proposals, I cast a final look at the book-filled paradise and stepped outside into the balmy spring air.

The Vivaldi piece continued to play in my head and I hummed along as I walked, enjoying the sunshine and the scent of freshly cut grass. Municipal groundskeepers were busy in the town park; mowing, pruning, and exchanging spent pansies for pink and white vinca, purple coleus, and sweet potato vines. Rich, dark mulch had been spread beneath the newly trimmed boxwoods and dwarf holly bushes, and all around the park's perimeter, onlookers sat on benches, their books or magazines forgotten as they watched the landscapers transform the flowerbeds.

I recognized a man sitting on a bench shaded by a magnolia tree. He had his elbows resting on the top of his thighs and his chin in his palms. A newspaper lay on the seat next to him and I knew what the headline read. Deciding to postpone my return to the office, I made my way to his side.

"Hi, Ryan," I greeted him quietly. He sat so still that I was afraid any sudden noise would make him jump.

Instead of being startled, he moved in slow motion, as if he were underwater. Glancing up at me through glassy eyes, he released a heavy sigh and said, "It's so beautiful here. I wish it weren't. I wish there was rain or snow and not a single flower. No birds singing. Right now I hate their songs. It's like they're mocking me—reminding me what happiness sounds like."

Gesturing at the vacant end of the bench, I said, "May I?"

Nodding absently, he reached over, folded the newspaper in half, and tossed it on the ground behind us.

I couldn't blame him for not wanting to see the photograph of Klara and the bold letters proclaiming her murder. Part of me believed that he couldn't bear to look at the article because it caused him pain. This would confirm the fact that he loved his wife and was in the initial throes of an awful grief. On the other hand, I still felt I had to view Ryan Patrick as a murder suspect. The front-page reminder that Klara had been poisoned might be causing him a different sort of agony: the kind created by intense feelings of guilt or regret.

Sean wouldn't approve of my conducting an investigation, but he had his hands full interviewing Bryce and figuring out the meaning behind the duffel bag of cash discovered in his hotel room. Things looked bad for Bryce indeed. Not only was he in possession of all that money, but he'd also been at the coffee shop when Klara collapsed and he could have put the arsenic in her coffee. And yet, he'd been the only one who'd tried to save her. Ryan hadn't. He'd sat in shock, watching another man attempt to resuscitate the woman he supposedly loved. So was Bryce guilty? Or had someone else poisoned Klara? Like the man sitting within inches of me?

I needed to know the truth about Ryan Patrick and I wasn't going back to Novel Idea until I had it.

"Do you really think it was him? Bryce?" Ryan asked as if he'd read my thoughts. "Is it possible that he was just using Klara to get to our nest egg? Those funds would be enough to keep that floundering restaurant of his afloat."

I could tell that it had been difficult for Ryan to speak Bryce's name. "If that's the case, the police will find out," I said by way of comfort.

"Sorry, but I don't share your confidence in the local law enforcement. Maybe if I were sleeping with one of the officers, I could show the same amount of faith," Ryan said snidely. And then he instantly shook his head. "Forgive me, Lila. You've gone out of your way to be kind ever since Klara and I arrived." He studied his hands as if they were unfamiliar to him. "Now she's gone, my kids are shut up in their rooms, and the members of the media are circling like sharks that have caught the scent of blood in the water."

"The press can be capricious," I said sympathetically. "One moment they're celebrating your success and the next, they're taking your most painful and private experience and sharing it with the world."

He grunted. "All those sycophants at the TV station. They'll attach themselves to another celebrity like *that*." After snapping his fingers, he laced them together so tightly that his knuckles turned white. "I know I'm the only one who'll truly mourn Klara's passing. Bryce was a fling, my kids never bonded with her, and she was too competitive to form any lasting friendships. Women either idolized her or wanted to supplant her. Take Leslie or Charlene, for instance."

I'd certainly learned that the visiting chefs were prone to petty squabbles and jealousy, but it was Ryan I wanted to focus on now. "You were her true companion," I said softly. "Her genuine other half."

"Yes," he whispered miserably. "She would never have risen to such heights without me, but I savored her success. Even though I was behind the scenes, we shared the spotlight. Her triumphs were mine as well."

I frowned. "I remember your saying something about Klara being nothing without you. Were you referring to her career?"

"It goes back to the day we first met," Ryan began, his gaze fixed on some point in the middle distance. "I was working at a small-town television station in the Midwest. I hosted a cooking show and did other kinds of on-location reporting to make ends meet. But it was the cooking I loved best."

This came as a surprise to me. "You're a chef, too?"

Ryan let out a humorless laugh. "I was an army cook, not a chef. Whatever my title, I've always had a way with food. What I could never develop was a television personality. Klara, on the other hand, was a natural in front of the camera. She was hired at the station to do general grunt work, but one day I asked her to assist during one of my shows. She didn't know the first thing about cooking, but the viewers loved her. So did I. We started dating and I groomed her to take over as host."

"What about her Dutch grandmother and all those stories about her heritage?"

"A fabrication," Ryan answered blandly. "I'm the one with the Dutch connection, not Klara. My audience, which became hers over time, loved the Dutch-inspired cooking angle. I know I'm using a silly pun, but they ate it up. It was foreign and homey all at once. So we gave Klara a Dutch grandmother. But she couldn't say the words correctly half the time. I'd sit with her and drill her on the proper pronunciation, but she always struggled with foreign languages. I even had to coach her on the pronunciation of French and Spanish dishes. She was hopeless, but it didn't matter." He smiled, lost in his memories. "She charmed her way to the top."

As I tried to take in this information, I wondered if anything about Klara Patrick had been genuine. "Was your family from the Netherlands?"

"No, I was stationed there. My base was American, but we abided by Dutch laws and regulations and interacted with the locals quite a bit. I was fascinated by their culinary history, of course, and picked up a few traditional dishes on my own, but what I really wanted was to learn from one of the townsfolk."

"And the Dutch *oma*? Where does she come in?"

He looked directly at me for the first time since I'd sat down. "That's how I viewed Mieke. As a grandmother. She was out late one night, walking home from a friend's house where she'd been playing cards with two other elderly ladies, when a man attacked her. I just happened to be passing by, interrupted the mugging, and gave the assailant such a shiner before he got away that he was pretty easy to identify the next day." Blushing a little, he stared into the middle distance. "The mugger had been assaulting women for weeks before I came along. Mieke was so grateful that she offered me a reward. When I found out she owned a small café, I begged her to teach me how to cook Dutch dishes."

Completely absorbed by Ryan's tale, I imagined the old woman and the heroic young Army cook standing shoulder-to-shoulder in the café's kitchen, talking and laughing as they chopped fruits and vegetables or stirred pots on the stovetop. "You two must have grown close."

"We did." His voice was full of tenderness. "When I got back to the States, we wrote to each other. She mailed me recipes for years. Almost every dish mentioned in *My Grandmother's Hearth* was hers. She passed away over a decade ago and I really miss her."

"So that's what you meant when you said that Klara could never have climbed onto a pedestal without you," I mused aloud. "You were the true chef, but she knew just enough to cook on camera."

Ryan nodded and then a look of panic surfaced in his eyes. "You're not going to tell anyone about this are you? It would destroy everything we've built over the years."

I didn't make any promises. After all, I'd have to tell Sean everything I'd heard. Instead, I said, "Klara was so convincing. How did she do it?"

"I walked her through each and every recipe at home. She was a quick study when it came to parroting my movements, and like I said, she could talk about anything while she was on the air and people would respond favorably. She was like a ray of sunshine bursting into their living rooms."

That couldn't be denied. After all, I'd tuned in to her show over and over, hypnotized by her charisma. "You're right," I told him. "She never failed to make me laugh and I'd been delighted by her anecdotes of cooking with her grandmother. Poor Klara. She didn't actually have a relationship with the wonderful woman she described so vividly on television and in her cookbook. And she clearly wasn't close with your kids. So you were everything to her. Until Bryce," I added hesitantly.

Ryan made a low, guttural noise. "It seems that I was a better manager than husband, but I gave her everything. *Everything!* And how does she repay me?" His eyes darkened with quiet fury. "Cleans out the safety deposit box. Sneaks out of our bed to have sex with her lover and then comes creeping back before dawn. How could she make such a fool out of me?"

I noticed he was using present tense, as if Klara were still alive. Ryan's hands clenched and his lips curled in a snarl. "I loved you, you stupid woman. What would you be without me? Nothing. Nothing. *Nothing.*" He practically spit the last word and I was frightened by how swiftly his tender reminiscences had changed into angry accusations. The man beside me was coming unglued. Or had that happened in the coffee shop yesterday? Had Ryan been filled with enough silent rage to murder his wife?

"I think you should be with Carter and Carrie," I said, trying to put an end to our conversation without upsetting him further.

He didn't seem to hear me. Staring down at the ground, he muttered under his breath. I caught Klara's name once or twice, but his words were otherwise unintelligible. I glanced around, wondering what would happen if I just left him here. Even though I continued to view him as a murder suspect, it seemed wrong to simply walk away from this broken man.

And while I didn't think he should be alone, I didn't want to place anyone else in a precarious position. Who could watch over him and be on guard against him at the same time? Suddenly, I had an idea. "Ryan?" I touched him briefly on the shoulder. "Have you seen Annie? Maybe you could—"

"Annie," Ryan whispered blankly. "She brought me breakfast. Strawberry jam on a croissant. It was flaky and warm from the oven. So sweet."

"That was nice of her," I said. "Have you had anything else to eat today? Maybe you and Annie and the kids could have supper together? I don't think you should be alone."

Something shifted in his vacant eyes. "Annie. She always knows what to do. She's always there for us. For me. She's an angel."

"Will you call and tell her where you are?"

He nodded and pulled his phone from his pocket. I waited until he dialed, spoke a few sentences, and then hung up. "She told me to wait here. She's coming to get me."

"That's good," I told him and forced the corners of my mouth to turn upward in a smile. "I'll see you soon, Ryan."

He didn't reply. I left him amid the mulch, flowers, and grass cuttings. As I walked the rest of the way to Novel Idea, I hoped I was right in my belief that he'd never hurt Annie. He was obviously unstable and, therefore, dangerously unpredictable.

I quickened my stride.

In the privacy of my office, I called Sean. I wanted him to assure me that the case was closed, that Bryce had been arrested and the entire town could rest easy. However, I couldn't think of a single reason why Bryce would have killed Joel. As the phone rang and rang, the flat tones reverberating through the earpiece, I had a horrible feeling that, although the festival was coming to an end, the chefs would be staying with us well beyond the closing ceremony.

AS BENTLEY HAD foreseen, this event was very low-key. Other than the Novel Idea agents and the chefs, there were barely thirty people in the audience at the Marlette Robbins Center for the Arts. This surprised me; I assumed that at least twenty-seven of them were the writers who had submitted stories to the contest. I supposed in the wake of two murders, most attendees from out of town had chosen to leave Inspiration Valley.

Despite all the empty chairs in the hall, Bentley assertively walked onto the stage, her pink heels clicking on its wood floor. She spoke briefly about the tragedies that had befallen Joel Lang and Klara Patrick, and concluded with, "These events are in no way a reflection of our beautiful town, or Novel Idea Literary Agency. Our agency is committed to our authors and to great books." She then held up an envelope. "I have here the recipient of the first Novel Idea Best Cookbook Award as voted by you, the readers. And the winner is . . ." She peered over her rhinestone-studded glasses at the expectant faces in the audience and dramatically ripped open the envelope. This was an act, of course, since Vicky had given us the results of the vote when we prepared for this final ceremony. Bentley leaned in to the microphone. "*My Grandmother's Hearth* by Klara Patrick."

The audience broke into applause. I regarded them from the wings of the stage. The thirty or so people clapped enthusiastically, but with their small number, the accolade was feeble. Among the group of visiting chefs, only Annie joined in with the acclamation. I could not see Ryan or his kids anywhere.

Bentley displayed a certificate. "Is Mr. Patrick in the audience? No?" She looked at me and raised her eyebrows, then turned back to the audience. "We bestow this honor upon Chef Klara posthumously. I would now like to call upon two of our agents, Jude Hudson and Lila Wilkins, to announce the winners of the short story contest."

Bentley stepped back, and Jude and I took her place at the podium.

"We were impressed by the quality of writing in the entries we received," began Jude. "Those of you who submitted a story should be commended for your efforts. In fact, could all the authors who entered the contest please stand?"

About twenty-five people rose from their seats. In the front row, Jay Coleman was smiling.

"You all deserve a hand." Jude began to clap. The rest of us joined in, and soon everyone in the hall was applauding. Jude nodded for the writers to sit, and the room quieted. Suddenly, the door to the auditorium banged open, and we collectively turned to see who had entered so late in the proceedings.

At the door, Bryce St. John held up his hands. "Sorry," he said to the assemblage, and took a seat in the back row. I couldn't keep from staring at him. The fact that he was here indicated that the police had released him, which meant that he was no longer a murder suspect. Although deep down I had not believed that he was the one, his presence nonetheless disconcerted me. It would have been a relief if Bryce had been guilty, because then the killer would be behind bars, all the chefs could go home, and Inspiration Valley would be safe and peaceful once more. But clearly, the murderer was still on the loose. Uneasiness crept over me as I recalled my conversation with Ryan Patrick and his overt instability. I wondered if my earlier suspicions about him being the murderer could be valid.

Jude nudged me with his elbow. "Lila!" he whispered. "You're on."

Drawing my gaze away from Bryce, I focused on the people sitting in the front row and said, "The third-place winner is . . ." I looked down at the sheet of paper in my hands. "Stephanie Miller for 'Cupcake Chaos.' Stephanie, please come up to receive your prize."

A tall, freckled teenage girl rose and climbed the steps to the stage. Jude handed her an envelope and a book, and shook her hand. "Congratulations, Stephanie. This is a gift certificate for Sixpence Bakery and a copy of Leslie Sterling's cookbook." Stephanie grinned.

I also shook Stephanie's hand. "Keep on writing," I said. "And perhaps one day we'll be signing you as a client."

Stephanie blushed. "Thank you."

When she'd left the stage, Jude spoke into the microphone. "The second-place winner is Donna Wainright for 'A Tale of Two Kitchens.' Donna, could you please come up?" A full-figured woman with rosy cheeks and a long gray braid hanging down her back joined us on the stage. Jude congratulated her. "You've won a gift certificate for dinner for two at the Nine Muses Restaurant and a copy of Joel Lang's new cookbook," he said and presented her with the prizes.

"Thank you, thank you," said Donna, bobbing her head.

She grabbed my hand and pumped it up and down. "Thank you, thank you," she enthused again.

"And finally," I said as Donna descended from the stage. "The winner of the first annual Books and Cooks short story contest is Jay Coleman for 'Diner in the Rough.'" The audience applauded while Jay came up on the stage. I shook his hand and handed him an envelope. "Jay's story will be published in Inspiration Valley's weekly newspaper, *Inspired Voice*, as well as in the weekend edition of *the Dunston Herald*. And he wins a gift certificate from the Magnolia Bed and Breakfast for a romantic night for two, including champagne and a selection of fine chocolates."

"Nice work, Jay," Jude added. "I hope you have someone special you can share that prize with."

At Jude's comment, Jay's cheeks flushed tomato-red and he shrugged lightly. "I might. Thank you," he said and returned to his seat.

Bentley approached the podium, and Jude and I stepped back. We were joined by Franklin, Flora, and Zach. Bentley spoke into the microphone. "And that concludes our first annual Books and Cooks festival." She gestured in our direction. "On behalf of all of us at Novel Idea, we thank you for coming and hope that, despite the unforeseen calamities this weekend, you enjoyed yourselves. Have a good time at the rest of the Taste of the Town events, and be sure to return next year."

People milled toward the exit. I looked over to where Bryce had been sitting but he had already left.

"Man, I'm glad that's over," Zach declared. "There was more tension at this festival than a twelve-string guitar!"

"The tension has yet to dissipate, Zach," said Franklin.

"A murderer is still at large, and we have the chefs to babysit until the police determine the killer's identity."

"*You* do," said Zach. "They're *your* clients. This bad boy has new clients to snag. Catch ya later!" He snapped his fingers and headed for the door.

"We won't have much to do with the chefs anymore will we?" asked Flora. "I mean, I know we invited them here, but now that the festival is over, they're not our responsibility. And one of them is a murderer!" She rubbed her forearms as if chilled. "Hopefully, the police will resolve all this very soon so life can get back to normal."

"Amen to that," said Jude and departed.

Stepping outside, I inhaled the fresh air, feeling a relief similar to Zach's. Although the murderer had not yet been caught, the festival was over. It had certainly had its glitches, but discounting those, the events that our agency had sponsored could be considered successful. While it seemed a bit inappropriate to celebrate, I felt like doing something special, so on a whim I decided to stop in at the Grape Escape for a bottle of wine to have with dinner. Trey was home, after all, and Sean was coming over. I had wild-mushroom lasagna in mind, and a robust red would go nicely with that meal.

The bell on the door jangled as I entered the Grape Escape. Bottles lined every wall, and the light that filtered through the stained-glass window gave the room the illusion of being in a wine cellar. A giant barrel served as a tasting table, upon which sat wineglasses and a few opened bottles.

"Good afternoon, Lila," said Jeff, the owner. He had opened this shop several months ago, and the residents of Inspiration Valley had come to rely on his expertise. "It's been quite a weekend for our town, hasn't it? And for your agency."

"Yes, it has. And today has been an especially long day. I need a good wine to go with mushroom lasagna. What do you recommend?"

"I have a lovely Barolo that arrived the other day. There's a bottle open. Would you like to try it?"

He led me to the barrel table, where he poured a half inch of dark red liquid into a glass and handed it to me. I took a sip. As the wine hit my taste buds, I felt warmth inch through my body.

"Do you perceive the overtones of raspberry and ripe cherry, with a hint of spice?" he asked, watching me closely.

"Yes, I do. It will go perfectly with the lasagna. I'll take a bottle."

Purchase in hand, I pulled the door open and almost ran into Annie.

"Ms. Wilkins!" she exclaimed. "I'm so glad I bumped into you. I wanted to talk to you."

I stepped aside. "Hi, Annie. I was just on my way home. Is it very important?" I didn't mean to be rude, but I was tired and yearned for this day to end.

"I only need a few minutes."

Through her stylish cat-eye glasses, her pleading eyes were hard to resist. "Let's go to that sidewalk bench, okay?"

Once we were seated, she began. "Ryan told me that you talked with him today when he was . . . well, when he wasn't feeling quite himself. Thank you for that." She gave me a sad smile. "Even though I was Klara's assistant, I was also Ryan's, you know? And he's been hit hard by all that's happened, so I feel like I need to take care of him."

"You truly take your responsibilities seriously," I said.

She nodded. "It's my job. And just because Klara is gone,

that doesn't mean that my job is done. Not until Ryan says so, anyway." She adjusted her glasses. "I heard they arrested Bryce St. John and then let him go. So I guess the police still don't know who killed Klara or Joel Lang."

I shook my head. "Not as far as I know."

"I don't want to tell tales, but I might know who did it."

"Annie, if that's true, you should go to the police immediately." My tone was gentle but firm.

She shrugged. "Well, I'm not sure, but I thought if I told you first, you could decide if what I know is worth telling the police. I feel more comfortable talking to you because you've been so kind."

"Okay. Tell me what you know." My pulse quickened in anticipation of what Annie might say. Did she really know the murderer's identity?

"Dennis Chapman is a bitter man," she began. "And he harbored plenty of resentment toward Klara. He can be quick to anger, too. And volatile. If he's in a foul mood, you have to walk on eggshells around him or he'll explode. I've had to calm him down many times on set." She exhaled. "I don't want to get him in trouble if he's not guilty, but I've been thinking about his personality and his bitterness toward Klara, and that combination just seems to add up to the probability that he poisoned her. Especially after what he said to me when she died."

I nodded in encouragement. "Go on."

"Well, you should know that Klara was not kind to him. Even though she appreciated his skills, she treated him badly. But then, she treated most of us badly at times." She picked at a fingernail. "Dennis believes that Klara sabotaged a job application he'd submitted for head chef in an upscale restaurant. He never forgave her for costing him his dream job. He vented to me about it all weekend. But that's just Dennis." She shrugged. "At least that's what I thought. But when we found out that Klara was dead he was actually happy. He kept saying things like 'She got what she deserved' and 'I'm glad she's dead.' He even said that poisoning was too good for her and that she should have suffered more." She slid a lock of hair behind her ear. "And there's something more. I think Dennis knew Joel Lang before he came to work for Klara. I don't know anything about their shared past, but from the way he talked, and the way he acted the few times he was in the same room as Joel, it was obvious that he hated Joel, too. So you see? He might be responsible for both murders." She looked up at me wide-eyed. "Ms. Wilkins, he scares me. I'm afraid to be near him."

I put an arm around her shoulders. "You need to share all of this with the police, Annie. If Dennis is a murderer, they'll take him into custody."

"That's what I thought. But I feel better for having told you. Could you call your policeman friend for me?"

I pulled out my cell phone and dialed Sean's number. He answered on the first ring, startling me. I'd grown accustomed to getting his voicemail.

"Sean, I'm sitting with Annie Schmidt, and she's been telling me some things about Dennis Chapman that I think you should know. Based on the information she's provided, I'd say he's a pretty solid suspect for Klara's murder."

"He's actually next on our list for questioning," Sean said. "I'll send a couple of uniforms out to collect him but will talk to Annie myself. Are you at your office?"

"No, we're on the bench just outside the Grape Escape."

"Lila, do you mind staying with Annie until I get there? I'll be about fifteen minutes."

"Yes, I'll wait." I slipped the phone back into my purse. "He'll be here soon." I hoped those fifteen minutes would go fast. "How did you end up with the Patricks?" I asked, trying to make conversation.

"I was a prep cook in a small restaurant in New York. One day I read an article about Klara and Ryan, and then I saw her on TV and decided I wanted to work for her. I liked the way she celebrated Dutch food. She was very unique."

"So Klara's food is what drew you to her?"

She nodded. "Yes. She wasn't always a good boss, but her food, and Ryan's, made it worth having to meet her endless demands. Ryan is a great chef himself."

"I found that out today." I wondered if Annie knew the secret of Klara's success. It was not my place to ask, however.

Annie pointed at the Grape Escape. "Is it okay if I go inside to buy a bottle of wine while we wait?"

I was surprised that Annie would ask for my permission. Perhaps since working for Klara, she'd become accustomed to having to ask for leave to do anything. "Of course," I said. "I'll let you know when Officer Griffiths arrives."

Alone on the bench, I reflected on how levelheaded Annie had been throughout this disturbing weekend. It was a character trait that no doubt saw her in good stead as an employee of Klara Patrick. What a contrast to Dennis Chapman, who had only ever shown belligerence, anger, and envy—the key ingredients in crafting a crime of passion.

Chapter 13

BY THE TIME I WALKED INTO MY HOUSE, LADEN WITH groceries and a bottle of wine, I was exhausted. All I wanted to do was kick off my shoes, turn on the radio in the kitchen, and get the lasagna in the oven so I could indulge in a really hot bubble bath. Just as I dumped the bags on the kitchen counter and wiggled my feet out of my heels, I heard the front door open and Sean called my name.

"In here!" I yelled, putting a jug of milk in the fridge and a quart of lemon gelato in the freezer.

I'd just closed the freezer door when Sean's arms slid around my waist. "Hi, honey," he murmured into my neck. I'd seen him outside the wine shop less than two hours ago, but it felt like forever since we'd been alone together.

Swiveling around, I kissed him briefly and then we held each other for a long moment. His body felt strong and solid beneath my hands. "What a day," I whispered tiredly.

"It's not over for me, I'm afraid." Sean stepped back and eyed the groceries on the counter. "I have time for a quick meal and that's all. Can I help you make supper?"

Smiling, I said, "The last time I let you loose in this room, you started a fire, remember?" Reaching into a cabinet, I pulled out a large pot and handed it to him. "This won't be fast-food quick, but I can have you refueled in a little over an hour if we work together. You're in charge of cooking the lasagna noodles. Fill this with water, add a tablespoon of salt and a splash of oil, and then bring to a boil. Add the noodles and cook for ten minutes. Got it?"

Sean clicked his heels together and saluted me. In return, I swatted him with the dishtowel.

"Hey, that's assaulting an officer!" Trey shouted from the doorway. "I'll be your witness, Sean."

Grinning, I tried to flick the towel at my son but he was too swift. He danced out of the way every time, taunting me with silly faces and jibes. Soon, I was laughing too hard to attempt any more attacks. The second I lowered the dishcloth, Trey grabbed me in a bear hug and squeezed me until I cried, "I surrender!"

Releasing me, Trey opened the refrigerator door and peered inside. "I'm starving. Espresso Yourself was insane from the second I got there until Makayla told me I was done for the day. It feels like lunch was a million years ago."

"If you pitch in, supper will be ready all the faster," I said and pointed at a plastic bag of field greens. "Grab stuff to fix a salad. Anything you want."

"You got it." Trey gathered the field greens, a tomato, a cucumber, and a red onion and carried the vegetables to the sink to be washed.

Sean and Trey fell into an easy conversation about the day while I prepared the white sauce for the lasagna. Gently nudging Sean to one side of the stove, I placed a saucepan on the back burner and brought four cups of milk to a simmer. In a different pan, I melted butter, humming along to a song on the radio as I added flour, the warm milk, salt, pepper, and nutmeg. While I was whisking the mixture until it turned thick and creamy, Trey asked Sean if he'd made any progress with the two murder investigations.

"I can't tell you much," Sean said. "We've brought Dennis Chapman in for questioning, and he's been very open and forthcoming thus far. It's clear that he bore a grudge against Mrs. Patrick, but we still need to gather evidence to prove that he's our man."

Trey paused in the middle of chopping an onion and gave Sean an inquisitive look. "Couldn't he just be playing you? Acting all up-front about hating Klara so that you believe him when he says he didn't act on his hatred?" He turned back to the cutting board.

Sean nodded and poked the noodles with a fork. They rippled and roiled in the bubbling water like flags in a strong wind. "Most people experience intense dislike for another human being at one point in their lives. But few channel those feelings into acts of violence. Whether Dennis is capable of pre-meditated murder is what I need to discover when I return to the station tonight."

"How will you do that?" Trey asked with genuine fascination. "Get past his defenses? And his lies? How can you tell what's the truth and what's a load of crap?"

"Strangely enough, silence is my best weapon. That, and common courtesy. If I question someone in a respectful manner and then sit back and watch, wait, and listen, the person I'm talking with will often fill the quiet with an answer. It's not always the one I'm looking for, but every answer brings me closer to the truth. And if I begin with questions I already know the answers to, it's easier for me to determine if and when a suspect starts lying." He glanced at his watch. "The process can take hours. All night sometimes. And it's grueling. For both the interrogator and the person being questioned. That's why I need one of your mom's hearty meals. She'll fortify me for the night to come."

I smiled at the compliment and asked Trey to pass me the cutting board. He scooped his cucumbers into a large bowl and handed it to me. Working rapidly, I sliced portobello mushroom caps and then sautéed them in a mixture of butter and olive oil.

Sean drained the lasagna noodles and asked Trey what it was like to work with Makayla.

"If I didn't already have a girlfriend, I'd probably have a huge crush on her," Trey admitted. "She's a great boss and is positive and patient all the time. She's totally awesome."

I spread some of the white sauce on the bottom of a baking dish and then arranged a layer of noodles on top. I repeated this step, adding mushrooms and grated Parmesan with every other layer, and topped the whole thing off with a generous sprinkling of cheese. After popping the lasagna into the oven, I set the timer and began to unwrap a loaf of fresh Italian bread. "While that's cooking, I'll prep the garlic bread. Would someone please pour me a glass of wine?"

"I'll do it," Trey offered. As he battled with the corkscrew, he told Sean how Makayla had shown him the bits of poetry left by her secret admirer. Sean listened with interest, rubbing his chin as Trey shared his theory that Makayla's mystery man was smart, shy, and didn't see himself as a good-looking guy.

The last statement piqued my curiosity. "What makes you say that?"

"He thinks Makayla's out of his league. You can tell because he won't talk to her in person. Or if he does, he just orders his coffee or chats about the weather or whatever. He hasn't asked her out because he's too insecure," Trey explained, handing me a glass of wine. He then offered Sean one, but Sean shook his head and reminded Trey that he would be returning to the station right after supper. Trey shrugged and kept the glass for himself, giving me a sly smile as he took a large sip. "This is good stuff," he said and took a bigger swallow.

"No refills for you, young man," I warned. "If it were up to me, you'd still drink milk with every meal."

Trey rolled his eyes. "Anyway, I think Makayla's guy isn't intimidated by her love of books. My guess is that he's into books, too. And he's creative. Did you see that cool origami thing he made?" I nodded and Trey continued. "But he doesn't believe she'll want to date him, so he's trying to make her fall in love with him using the words of these poets instead of his own. The thing is, that's not going to work. Sooner or later, he needs to use his voice."

"An astute hypothesis," Sean said. He'd begun to set the table while Trey was talking and now sat down at one end, rubbing his chin in thought. "And have the clues been escalating?"

Trey carried the salad bowl to the table and also took a seat. "Yeah, Makayla said he's leaving them more frequently. Do you think he's working up his courage to reveal himself?"

"Maybe." Sean looked at me. "Has Makayla shown the poems to many people?"

I crushed a garlic clove with the back of a spoon and scooped the pieces into a small bowl. "No. She's been pretty private about them. I'm surprised she told Trey. On one level, she wants to discover this guy's identity, but I also think there's a part of her that doesn't want the mystery man aspect to come to an end."

"She told me because she wanted a man's take on the whole thing." Trey squared his shoulders and thrust out his chest. "And this manly man thinks her masked poet is basically a good guy. He over-tips, makes Makayla happy, and hasn't been creepy or weird. Still, I sense that she's getting a little frustrated. I need to catch this guy in the act and pull him aside and tell him to go for it. Ask the lady out."

Waving the serrated knife I'd just used to slice the loaf of crusty Italian bread, I scowled. "Unless he's married. Then you'd better convince him to buy his coffee elsewhere."

Trey popped a tomato slice in his mouth and nodded. "Don't worry, Mom. If there's anything about this guy that I don't like, I'll tell him not to go near Makayla again."

"Good." Satisfied that my son was looking after my best friend, I put the bread in the oven to toast and joined my men at the table. The wine, conversation, and scent of cooking food had eased all the kinks from my shoulders and I felt relaxed and content. Twenty minutes later, I took the lasagna and the garlic bread out of the oven and served them to Sean and Trey. While we ate, the guys talked about Dunston's Triple-A baseball team and I thought about how the three of us had prepared tonight's meal together. Like a well-written novel, we'd blended the ingredients until they created something worthwhile. Something rich and colorful and memorable.

"You're miles away," Sean said, putting his hand over mine.

I smiled at him tenderly. "I was thinking of how we worked together in the kitchen tonight. It was smooth and natural and made me feel really happy." I turned to Trey, including him in my smile. "From there, my thoughts drifted to the celebrity chefs and I began to wonder if they were all still amazed by how it feels to move in synch around a kitchen with the steam rising and water running and the knife blade hitting the cutting board. The sizzle of a hot frying pan, the rush of heat from an open oven, people spinning around each other like dancers." I paused and suddenly thought of the young man waiting for Sean at the police station. "That's the life Dennis wants. It's his dream. Klara denied him his chance. By holding him back and tying him to her, she fostered that hatred inside of him."

Sean nodded, but I could see from his closed expression that he didn't want to discuss the case anymore, especially in front of Trey. "Anyway, I can see why they're so passionate about the profession, and tonight I think we were as good as any of them," I said with a breeziness I didn't feel. By speaking Klara's name after we'd already set the subject of the investigation aside, I'd involuntarily invited a ghost into the room.

Hoping to restore the atmosphere of tranquility and relaxation, I stood and cleared the plates off the table. "There's lemon gelato for dessert. Who has room?"

Sean got to his feet and carried the lasagna dish to the

counter. "Not me." He gave me a kiss on the cheek. "Thanks for supper, Lila. It was exactly what I needed, but I've got to go."

I wanted to throw my arms around him, to whisper that I believed in him and had faith that he'd discover the murderer's identity soon. I wanted to kiss him with abandon, to let my body convey how much he meant to me. Sometimes words just aren't enough. But he was already saying goodnight to Trey and moving toward the front door. I followed him and before he could step into the darkness, I grabbed his hand.

Usually, this is when a quote from a famous writer would surface in my mind, but now I couldn't think of a single one, so I looked him in the eyes and said, "If there is one thing I'm certain of in this world, it's you. No matter how scary and upsetting things become in this town, I know that you're here for me. For all of us. That you're going back to work and that you'll keep going back until we're safe again. Thank you, Sean. Thank you for giving me certainty when so many things about life in the last few days have felt as insubstantial as quicksand."

He pulled me to him and kissed me deeply. I could feel the love and gratitude in his embrace. Then he broke away abruptly, smiling, and caressed my cheek with his palm. "If I can come back tonight, I will. That is, if it's okay with you. I'm sure you'll be asleep."

"I'd prefer to wake with you next to me than alone," I whispered. "I'll let Trey know that you have your own key and might come in at any time. I don't want him down here at three in the morning wielding a baseball bat."

After one final kiss, Sean jogged down the steps, down

the path, and out to his car. I stood on the porch, happy and hopeful, and watched his taillights cut thorough the dark night like a pair of bright red stars.

INEXPLICABLY, I SLEPT solidly that night and greeted Monday with fresh intentions for a productive week. Waving good-bye to Trey as he headed out into the fresh early morning air, I tightened the belt on my dressing gown. Although the sun was up, the grass was still damp with dew, causing his footsteps to leave imprints in the lawn. I marveled at his maturity. He'd been the first to rise. He set the coffeepot on and before I was even dressed he was out the door to help Makayla open her café.

"Your son has grown into a wonderful young man," Sean said behind me. He wore his uniform and his hair was still damp from the shower.

"I was just thinking the same thing. Do you have time for breakfast before you go?" I touched his arm.

"Maybe some toast," he said. "And coffee. It smelled so good when I stepped out of the shower."

"You smell good, too." I kissed his smoothly shaved cheek.

While Sean slathered black currant preserves on his bread, I spread peanut butter on mine. I bit into the crunchy rye toast. "So how did the interview with Dennis go?" I asked tentatively, hesitant about disturbing our cozy ambience. Sean hadn't come to my house until late yesterday evening and we were both too tired to discuss it then. "That is, if you want to tell me."

He took a sip of his coffee. "That guy is very volatile, and he's angry with a lot of people. I'm not convinced that he's the murderer, but he certainly has the personality for violence. And the motive. He told me that he has dreamt many times about killing Klara, and that he'd like to shake the hand of the person who did it. But no matter how we pushed him, he would not admit to having done the deed." Sean shook his head.

"So you believe Dennis had a motive to kill Klara, but do you think he could be responsible for Joel's death, too?"

He nodded. "Dennis bore a grudge against him as well. Just like he blamed Ms. Patrick for costing him that job, he also held Mr. Lang responsible. Apparently, their connection goes back to a food competition. Something to do with fish and fruit fusion, and Dennis beat out Mr. Lang. According to Dennis, his win humiliated the Asian fusion chef, and because of that, Mr. Lang would not write him a letter of recommendation. You should have heard him rant, Lila." Sean squared his shoulders and clenched his fists. Mimicking Dennis's voice, he bellowed, "'I told him he could have the damn trophy if he just wrote the damn letter. It's as if those snobby-assed chefs forget how they started.'"

I recoiled at the intensity with which Sean shouted while marveling over his impersonation of Dennis. "You sound just like him. I can easily imagine him yelling that at you. His interview must have been rough." Despite Sean's freshly showered appearance, his eyes were rimmed with dark smudges.

"It was. Dennis Chapman is not a pleasant man. And from what we've learned about Mr. Lang, Dennis's account of his pettiness seemed a bit out of character. Later, when I went through my notes, I discovered that the fish and fruit competition occurred just around the time that Mr. Lang and Mr. Bruneau parted ways, so I imagine that Mr. Lang was emotionally fragile then. Dennis Chapman's demands and abrasive personality would understandably be too much for him to deal with in that period of his life."

"And of course, Dennis would take the snub very personally."

"Yes," Sean said as he stood and picked up his cap. "And he's very bitter about it all. He viewed that potential job as his ticket to success and he blames Ms. Patrick and Mr. Lang for his not getting it. His motives for killing both chefs are not to be ignored, but we can't yet prove that he's responsible for either of the murders. Still, we're holding him for the time being."

ESPRESSO YOURSELF WAS bustling. All the tables were filled and a line of customers waited to give their orders. As I took my place at the end, I waved at Trey, who was busy restocking and wiping the fixing bar.

"I am so thankful for that boy of yours," Makayla said when she handed me my latte. "He was such a lifesaver during that madhouse Sunday and since I've got a to-do list longer than a rat snake, I went ahead and hired him for the rest of spring break. He's a damned fine worker."

Although Trey didn't respond, it was obvious that he'd heard her comment because his cheeks flushed and he broke into a grin as he scrubbed a pastry tray.

I, too, was smiling as I opened the door to Novel Idea. I began to hum "Walking on Sunshine," but pulled up short when I saw a girl sitting halfway up the steps leading to the lobby. It was odd to see someone there and I had a quick flash of memory about Marlette Robbins visiting the office day after day, desperate to have someone read his query letter. Did this girl feel unwelcome, too? Before I could ask if I could help her, she stood and spoke.

"Ms. Wilkins, I've been waiting for you." At her full height, she was taller than me, and very thin. Her hair was cropped close to her head. Pale blue jeans encased her long legs like skin and she wore a bright green batik-printed blouse. A silver wire with various stones and crystals hung around her neck, and a large red felted bag hung from her right shoulder.

"Do I know you?" I asked. She had called me by name so somehow she must be acquainted with me, but her face wasn't familiar.

"We've never met, but I see you around town all the time. On your Vespa. In the shops. At the festival this weekend." Her reply unsettled me. So did the fact that she was blocking my way. I frowned and was about to respond when she continued. "And you would certainly know me through my writing. I'm Zoe Bright. I sent you a query about my novel, *The Crystal Color Wheel Witch*."

I wracked my brains, sifting through the titles mentioned in queries that I could recall. "I'm sorry, I don't remember at the moment. I receive dozens of queries every day. Did you get a response?"

Her eyes darkened. "Just a form letter rejecting me. You didn't even send it yourself! After I gave you a gift and all." She fingered the stones around her neck. "I see that you don't have the necklace on. That crystal pendant is meant to enhance your well-being and you should wear it all the time."

My uneasiness increased as I recalled finding the gift

bag hanging from the handlebars of my Vespa along with the query letter. Her approach seemed creepy then; amid this confrontation it was even more unsettling. Inadvertently, my hand went to my neck, where her necklace would be if I had been inclined to wear it. "It is inappropriate to send a gift with a query," I said assertively. "The words should speak for themselves." I tried to soften my tone. "And a rejection letter does not mean that there is no hope for your manuscript. Only that you need to go back and work on it. Improve it before you resubmit it."

"But it's already good!" Her eyebrows knit together in anger. "I'm sure if you'd worn the energizing amethyst when you read my synopsis, you wouldn't have put it in the rejection pile for your secretary to reply to." She reached into her bag.

I tried to pass her. "Excuse me, Zoe. I need to go upstairs. I'd be happy to read your next query if you send it in the appropriate way, through email or post." Instead of stepping aside, she thrust a wad of papers at me.

"Please, take it now. Read my query again. And the manuscript. Give my novel a chance. It's good." Her eyes flashed hope. And desperation. "I didn't mean to offend you before."

I stared at her. "This is not the way we do things. You are making me uncomfortable. Go home and work on your query. Don't bring your submission in person, but send it to me via the process outlined on our agency's website. If you do that, I promise to consider your query."

She pressed her lips together. "Fine." Shoving the papers back into her bag, she stomped down the steps. I stared after her until she was gone, slamming the door behind her. This was not a great start to my workday.

* * *

THE DAY DID improve, however. I managed to catch up on the pile of queries in my inbox and I offered representation to an author whose joy burst through the phone. At the staff lunch meeting, Franklin reported with relief that the chefs remaining in Inspiration Valley had resigned themselves to staying in town for the time being. Both Bentley and Franklin had been contacted by several enterprising editors probing the idea of one of the chefs penning a tell-all about the weekend. Vicky indicated that she had been fielding calls about the murders all morning from the media, and that the number of email queries in her inbox was double the usual amount. I was thankful that Vicky was around to screen calls and queries; otherwise I would be the one having to cope with the increased interest in our agency. But it felt good to be back on track, doing the work that I loved. My morning encounter with Zoe Bright faded into memory.

I was in the midst of compiling a list of points to negoti-ate for a publishing contract when there was a knock on my door.

"Mom? Sorry to bother you." Trey approached my desk, his face alight with excitement.

"You're no bother, Trey. I like it when you drop by my office." Noticing that he was bouncing on the balls of his feet, I said, "You look as if you have something to tell me."

He grinned. "I know who Makayla's secret admirer is." He held out a five-dollar bill. "This is what he left today."

I barely glanced at Lincoln's face before noticing the hand-written lines in small script around the edge. "*'Happiness held is the seed; happiness shared is the flower,'"* I read aloud. I looked up at Trey. "It's beautiful, but I don't recognize it."

"The author is unknown, but often the quote's attributed to John Harrigan."

My jaw dropped. "You're familiar with it?"

"Naw. I looked it up on Google. Read what's on the other side."

I turned the bill over. Written across the top of the Lincoln Memorial was, "Makayla, I wish to share my happiness with you."

"Wow," I said. "That's the most personal of all his messages. Do you think he's ready to reveal himself?"

"He's definitely getting closer. I saw him during the mid-morning rush. Makayla was busy filling an order of two mocha hazelnut *macchiatos* so she wasn't paying too much attention at the front. I was in the book corner rearranging the shelves, but keeping an eye on her tip jar. Her admirer had already gotten his coffee, had been to the fixing station, and kept staring at Makayla. When he thought no one was looking he stuck the bill in the jar and hurried out to the street. I rushed right over to the counter and fished it out and voilà!" He pointed at the bill in my hand.

"So who is it?"

He laughed, deliberately stretching out his story. "Guess."

"I don't know, Trey. Just tell me."

"There's a clue in the message, if you think hard." He grabbed the bill from my hands and read, "*'I wish to share my happiness with you.'* Who recently received some awesome news?"

Puzzled, I shrugged. The only person who came to mind was my excited joyous author to whom I'd offered representation this morning, and she was female and lived in Virginia. Then I remembered Jay Coleman, on the verge of a potential author's career. "Jay Coleman?" I asked. "Was it Jay?"

"Mom! You *are* a detective." He sat down. "Yes, it was Jay."

"Really?" I was thrilled beyond measure. No other name could have made me happier. I loved the idea of Makayla being matched up with sweet, gentle Jay. "Does he know that you know?"

"I'm pretty sure he doesn't, but he will soon. I'm going to the bookstore to encourage him to reveal himself to Makayla." He scratched his head. "I'm just not sure if I should tell her who her secret admirer is before or after I go see him. What do you think?"

I pondered. Although Makayla wanted to know the identity of her poet, she also enjoyed the game that Jay had set in motion. And Jay, while shy and insecure about approaching Makayla openly, seemed to have a plan. It would be a shame to spoil that. "Don't say a word to anyone. Let Jay reveal himself in his own way."

"Yeah, that's what I thought, too." He stood. "But I'm going to strongly encourage him to do it sooner rather than later."

"Just be gentle with him. People in love can be unpredictable!" I called as Trey headed out on his mission.

Unwittingly, my thoughts turned to Ryan and Klara Patrick. Their relationship had seemed so straightforward, but Klara had fallen in love with Bryce, and they'd been exposed here, in Inspiration Valley. Unexpectedly, all three of them were connected by a tangle of secrets and passion. "Yes," I said to the stack of papers on my desk. "Love has a tendency to make people more than a little crazy."

Chapter 14

IT WAS NEARLY QUITTING TIME WHEN VICKY'S VOICE came through my phone's speaker.

"Your mother's on line one. She said you'd forgotten to charge your cell phone again. Should I put her through?"

"Absolutely," I said. I could use a dose of my mother's unique humor and wisdom. And she was right about my cell. It had gone dead an hour ago and the charger was sitting on my kitchen counter.

"Lila? I've had the most wonderful idea!" my mother declared after I said hello. "Since your policeman won't let those chefs of yours leave town just yet, they must be feelin' as cagey as racehorses in the startin' gate. What they need is some stress relief. A bit of mountain air and good old-fashioned exercise is sure to loosen their tongues."

"What did you have in mind?"

"I thought I'd volunteer to take them on a hike up Red

Fox Mountain. We could have a picnic at the top and I'd be pleased to do a readin' for anyone who's interested."

I couldn't help but smile. "So this offer isn't purely altruistic?"

"Well, a gal has to make a livin'."

My smile vanished. "You can't go on a mountain trail with this group, Mama. There could be a murderer among them. Dennis Chapman was brought in for questioning but I guess he hasn't officially been charged with a crime. If he had, or better yet, if he'd confessed, Sean would have told me by now." My mother didn't respond and during the lull in our conversation, I had an idea of my own. "Still, a hike might create the perfect scenario for a little sharing between our out-of-town guests. In such a remote location, they might feel more comfortable showing their true natures. And if your happy hikers were accompanied by a couple of park rangers—"

"Who are really cops in disguise," my mother finished for me. "Just in case someone doesn't behave or blurts out somethin' real juicy."

"You're brilliant! I'll call Sean right away. What time do you want to get started?"

"Drag 'em to my place early tomorrow. I'll fix the folks some of my killer coffee and then we'll set out. And Lila? You can't come. I've got a strong feelin' that you need to stay in town tomorrow. You're meant to work on this puzzle from there, ya hear?"

I was about to argue, but something prevented me from speaking. I'd spent my entire life doubting my mother's gift and had always hesitated to follow her advice, but this time I would heed her counsel. "Fine, but only if Sean assigns two of his best to guard you."

"Oh, he will," she said with her usual confidence and said good-bye.

My finger was hovering over the phone's number pad when Franklin appeared in my doorway. His cheeks were flushed and he was dabbing at his forehead with a handkerchief.

"They've started again," he said, collapsing into the chair facing my desk. "I got only a few hours of respite today from Bryce, Leslie, Charlene, and Maurice. Lord save me from having so many of my clients in town at the same time. For the last two days, they've been calling, emailing, and sending me texts, wanting me to do something about their forced sojourn in Inspiration Valley." He brandished his cell phone and pointed at the screen. "I didn't even realize I had a texting plan. I prefer to communicate with my clients in a more personal manner. And some of these messages?" He cleared his throat. "Let's just say that I'm not accustomed to such vulgar language. All I want to do is go home, sit in the garden, and enjoy a nice glass of chardonnay, but I'm worried that one of them will follow me to the house. I feel completely harassed. What can I do?"

Franklin's anxiety was nearly palpable. He never discussed his personal life at work, so he'd undoubtedly view an agitated client showing up on his doorstep as a gross invasion of his privacy.

"I'll talk with them," I promised. "My mother's offered to lead all of our guests on an invigorating hike up Red Fox Mountain tomorrow morning. That should keep them out of your hair for at least half a day."

"That woman is a saint." Franklin's shoulders sagged in relief, but then his expression turned grim. "Oh, no, no, no.

We can't allow her to be alone with that group. One of those people could be a homicidal maniac."

I nodded. "Exactly. If Dennis Chapman isn't responsible, then the real murderer is still enjoying his freedom." My voice had gone quiet with anger. "This person has stolen two lives, done his best to ruin Books and Cooks, and has spread distrust, dread, and unhappiness through Inspiration Valley. I'm tired of this state of limbo, aren't you?"

Franklin looked confused. "Certainly, but how could you put your mother in harm's way? It's simply unconscionable, Lila."

"Don't worry, she'll have protection," I said and outlined the plan.

Mollified, Franklin waited while I phoned Sean.

"I don't know, Lila." Sean was less than enthused about the outing. "What if they don't want to go?"

I hadn't considered this. "Then I'll take those who pass on the hike to a leisurely lunch. Someone's got to crack sooner or later, Sean. Besides," I plodded on. "What could happen to me over a sandwich and a side of chips?"

"Do I need to remind you how and where Ms. Patrick was murdered?" Sean growled.

"No," I replied feebly and quickly changed the subject. "How are things going with Dennis?"

Sean let loose an exasperated sigh. "He claims to have an alibi for Mr. Lang's murder. According to his statement, after the group tour of the Marlette Robbins Center for the Arts, he had dinner at the Piggy Bank in Dunston. We're checking that out. He can't really account for his time afterward, but neither can most of the chefs since they were all in their rooms getting ready for the dinner. Anyone could have planted those cans in the oven during those hours. Meanwhile, Mr. Chapman earned himself some extra time with us by clocking an officer in the jaw. Fortunately for Officer O'Brien, the young man has a weak left hook."

"So he hasn't calmed down at all?"

"No. If anything he's more volatile. And yet, I don't think he's our man. This is just my gut talking, but despite Mr. Chapman's explosive combination of hatred and pent-up rage, he doesn't act like someone who has exacted revenge on his enemy. He's still angry. He's still directing that anger at Klara Patrick even though she's dead. If he'd killed her, the strength of this emotion should have ebbed to some degree."

As much as I wished otherwise, Sean's hypothesis made sense. Dennis was a young man whose dreams had been ripped to shreds. The deaths of Joel and Klara had done nothing to improve his fate and, to him, the future must look pretty bleak. I bet he was just as angry as he'd been before the two chefs were murdered. "Are you going to interview everyone else all over again?"

Sean hesitated. "I was until I talked to you. Now I'm actually considering your mother's wild idea. We've tried it my way and that hasn't led to an arrest. This time around, I think I'll let Amazing Althea do her thing."

"And what about me?"

"You can have lunch with the remaining suspects as long as I can watch over you. If you sit at one of the outdoor tables at Catcher in the Rye, then I'll keep an eye on you from inside."

"That sounds reasonable. Will you be coming over tonight?" I knew he had important work to do, so I tried to keep my tone casual. In truth, I really wanted to spend the evening with him. Franklin's fantasy of sitting in the garden with a glass of wine sounded lovely to me. I longed to watch the sunset paint the flowers a burnished gold while talking with Sean about pleasant, positive things. Books and food and friends. Movies and vacations and weekend plans. Anything but murder.

Despite my attempt to conceal my desire for us to be together, Sean picked up on my feelings. "I'd love nothing more, Lila, but I can't. I'll see you at noon tomorrow and remember, don't leave your food unattended."

I groaned. "If I dwell on the fact that one of my dining companions might have a pocketful of arsenic, I won't eat a thing. Guess that's one way to start a diet."

After we said good-bye, I asked Vicky for a list of cell phone numbers so I could contact the chefs and the rest of our out-of-town guests without going through their hotel operators. All of them leapt at the chance to go on the Red Fox Mountain excursion except for Ryan and Annie, so I invited them to join me for lunch. The moment the other agents heard what Franklin and I had plotted, most of them asked to be included. Flora volunteered to come with me to Catcher in the Rye and Jude insisted on accompanying my mother, for which I was grateful. Even Vicky wanted to help but I told her Novel Idea needed her right where she was.

"Well, the Zachmeister is staying here!" Zach folded his arms across his chest. "Someone has to keep this agency going and I've got big fish to hook. Big fish!"

Franklin gave him a pat on the shoulder. "Of course you do, son. I'm drowning in phone calls and proposals as well. It seems like every chef in the northern hemisphere wants me to represent their cookbook. A lady even overnighted her seven-layer coconut cake for me to try. When she emailed to ask whether I'd received it, I didn't have the heart to tell her that the delivery man had neglected to notice the *This Side Up* sticker."

We all laughed heartily. It felt so good to be among my coworkers, sharing this moment of levity following the weekend's unexpected horrors. Like me, my colleagues were obviously eager to focus on their jobs once again. And when I fondly gazed at their faces, my determination to help the police discover the murderer's identity became stronger than ever.

"Oh, wouldn't it be wonderful if our town was itself again by the end of the week?" Flora asked dreamily. "We could all meander around the farmers' market or browse the paintings and handmade pottery sold by the sidewalk vendors. The reporters would be gone. The chefs, too. We could have a frozen yogurt on a park bench while reading a steamy erotica novel."

This statement caused more laughter. Still smiling, I collected my things, waved at Vicky, and left the office. However, my smile vanished the moment I saw my scooter. It seemed to have shrunk, its two tires spread out sideways like deflated balloons. Upon closer inspection, it became clear to me that they hadn't gone flat on their own. Someone had slashed them.

Touching the edge of one of the jagged gashes, I wondered who'd be crazy enough to vandalize my scooter in broad daylight.

"It could have been a writer who can't handle rejection," I murmured angrily and took out my phone to report the incident to the police.

* * *

HOURS LATER, I was still fuming over the assault on my scooter. Though I filed a report with the police substation in town, I was told there was little they could do as no one had witnessed the vandalism. I knew their hands were tied. I had no evidence with which to accuse an individual of the crime and the cops weren't about to dust my scooter for fingerprints, seeing as they couldn't spare the time or resources on the loss of two tires. Still, I hated that nothing was being done to find the culprit, whom I strongly suspected was Zoe Bright, the writer who'd given me the necklace with the crystal pendant.

During dinner, Trey helped to take my mind off my troubles by describing his visit to Jay.

"He was sort of embarrassed that I'd discovered his secret," recounted Trey as he speared a piece of red pepper from his salad. "He was blushing practically the whole time I was there."

"I hope you were tactful about it," I said, cutting off a piece of grilled pork chop. "Jay's a sensitive guy."

"I was, Mom. He thought it was kind of cool that I was looking out for Makayla. And he completely understood that his game shouldn't go on much longer. He said he would soon reveal himself to her, but didn't want to share any details in case I gave his plan away."

I smiled at my son. "Well, I think Jay is a perfect match for Makayla. But why does he use poetry written by others to express his feelings for her, and why anonymously?"

"He said he was afraid that if he just asked her out she'd turn him down. Since she's a fan of literature, he decided that poetry was the best way to tell her how he felt because poets describe their love so much better than he could. He said that true word crafters express so much emotion in few words."

I nodded, remembering Jay's comment when I asked about the poetry book on his desk. "He conveyed a similar thought to me."

"And then he told me that he knows how much Makayla loves a good mystery. I think he was basing this on her book collection at the café. Anyway, he figured that leaving poems in the tip jar would increasingly pique her curiosity, so that by the time he was ready to reveal himself, she would be dying to meet him and it wouldn't matter to her how shy or nerdy he was." Trey put his hands up. "His words, not mine. I told him he wasn't nerdy at all. Anyway, he did tell me that she'd discover who he was within the week. So it's all good. I'll butt out now and leave them to it." He took his dishes to the sink and headed for the door. "I'm going to my room, okay? I told Iris I'd Skype with her tonight."

That night, my sleep was plagued with dreams involving violent images of knives sinking into tires, ovens disgorging orange and yellow flames, and Klara's anguished face. I awoke groggily to the aroma of freshly brewed coffee, courtesy of Trey. By the time I was dressed and downstairs, he had left for Espresso Yourself, having propped a note against the coffeepot that read, "From your personal barista. See you later. T."

I walked to work with a light step, marveling at how my once rebellious and surly teenager had turned into a fine young man right before my eyes. I was incredibly proud of him and loved having him around the house again.

When I reached my office building, I was surprised to see a throng of reporters with cameramen in tow assembled outside again. I quickened my pace, fearing that something terrible had happened at Espresso Yourself or at Novel Idea.

"What's going on?" I asked the closest journalist.

"The police are going to have to charge Dennis Chapman with murder today or let him go," she replied in a bored monotone. "They can't keep holding him. We want to get sound bites from the other people who were in the café when Klara Patrick died to accompany our footage from the Dunston police station." Suddenly, her eyes narrowed. "Hey, weren't you—"

I dashed away before she could finish her sentence.

The morning at work passed quickly. I buried myself in an assortment of tasks, trying not to think about my mother leading Bryce, Charlene, Leslie, Carter, Maurice, and Carrie up an isolated trail on Red Fox Mountain. When Flora knocked on my door at a few minutes before twelve, I was surprised that it was already so late.

"Are you ready for our lunch, dear?" asked Flora as I grabbed my bag. "We're fortunate that we've got the easy task of entertaining Ryan Patrick and Annie Schmidt," she added. "Of all the out-of-town guests, they seem to be the least theatrical."

"I agree," I said, holding open the door at the bottom of the steps. "I'm sure Ryan is still emotional about his wife and that can make him a bit unpredictable, but otherwise he's easygoing. And Annie is sweet. I feel most comfortable around them as well."

"I feel sorry that Jude and your mother are stuck on the

mountain with the others. I've been worrying about them all morning."

I nodded my head emphatically. "Me, too. But remember, they're not alone. Now, let's enjoy a pleasant meal alfresco."

Catcher in the Rye was in the midst of its usual lunchtime bustle. Ryan and Annie were already seated on the patio, and Ryan waved us over.

"We saved you a spot," said Annie as she removed her purse from the chair beside her. "But we haven't ordered yet."

Flora pulled her wallet out of her bag. "That's good, because we're treating you." While Flora discussed the sandwich selections, I caught sight of Sean sitting at a table inside. He nodded at me and I shot him a quick smile before turning back to the conversation.

"So let me see if I have this right," said Flora. "A Pavarotti for Ryan—"

"That's with the Genoa salami, right?" Ryan interrupted.

"Yes. And Annie, you're having the Hamlet—ham and Havarti on rye, correct?" At Annie's nod, she asked, "Lila, what are you in the mood for?"

"I'm not sure yet, so I'll just come in with you."

"Nonsense, dear. I can manage to get four sandwiches. You stay here with our guests." She directed a meaningful look in my direction.

"All right. Let me see. I'll have . . ." I stared at the menu board posted beside the entrance even though I came here so often that I practically had it memorized. "A Van Gogh."

"Oh, that sounds good," said Annie, reading from the menu. "Turkey, sliced Brie, and apples with honey mustard on a French baguette. I think I'll change my order. Is that okay, Flora?"

"Of course," replied Flora as she headed inside.

"Say hi to Big Ed for me," I called after her and took a seat. "I guess you guys must be eager to leave Inspiration Valley and go back home."

Ryan nodded. "Definitely. This place is full of bad memories now. Sorry. I know it's where you live and work, but I hate it here," he added. "I need to get my life in order after . . . after what happened this weekend."

"I understand," I commiserated.

"And I really have to get home to Paddy, my kitten," said Annie. "My neighbor is looking after him, but I know he's missing me."

"You have a kitten?" Thankful to have a pleasant topic to discuss, I asked, "How old is he?"

"Six months. He's the sweetest calico." She showed me her cell phone. "Here's a picture of him tangled up in my laundry. Isn't he cute?"

I chuckled over the photo of a brown, white, and ginger cat in a basket, entwined with socks and T-shirts. "He's adorable."

"I know. I can't wait to see him again." She touched Ryan's hand. "You like cats, don't you, Ryan?"

Ryan pulled his hand back and placed it on his lap. "I'm more of a dog person myself. But Klara never wanted a pet. Couldn't deal with the mess. Carter and Carrie begged for a puppy when they were younger, but Klara always said no."

"She did like to have things her way," said Annie, adjusting her glasses. "Maybe you can get a dog now."

He directed a pointed stare in her direction. "That's certainly not on my radar. Klara's barely—"

"Here we are!" Flora burst into the conversation like the sun breaking through a cloud. She placed a tray containing paper-wrapped sandwiches and four cans of sparkling fruit juice on the table.

"Great," I said, distributing the food. "I'm starving." As I bit into my baguette, the fusion of flavors from the salty turkey, the creamy Brie, and the sweet apple filled my mouth. The others tucked into their sandwiches. "Flora, Annie has the cutest picture of her kitten. You should see it."

"I just adore kittens," Flora said, taking the phone Annie handed her. She giggled as she looked at the photo. "Oh my, how precious. It's been a long time since my Skimbleshanks and Fiddle were that small. They're both seventeen years old this month, and although they mostly sleep now, they still like getting into mischief every now and then."

"Those are interesting names," Annie said. "How did you come up with them?"

"From one of my favorite books of poems, dear, by T. S. Eliot: *Old Possum's Book of Practical Cats*. We kept Skimbleshanks's name as it was, but shortened Firefrorefiddle to just Fiddle, because our tongues kept getting tied up in those f's and r's."

"Wasn't the Andrew Lloyd Webber musical *Cats* based on that book?" Ryan asked.

"That's right," I said. "I loved the songs from that show. Do you think your cats resemble any of the felines onstage, Flora?"

Flora shook her head and smiled. "I remember when they were smaller than your kitten, Annie. We found them under our porch when they were just four weeks old." She took a sip of her drink. "Skimbleshanks and Fiddle have since grown into fat happy adults. We think of them like our children."

"I'll vouch for that," I said, remembering having dinner at Flora's house and seeing how she and her husband doted on them. "They are very pampered." I popped the last bit of sandwich into my mouth.

A digital rendition of "Hedwig's Theme" intruded on our conversation. Flora pulled her cell phone out of her purse. "Excuse me," she said as she turned away from the table and spoke into it.

Ryan crinkled up his sandwich wrapper and downed the rest of his beverage. "That was delicious. Thank you. It was nice to get out of the hotel and have an innocuous conversation with someone who isn't a chef."

Flora finished her call. "I'm sorry to have to leave so abruptly, but I need to return to the office right away. A client of mine is rather anxious about something and wants to speak with me." She wrapped up the remainder of her sandwich. "I'll take this along. Bye for now!" she called over her shoulder as she hurried away.

"I should get back to the hotel and see if Carter and Carrie have returned from their hike yet." Ryan got to his feet.

Annie finished the last of her food. "I'll go with you." A look of desperation crossed her face. "I need to talk to you about something."

Ryan raised his eyebrows.

"You two go ahead. I'll clean up," I said, gathering the refuse from our meal.

Annie turned to me. "Thanks, Ms. Wilkins. It was nice

to chat with you. Please thank Ms. Meriweather for treating us to lunch."

They headed away and impulsively, I decided to follow, wondering what Annie wanted to tell Ryan. Normally, it wouldn't be any of my business, but with a murderer loose in Inspiration Valley, I didn't know what useful information I might glean from eavesdropping. As I tossed the trash into the can, I glanced briefly through the window where I'd seen Sean, but he was no longer there.

Staying several yards behind Annie and Ryan, I pretended to stroll unhurriedly back to the office, all the while keeping a focused eye on the pair as they approached the park in the town center. They walked with their heads down, Annie leaning slightly toward Ryan. I scurried closer in order to hear what they were saying, but stopped when Ryan abruptly halted.

"What?" he exclaimed, clearly astonished. "Is it really you? How can that be?"

Annie grabbed his hand and pulled him toward a bench on the corner of the sidewalk. Trying not to appear obvious, I hastened to Ginny Callaway's metalsmith shop directly behind them and looked in the display window.

Annie was midsentence when I was finally able to tune in to their conversation. I feigned interest in the array of sculptures and jewelry, but was in actuality observing their reflections in the glass. ". . . the job to be near you." Annie clung tightly to Ryan's hand. Taking off her glasses, she gazed directly into Ryan's eyes. Yearning and adoration radiated from her whole being. "Do you remember me now?" she asked, her voice a plea.

He yanked his hand away. "No, I don't. I told you, I barely noticed you then."

Her shoulders slumped, but then she straightened and moved closer to him so that their knees touched.

"Ryan, I love you. I've always loved you. Can't you see that?"

He pushed her away and stood. "Annie, I can't do this. I don't want to hear this. Klara is only just—"

"But in time, Ryan," she implored, her eyes large and pleading. "Once everything is settled, you and I can be together."

"No, we can't. I don't love you. I never will. I'm sorry." He turned and strode quickly away. Annie watched him disappear around the corner, and then collapsed back on the bench. Her chin fell to her chest.

Saddened to see such heartbreak, I rounded the bench and sat beside her. "Are you okay, Annie?"

"Oh, Ms. Wilkins . . ." She exhaled loudly as she wiped her eyes. "The only man I have ever loved just rejected me. Now I have no one."

"Annie, he is unworthy of you. You are such a special person. You'll find someone who deserves you more."

She glared at me, her eyes flashing anger. "How can you say that? You don't know me. And you don't know Ryan. He is the *only* one for me."

"I'm sorry, I didn't mean to offend you," I said, taken aback by her rapid transformation from heartache to outrage. Abruptly, an unwelcome thought crossed my mind. Was it possible that Annie murdered Klara to get her out of the way?

She frowned. "You have no idea how much he means to me. Ryan's a wonderful man." Her eyes shining with tears, she said, "I just need to be alone now, okay?" Pushing herself off the bench, she trudged in the direction of the hotel.

I stared after her. It was impossible to believe that Annie

was a murderer. And what reason would she have to kill Joel? I shook my head. Her passion and love for Ryan brought forth her anger with me. I'd been insensitive to suggest she put aside her love for Ryan so swiftly. A line from Elle Newmark's novel *The Book of Unholy Mischief* came to mind: "Unrequited love does not die; it's only beaten down to a secret place where it hides, curled and wounded." Annie's hurt was still so fresh. She needed time to heal.

I would call her later to apologize, and invite her to my house this evening. I imagined us sitting together on the porch swing, sipping glasses of sweet tea, admiring the vibrant hanging fuchsias, and chatting about her kitten. Perhaps I could play a small part in healing the fractured heart of a sweet soul.

Chapter 15

BY THE TIME I GOT BACK TO MY OFFICE, THE DAY HAD grown quite warm. The breeze was no longer refreshing, but carried hints of summer on its breath. I thought of my neglected garden and of all the plans I'd had to transform it into the image of a Monet painting. The last time I'd visited the Secret Garden the head horticulturist had said, "Work hard in the spring and you'll enjoy the fruit of your labors all summer," but I'd barely gotten my hands dirty.

I was so caught up in visions of weeds threatening to overtake my herbs and crabgrass spreading through my perennial beds that I nearly walked right past the entrance to Espresso Yourself without noticing that something unusual was going on inside.

Luckily, I heard the sound of music coming from within and paused. It didn't sound like the bubbly jazz Makayla typically played during the afternoon. The notes were too loud and came from a violin. Curious, I stepped into Espresso Yourself and gaped in surprise. For there, standing on top of a table, was a violinist. The young woman was attired in formal concert dress. Her long black skirt swished against the tabletop as she swayed in time to the music.

The patrons looked as stunned as I felt. No one moved. The entire place was like a scene from Madame Tussauds wax museum. Trey stood behind the counter, his fingers resting on the cash register keys, and Makayla was positioned near the espresso machine, a stainless steel pitcher of steamed milk held aloft in her right hand.

As the musician continued to play, I recognized the haunting melody of the song. It was "Somewhere in Time," from the movie starring Christopher Reeve and Jane Seymour. No wonder everyone was spellbound. It was a beautiful and moving piece.

When the violinist finished, everyone in the room applauded. She gave a little bow and allowed a man to help her down. She then took a red rose from her violin case, walked over to Makayla and presented her with the flower.

"Thank you," Makayla said. Her eyes were sparkling and her cheeks were flushed. "An impromptu concert! That was lovely."

Wordlessly, the young woman gestured toward the door leading to the street. Makayla hesitated and the violinist repeated the motion, waiting patiently until Makayla came out from behind the counter and cautiously stepped outside. A matronly woman winked at her before raising a flute to her lips. She began to play "Unchained Melody" while Makayla smiled in delight. Further down the sidewalk, a man leaning against a streetlamp took up the song on his clarinet. The flutist lowered her instrument and handed Makayla a red rose. Like the violinist, she said nothing, but pointed at her colleague, indicating that Makayla should walk toward him.

Makayla looked back over her shoulder, spotted me, and waved for me to join her.

"I'll watch the shop!" Trey called out from behind me and I turned and gave him a thumbs-up.

By the time we neared the man playing the clarinet, an elderly gentleman dressed in a tuxedo appeared from the interior of a car parked at the corner. He waited for the clarinetist to give Makayla her rose before blowing into the mouthpiece of his French horn. It took me a moment to identify the song.

"It's 'When a Man Loves a Woman,'" I told Makayla.

"Do you know what's going on here? Because if you do, you need to tell me right now!"

"I have no clue," I said, keeping my face bland. Of course, I suspected this was Jay's doing, but I wasn't going to be the one to spoil his big moment. "I'm as surprised as you are."

The patrons from Espresso Yourself had followed us down the sidewalk and a dozen more townsfolk joined our little band as we walked from musician to musician. We'd formed a small parade. Without a leader, none of us seemed to know where we were going, but we were all too curious not to continue on.

The next musician was on the other side of the street, standing on the path leading to the fountain of the Nine Muses. He held his saxophone in the air until the traffic light turned red and the moment it did, the French horn player bowed and handed Makayla a rose.

"Who arranged all this?" she asked, but he only smiled and gestured for her to hurry and cross the street.

As soon as we reached the opposite side, the saxophonist began to belt out, "You Are So Beautiful." This time, he led us forward and we fell into step behind him. Musicians began to pop up all over the place. Two trumpet players appeared from behind the bushes and a cellist got up from a park bench nearby. The violinist from the coffee shop had somehow beaten us to the fountain and she and another flutist had taken up the song. Then, to my utter astonishment, we heard the sounds of a piano.

"No way," Makayla breathed.

But there, on the side of the fountain where Erato, the muse of love poetry, stood forever strumming her lyre, was a baby grand piano. Its entire surface was covered with red rose petals.

The moment Makayla and I drew close to the pianist he abruptly stopped playing. "Who are you?" Makayla asked. "Why are you doing this? Please, don't get me wrong, I'll be smiling for a year just thinking about today, but I am one confused barista right now."

The man simply handed her a rose and pointed at the fountain. There, sitting on the edge between Erato and Calliope, was Jay Coleman.

"I have something to say to you," he said and picked up an acoustic guitar from the ground. He strummed the strings once and began to sing the opening lines of "The First Time Ever I Saw Your Face."

The rest of the musicians accompanied him, but his voice soared above all of them. He wasn't an accomplished singer and some of his notes were off key, but he looked at Makayla with such tenderness and infused every word with such passion that it didn't matter. It was as if they were the only two people on earth. I was overjoyed to see my friend's eyes were filling with tears of happiness. She clutched her roses to her chest and stared at Jay in amazement.

When the song drew to a close and the crowd broke into thunderous applause, Jay laid his guitar aside and got down on one knee. Holding out a red rose, he said, "I'm your secret admirer. I'm sorry that I've borrowed other people's words to tell you how I feel. Now it's time for me to use my own, and all I need to say is that I've loved you since I first saw you. You're the most beautiful person I've ever known, Makayla. It's not just your green eyes or glowing skin or supermodel body, either. It's your kindness, intelligence, your love of art and books, and the way you care about the people of this town that make you so exquisitely beautiful. I would be honored if you'd have dinner with me."

Collectively, we held our breaths and stared at Makayla. She took a step forward, accepted the rose, and said, "Would you mind standing up for a second?"

It was obvious that Jay was desperate for an answer, but he was too much of a gentleman to deny Makayla's request, so he slowly got to his feet. He gazed at her with a look of such keen expectation that I wanted to shout at her to say yes.

She leaned in, whispered something in his ear, and then took his face in her hands. With all of us looking on, she inched even closer, erasing the space between their bodies, and kissed him hard.

The crowd went wild and I was right there with them. I hooted and clapped, smiling with joy at the romantic scene. The musicians broke out in song again, and when the peppy strains of "Happy Together" by the Turtles floated over the small park, people began to dance.

I gazed around and saw the cheerful, grinning faces of Inspiration Valley's merchants and residents. After the violent deaths that had occurred here last weekend, I'd forgotten how magical our town was and how spontaneous and wonderful life could be.

It was with no small measure of regret that I left the jovial gathering around the fountain to return to Novel Idea, but I had to get some work done. I almost stopped by Espresso Yourself to tell Trey what had happened, but decided that I'd let Makayla share the story with him. It would sound richer and more colorful coming from her, and besides, it was her story.

The rest of the afternoon passed swiftly. With Jay's musical montage still playing in my head, I read through two days' worth of queries in a couple of hours. I was in the middle of emailing an author a request for a partial manuscript when Jude knocked on my open door.

"What a day!" he exclaimed and collapsed into my guest chair. "I never knew a leisurely hike through a pristine forest could be so easily ruined, but between the chefs and those miserable twins, it was a disaster."

"Hold that thought," I said. I finished the email, hit the send button, and then gave Jude my full attention. "Did you learn anything?"

Jude shook his head. "Other than Leslie hates bugs of every size, shape, and color? Or that Charlene is in terrible shape and needs to hit the gym more often? That those kids of Ryan can argue about what shade of blue the sky is?" He rolled his eyes. "No, nothing important was revealed, though your mother may have had a better opportunity to gather intel during her palm-reading sessions during lunch. I asked her about them on the way down, but she said they were confidential." He shrugged. "Maybe she'll tell you more."

"I sure hope she got something out of that group. Flora and I spent most of our lunch with Ryan and Annie talking about cats."

"Cats?" Jude laughed. "You're a sly detective, Lila."

I couldn't help but smile. "Yep, that's me. I just bring up the subject of kittens and people confess all their dirty little secrets."

All traces of humor vanished from Jude's face. "Did you know that Dennis Chapman was released?"

"No. I've been completely engrossed in my work." I ran my hands through my hair in exasperation. My buoyant mood had evaporated like an early morning mist. "Back to square one. Murderer on the loose. No leads. No arrests. No—"

"Chefs packing their suitcases and leaving us in peace," Jude moaned. "But we have to keep forging ahead, Lila. We have lives to lead and clients to sign. We can't let this one twisted individual hold us back or define how we behave."

His words were inspiring. "You're right," I said and thought of Annie. The poor young woman had already lost years loving a man who wasn't available. Ryan's rejection shouldn't hold her back. I needed to convince her to live her dreams without him. "Thanks, Jude. Now I know exactly how I'm going to spend my evening. I plan to enjoy my little corner of heaven regardless of what's happened."

"I'm sure you and I have different definitions of heaven." Jude gave me an impish wink and left my office.

When I was alone again, I dialed Annie's cell phone number. Her hello was thin and fragile and when I asked her to come over to my place for supper, she hesitated.

"You've had a terrible day and I'm sure that my insensitive comments did nothing to help," I said. "Let me make it up to you. I'm a good listener and I've been in your shoes before, so I know exactly how you're feeling right now."

After a lengthy pause, Annie accepted my invitation and I gave her directions to the house. "Can I bring anything?" she asked when I was done.

"Absolutely not," I said. "You've been taking care of other people for far too long. Let me spoil you for a change."

"That sounds really nice." Her voice sounded a little brighter. "See you in a bit."

After tidying my desk, I said good-bye to Vicky and headed downstairs to tell Trey that we were having company for supper.

"I already made plans, Mom. I'm catching a movie in Dunston with a few guys from high school. I won't be home for supper."

"Oh, okay." It would have been nice to have someone closer to Annie's age at the dinner table, but Trey had been working so hard that I didn't want to ask him to change his plans. "How's Makayla been today?"

"I don't think her feet have touched the ground." Trey grinned and we both stared at her. She was talking to a customer by the fixing station and was so animated that she seemed to have forgotten that she was holding the cinnamon shaker. As she spoke, brown sprinkles rained onto the floor. "Jay figured out how to get the girl all right," Trey said. "He totally pulled out all the stops."

Makayla finally noticed what a mess she was making and laughed. After dusting off her customer's sleeve, she excused herself and headed down the back hall, undoubtedly in search of a mop.

"Have fun tonight," I told Trey and followed Makayla.

I found her waltzing with the mop in the storage closet. "Jay's a handsomer partner," I teased.

She examined the cleaning tool. "I do believe you're right. I always thought he was cute. And smart as a whip. And funny. I just assumed he was involved with someone. He never talked about anyone in particular, but I figured there was no way such a catch could be available."

"You were," I pointed out.

"Not anymore." She beamed. "I don't even need to have a first date to tell you that I am officially off the market. Do you know how many times I've chatted with Jay at the Constant Reader? I liked him from the get-go, Lila. I just didn't know how much until today."

I smiled at her. "I'm thrilled for both of you."

She dropped the mop, threw her arms around me, and squeezed. "I only hope we can be as happy as you and your man. Are you seeing Sean tonight?"

"I wish, but no," I said. "I have a different kind of date. I'm going to try to make a young woman forget her troubles for a little while."

Makayla pointed at the mop and frowned. "Who's the girl? And does she have man problems?"

I nodded. "The worst kind. It's Annie, Klara's assistant. She loves someone who doesn't love her back."

"Nothing hurts quite like that." Makayla's fern green eyes filled with sympathy. "A homemade meal and a glass of chardonnay will go a long way toward making her feel better. You're a real gem, Lila. A diamond in a pile of cubic zirconia."

I swatted her lightly on the arm. "You must be in love. I've never heard you utter such a bad metaphor."

She laughed again. "Lord, have mercy, I must be!" She picked up the mop and drew it against her chest. "Come on, you sexy thing. We have memories to make together."

When I left the coffee shop, Makayla was pirouetting around the floor while Trey looked on in amusement. I carried the image in my mind as I shopped for groceries and started to prepare a meal of lemon chicken, butter beans, and wild rice. As day gave way to night, I closed my eyes and wondered how long it would be before Sean would be free to dance with me on the lawn under the bright gaze of a million stars.

THE PHONE RANG just as I was placing a vase with lilacs from the garden on the table. The centerpiece was the final touch. Everything else for my dinner with Annie was ready.

"Oh, sweetie," my mother said before I'd barely had a chance to say hello. "I meant to call you sooner, but I had to take a catnap after traipsin' up the mountain with those ungrateful out-of-towners. I was plain tuckered out."

"I'm not surprised. You were a real trooper for volunteering. Did you happen to learn anything useful?" I asked as I adjusted one of the lilac blossoms.

"Maybe. I'll tell you one thing though. That Jude is a darlin' boy, and ever so patient. The way he handled those twins—"

"Mama, Jude already gave me his report. I don't mean to rush you, but I'm expecting company any minute."

"Shoot, I don't want to keep you from gettin' ready for your man," she said contritely and I didn't bother to tell her that it wasn't Sean who was coming to dinner. My mother took a quick breath and continued right where she'd left off. "Jude was a doll, but doesn't know a thing about the intimate confessions I heard durin' my one-on-one sessions."

My heart thumped in anticipation. "You mean you discovered something that might help solve the murders?"

"I found out lots of things in every readin', but I still can't say for certain that one of our little band of hikers killed Klara or Joel."

Disappointment edged its way into my tone. "What did you learn then? Could we at least cross a name or two off the list of suspects?"

"That would be mighty risky because they're all capable of serious wickedness. Charlene has a deeply etched fate line, which means that she's strongly controlled by destiny. If destiny compelled her to eliminate her competition, then she could have done the deed. Leslie has a very shallow life line, meanin' she's easily manipulated by others. She could be someone's puppet. And the shape of Carrie's hand, where her palm is shorter than her fingers, tells me that she's got a big ego and is impulsive and insensitive—just the kind of person who would do away with a step-mama."

I didn't see how my mother's assessments of these people based on their palms would be of much use, but she'd tried her best to help, so I thanked her and then insisted that I had to go.

"Lila, I'm not done yet. I wanted to tell you that when I looked at your cards this mornin', I saw real danger in the—

The peal of the doorbell drowned out the rest of her sentence. "Mama, my company is here. I'll call you back later, okay?"

I hung up and opened the door. Annie stood at the threshold holding a clay pot containing three clusters of plants with dark textured leaves. Delicate blue flowers grew in a posy at the center of one of them, the second had white blossoms with magenta edges, and the third had vermillion blooms. Their centers were all a friendly yellow.

"I stopped in at Secret Garden and bought some primroses for your garden," she said, extending her gift to me. Her eyes were red-rimmed behind her glasses and her face pale.

"They're lovely, thank you." I took the pot. "I'll set it here on the porch for now. Come on in. I've got a bottle of sauvignon blanc chilling."

She hesitated on the threshold. "Can we sit out here for a bit? It's such a warm evening." She gestured in the direction of the porch swing.

"Sure. Dinner's not quite ready yet. I'll just get our drinks." In the kitchen, I checked on the rice cooker before putting the lemon chicken in a preheated oven and set the timer for twenty minutes. When it buzzed I'd have time to steam the butter beans before the chicken was done. Pouring two glasses of wine, I placed them on a tray along with a dish of roasted almonds and carried it out to the porch.

Annie was swaying back and forth on the two-seater swing, her fingers entwined on her lap. I set the tray on the glass-topped table, handed her a glass, and took a seat in a white wicker rocker.

She took a sip. "Have the cops gotten any closer to finding out who murdered Klara and Joel? I noticed that Dennis was back at the hotel, so I guess I was wrong about him. I feel really bad about pointing the finger at him."

"The authorities didn't have enough evidence to hold him," I replied. "But that doesn't mean he's no longer a suspect."

Her swinging slowed a bit. "It's nerve-racking, having to stay in this town, knowing there's a murderer on the loose. I just want to go home."

"Yes, I know. But I'm confident he'll be apprehended very soon," I said, sipping my wine.

"Or her." Annie stared vacantly out at the garden. "You have a pretty spot here."

"I still have a ton of work to do in the yard before it lives up to my vision," I said, thinking about the mental list I'd concocted earlier today.

"The primroses would look good under that tree, in that bare patch beside the hostas." She pointed at the maple in the corner of the yard. "They do best in shade. My grand-mother used to have multicolored primula beds under the trees in her garden."

"That's a great idea. I'll plant them there." I gazed at the pot of flowers she'd brought. They looked like such congenial little blossoms. "Were you close to your grandmother?"

She nodded. "My parents worked a lot, so I went to her house after school almost every day. That was in Holland." She smiled slightly. "Did you know I was Dutch?"

I raised my eyebrows. "No, I didn't. That's a remarkable coincidence, considering Klara's . . . *oma* was also Dutch." I wondered if Annie knew the truth about Mieke, the woman Klara had pretended to be related to.

Annie pressed her feet to the porch floor, jerking the swing to an abrupt stop. Wine splashed over her hand and dripped onto her pants, but she didn't seem to notice. "Klara was no more Dutch than you are, Ms. Wilkins. The *oma* who created the recipes that deceitful crook stole was *my oma*." She rubbed a trembling hand on her jeans.

My eyes widened. "Mieke was *your oma*?"

She nodded, pressing her lips together.

I touched her arm. "I know the story about Mieke. Ryan told me the truth about how he'd come to know her, but he never mentioned that she was your grandmother."

"He didn't know. He didn't remember me and I never identified myself to him." Angrily, she wiped her eyes under her glasses. "Not until today. I was just a girl when he used to visit Oma for his cooking lessons. I look nothing like I did then and as you can hear, I managed to get rid of my accent. To him, I was just another New Yorker. And I wanted it that way. If I'd revealed myself too soon, he would have made me leave, so I wouldn't give away Klara's secret." She stood and paced, seemingly unable to sit still. "I adored Ryan from the first day he walked into my *oma*'s kitchen. He was so handsome, so confident, so American. I'd sit at the table with my homework and watch him learn how to make our family recipes. I loved listening to him speak his broken Dutch. He was sweet to Oma, but he rarely acknowledged me. I was just a gangly twelve-year-old kid with pigtail braids, buck teeth, and glasses."

She put her wineglass on the table and sat back on the swing, setting it in rapid motion.

"I might have been young, but I loved him. Through all these years, I never stopped loving him." She pushed the swing harder. Faster. Her cheeks were flushed and her eyes glistened. "A few years ago, I saw him on television with

Klara. I recognized him right away. That smile. Those beautiful eyes. Seeing the love of my life on that screen was like a sign that I was meant to go to him. I gave up everything to come to America to make that happen—to give us a chance to be together. I gave up everything!"

Her agitation was unnerving. I needed to calm her down or the evening would be a total disaster.

"Annie," I said, gently stopping the swing with my foot. "Let's plant those primroses now. It'll take your mind off Ryan. Come on, I have an extra pair of gloves." After waiting for her to stand up, I picked up the pot and carried it to the maple tree. I then retrieved the garden gloves, a trowel, and a hand rake from the garden shed and brought them to the tree where Annie stood staring down at the pot of flowers.

The moment I handed her the gloves, the oven buzzer went off. "I'll be right back. Our entrée is calling," I said. Hurrying inside, I quickly turned off the oven, made sure the rice cooker was on the keep warm setting, and rushed back out to the garden.

Annie was kneeling at the base of the tree, clawing at the dirt with the hand rake. The sun was sinking toward the horizon. Its light filtered through the branches, creating splintered shadows on the lawn. The tranquility I usually felt in my garden was absent. Somehow, Annie's discontent had tainted the atmosphere and I longed to purify it again.

"Dinner can wait until we finish here," I said with forced cheerfulness, but Annie didn't seem to hear me. I knelt beside her and started to dig a hole next to the dirt she was loosening.

"How could he not want me once he knew who I was?" she said in a voice tight with anger. "How could he not know how faithfully I loved him for all these years? And how much he owed me and my family?"

"I guess when he met you as an adult it was in a different context. When he last saw you, you were just a little girl. It was a different chapter in his life. He was a single man in the army," I offered. "When you were hired to be Klara's assistant, he was a married man with teenage kids. And he was in love with Klara," I said very gently. "He wasn't looking for anyone else."

"Oh, yes. Klara." She attacked the dirt aggressively. "Klara. Klara. Klara." She stabbed at the ground, gouging the soil until it was riddled with holes. "I got rid of her, now didn't I?"

She began to laugh.

My hand stopped in the midst of removing a primrose from the pot. "What do you mean 'got rid of her'?" I asked quietly, fighting to keep my voice even.

In the twilight, the shadows lengthened and fell over both of us. I felt a chill in the air as Annie's laughter grew louder and more hysterical.

Was I gardening beside a murderer?

Chapter 16

ANNIE STOPPED LAUGHING AND EXHALED LOUDLY. "I made so many sacrifices for Ryan Patrick. So many. Klara was just one of them."

I put down the plant I was holding and shifted sideways, increasing the distance between us. My fingers closed around my spade and I brought it behind my back and held it at the ready. "Tell me about these sacrifices."

She turned to me. Her face was cast in gloom, but her eyes blazed with a cold light. "I didn't mean to kill Joel. The explosion was meant for Klara. She had to look perfect on camera and she always practiced her dishes the night before each show. I figured she'd do it that night, too."

"So Joel's death was a scheduling mix-up?" I couldn't disguise my disbelief.

She shrugged. "Yes, it was. I had no idea Joel would do what Klara usually does. If she hadn't made him feel so crappy about his menu, he would never have been there. I heard about what she said to him over dinner that night. The way she made him doubt his choices. That's the kind of nasty person she was. The world's better off without her." Annie stood up, the hand rake dangling at her side, and gazed down at me. "I may have screwed up killing Klara the first time, but I got her on my second try. At your friend's café. I hope it didn't hurt her business too much. She seems nice. I even disposed of Klara's coffee cup in a trashcan down the street so she wouldn't be implicated. Remember when I ran after the ambulance?"

My mouth went dry and dozens of conflicting thoughts crowded my mind. I knew I needed to get away from Annie. I had to get to a phone and call the police. Slowly, so as not to startle her into reacting, I got to my feet. Refusing to show her any fear, I said, "You can tell me everything over dinner. I'll go check on the food and bring our wineglasses out here. I could really use something to drink." I gestured toward the house with my free hand and even managed a wobbly smile.

Annie moved with lightning swiftness. She grabbed my outstretched wrist, her fingers digging into my skin. "No, wait! You need to hear the rest of it. You need to understand." She tightened her grip. For someone so slight, she had remarkable strength. Pain surged through my arm and I instinctively brought up the other hand, the one holding the trowel, and swung it at her. She ducked, seized the tool, and yanked it away. She gazed at it curiously and then tossed it into the bushes.

"I know you'll sympathize with me," she continued as if I hadn't just tried to strike her. Her face was a mask of calm.

Her eyes had gone cold and dark. "Once you know the whole story you won't blame me. I know you won't. Sit on the ground and listen to me."

I eyed the hand rake that she still held. "But I really need to—"

Without warning, she pushed down on my shoulders and I let my knees fold. I didn't dare put up a fight as long as she had the rake. It was a small tool, but it could still do plenty of damage.

"Look," she said. "I don't want to hurt you. I really don't. I just need to explain. I need someone to listen to me. Someone to be *my* audience."

I nodded agreeably. If I kept her talking, I'd buy myself more time to figure out how to get her weapon away from her. "I can do that. I can listen to your story."

As if she didn't trust me to comply, she brandished the hand rake and pressed her fingertips against the tines.

"I'm not going anywhere," I assured her.

"I've been waiting for years for everyone to know who I really am. Especially Ryan." She took a step closer, looming over me. "I didn't tell Ryan I was Mieke's granddaughter when he first hired me because I wanted him to fall in love with the person I had become. I wanted him to see me as a pretty, chic, hardworking, and interesting woman. I could have replaced Klara. I could have been so much better than she ever was. But I never got a chance to prove that to him. He only talked to me about *her*. It was always Klara this and Klara that." Her brow furrowed. "I got rid of her for Ryan's sake. She wasn't good enough for him. She was cheating on him!"

"Why didn't you just tell Ryan about Klara cheating? Wouldn't he have left Klara then? Wouldn't you have had a chance then?"

She shook her head rapidly. "You don't really understand the kind of person he is, do you? He was so loyal to Klara. If I'd told him about her and Bryce, he would have always associated me with Klara's betrayal. He would never realize what I've always known. That he and I belong together."

"But Ryan doesn't love you," I reminded her softly. "Annie, you need to start thinking of a different future. Ryan isn't going to come around to your way of thinking. You should move on. As you said yourself, you have so much to offer."

Her chin dropped to her chest. "He's still upset over that whore Klara, but he'll get over her. He'll soon realize that he does love me. That he can't have a career without me. I'll do everything she did and more. And I'm no crook. Those Dutch recipes belong to *me*. All the money they've made from those cookbooks belongs to *me*." She swung the rake back and forth, her lips thinning in anger.

Raising my hands in a gesture of surrender, I said, "You're absolutely right. They've gotten rich off your grandmother's recipes and your family stories." Dropping my arms, I changed tactics. "You told me what happened to Joel and that you poisoned Klara's coffee with arsenic. But what I can't wrap my head around is how a nice girl like you managed to get her hands on arsenic. How did you do it?"

She smiled. I think she wanted to impress me. She liked that she could surprise people with her intelligence and daring. "You should see the dumpy apartment building I live in. I have to do my laundry in a huge creepy basement. Imagine a place that hasn't been cleaned out for decades. Bare lightbulbs and spiderwebs and tons of old crap." She grimaced. "In the tool room, there's a set of shelves full of pesticides and mousetraps and boxes of rat poison. I'm talking about the old-fashioned kind. It's probably as old as the building and its main ingredient is arsenic. It was right on the label. I took it as another sign. Just like when I saw Ryan on TV when I was still living in Holland."

"Yes, another sign." I nodded, encouraging her to keep talking. My gaze darted to my back door and I wondered if I could beat her inside. I'd need a distraction because she was certain to be the faster runner. Annie was much younger than I was and in far better shape.

"I've been carrying a small container of poison in my purse ever since we left New York," she continued. "This weekend seemed like the perfect opportunity to take action. I've stayed in the background for far too long and when I saw the cover of Klara's new cookbook, I knew it was time to punish her. I didn't really want to use poison, though. I wanted her to die cooking."

I made a sympathetic noise. "You couldn't have known that Joel would use the stove reserved for her demonstration."

She shook her head. "No. I wouldn't have rigged the oven if I'd known he'd use it. Poor Joel. He didn't deserve that kind of ending."

That was too much for me. The anger I'd been suppressing since she'd begun her twisted confession welled up inside of me. "Nobody deserves to be murdered," I said. "You could have brought Klara down by proving that she and Ryan were using your grandmother's recipes. You could have told everyone that she was a fraud. She would have been ruined."

"And so would Ryan. I wouldn't do that to him!" Annie began to scrape bark from the tree trunk using the hand rake. "Klara had to pay for stealing the recipes." She scratched off another chunk of bark. "For stealing my *oma*." The scratches bit deeper and deeper into the flesh of the tree. "For stealing my future. For treating Ryan like crap. For treating me like I was lower than dirt. She had to be punished."

"There are other ways to bring people to justice." I put my hands on the grass behind me, preparing to push myself off the ground and dash for the house. "Listen, Annie. You should turn yourself in to the police. If you did, things would go better for you. You were able to talk to me about this. Don't you want to tell your story to everyone? Don't you want people to know how you've been mistreated?"

"You obviously don't understand me." Abruptly, she crouched in front of me, bringing her face close to mine. "I did it all for love. Why can't you see that?" Annie's hot breath, tinged with the odor of wine, wafted across my face. Her wild eyes pleaded for me to take her side, but I was done listening. I was through pretending to sympathize. She'd killed two people. She'd wreaked havoc on my town and created an atmosphere of fear and distrust for days. I was through with letting her be in charge.

I pushed against her chest with both hands, putting my body weight behind the thrust and she fell to the ground. The hand rake landed a foot away from her fingertips and I reached for it. That was a mistake. I should have just run.

Annie grabbed me by the ankle and I lost my balance. My face and chest slammed on the grass, knocking the breath out of me. Before I could inhale more than a shallow gulp of air, she straddled my back and placed the tines of the hand rake against the skin of my neck. The bite of cold steel on my flesh forced me to go still.

Annie leaned down and whispered into my ear. "I can't go to jail. Ryan needs me. And I can't let you tell anyone about me. I know who your boyfriend is. I'm not dumb." She tapped the tines once, twice. "You pretended to be my friend, Ms. Wilkins. You're a fake, just like Klara."

Her comparison frightened me. I had to get out from under her. I knew I'd need to gather a surge of power to throw her off and I used a few precious seconds to garner strength from the people who meant the most to me. Images flashed in my mind. Trey and his impish smile. My mother and her twinkling eyes. Sean's face on the pillow in the morning. Makayla throwing her head back as she laughed. Empowered by these visions, I gave an immense thrust and rolled to the side.

The sudden shift was too much for Annie and I felt her weight slide away. Scrambling to my feet, I ran.

I'd just made it into the kitchen when her hand closed around my hair. I jerked backward, unable to close the door.

"I can't let you get away," Annie hissed.

I grabbed the phone cradle from the wall and brought it behind my head with all my might. It connected with her hand and she let go with a snarl of rage. A second later, she swung at me with the hand rake and I ducked, lurching farther into the room and barreling against the kitchen table. I'd barely regained my feet when Annie raised the rake above her head, preparing to come at me again.

"I'm home!" Trey's voice, followed by the door slamming, burst through the house.

Annie hesitated and I shot forward. "Trey! The killer's here!" I shouted. No matter what happened to me, she would not hurt my son. "Run! RUN!"

The awareness that another person was in the house must have sent Annie into a panic. She dropped the garden tool and vanished through the kitchen door.

I nearly collided with Trey in the hall. "Mom! Are you okay?" He looked me up and down, his eyes filled with fear and worry.

"Yes. It was Annie. She's outside. I need to call the police."

Before I could make a move to stop him, Trey dashed out of the house. "NO!" I yelled and reached for my cell phone. I spoke as swiftly as possible to the emergency operator and then hung up. Grabbing a carving knife, I followed my son into the darkness.

"Trey!" I called desperately. "TREY!"

"We're here!" he bellowed from the front.

I ran around to find Trey on the porch. Trey had used his belt to secure Annie's wrists to the swing's chain and though she struggled for a minute, the fight ebbed out of her with amazing speed. Suddenly, her entire body went limp and she began to cry. I heard her whimper for Ryan over and over.

"She's a murderer?" Trey whispered when he'd recovered from the initial shock of subduing Annie. "I can't believe it."

"She told me everything," I said wearily. "It's over now."

Trey pried the knife from my hand and pulled me to him. "You sure you're all right? You're not hurt?"

I shook my head. "You're my hero," I told him with a smile. "You came home just in time."

Trey looked pleased. "Yeah, it's all in a day's work."

We stood like that, arm in arm, until the sound of sirens cut through the night.

LESS THEN FIFTEEN minutes later, a police officer Mirandized Annie and helped her into the back of his cruiser. Trey and I rode with Sean and we were all quiet on the drive to Dunston. Trey held my hand the whole way and I closed my eyes and rested my head against the leather seat. I knew the ordeal was far from over and I couldn't relax until our statements had been given and Sean had Annie's signed confession in hand.

When Sean got to the station, he put the car in park and swiveled around to face Trey. "You're a fine young man, Trey Wilkins. I'm grateful for your assistance in apprehending a dangerous criminal and for protecting the woman who means more to me than anyone else in this world." He stretched out his hand. "I wanted to say something to you at the house, but I had to maintain a professional demeanor."

Trey smiled and accepted Sean's hand. "Understood, Officer Griffiths. And I'm going to turn Mom over to your care when I head back to school at the end of the week. Do you think you can keep her out of trouble?"

The two men grinned and I feigned offense. "Hello. Stop talking about me like I'm not here. Can we go in and do what needs to be done to put an end to this thing?"

Trey got out of the car, but Sean lingered for a moment. "I have a plan to make sure you stay safe, Lila. In the future,

I don't want to come to your house with my weapon and cuffs. I'd like to show up bearing wine and roses."

"Well, it just so happens that my calendar is wide open, so bring on the wine and the roses," I said and leaned forward to kiss him.

That was the only highlight of the next two hours. I gave my statement to an extremely thorough female officer who made me repeat every word of my conversation with Annie over and over again until I couldn't take it anymore. When she asked me to review the entire evening for the fifth time, I pushed my cup of cold decaf away and folded my arms over my chest. "No," I said firmly. "I'm done. I'd like someone to drive my son and me home, please. Now."

The woman tried to stare me down but failed. "Of course." She handed me a pen. "If you could just sign and date the bottom of your statement, I'll see if your son is ready."

I followed her out to the lobby where Trey sat on one of the chairs, his gaze fixed on his iPhone. Looking up, he said, "I wasn't sure if they arrested you by mistake. Iris and I have been texting for like, an hour."

"Officer McBride here knows how important it is to cover all the bases in this case." I turned to the female policewoman. "Is Officer Griffiths free?"

Her frosty composure melted a little. "He's still in with the suspect, but he told me to see you home. He also wanted me to tell you to leave the lights on the front porch on."

I nodded and Trey and I followed her out of the building.

"What's with the porch light? Is that a secret code between the two of you?" Trey asked.

Smiling, I said. "Not really. It's just his way of saying that no matter how late it is, he'll be coming over tonight."

"He's really into you, Mom," Trey said and nudged me playfully in the side.

I linked my arm through his. "I'm a lucky woman. Tonight, I'll have a cop and a hero under one roof. What more could I ask for?"

"Supper," Trey replied and handed me a granola bar. "I know you didn't get a chance to eat, so I bought that from the vending machine."

I stood on tiptoes and kissed his cheek. Unable to help myself, I said, "This reminds me of a cute little poem by an unknown author. It goes:

'A rose can say "I love you,"
orchids can enthrall,
but a weed bouquet in a chubby fist,
yes, that says it all.'

The policewoman stopped in the middle of unlocking her car. Her eyes were moist with unshed tears. "That is so sweet," she said. "As soon as I drop you off I am going to call my mother."

"Oh!" I exclaimed to Trey. "I need to do that, too. I think your grandmother was in the middle of trying to warn me that I was in danger when I hung up on her to answer the door bell."

Trey opened the car door for me. "Guess she was right, considering you were about to invite a killer inside."

I WAS SO exhausted that I didn't hear Sean come into the house. In fact, I slept so deeply that it wasn't until I heard the murmur of low voices in the kitchen the next morning that I realized he'd lain beside me for hours without my even knowing it.

It was after eight when I tiptoed to the kitchen. The house felt quiet, as if it were holding its breath, and I didn't want to disturb the tranquility. However, when I heard Sean say, "I need to ask you something really important, Trey, and I don't want you to tell your mother about it," I stopped in the middle of the hall. Why would my boyfriend want to talk to my son in secret?

"Trey, I love your mom. I've never felt this way about a woman before. She's smart, kind, generous, and incredibly beautiful. And seeing as you're the man of the house, I'd like to ask for your permission to marry her."

My breath caught in my throat. When Trey didn't answer right away, I felt the stirrings of panic. But then I heard, "That's so cool, ah, Sean. I can tell she totally loves you back. You guys are good together. So yes, I'd be happy if you got married."

"Thanks, Trey. I'm really looking forward to starting a new chapter with your mom. She makes me a better man in every way."

I rushed back to my bedroom, flopped onto the bed, and shouted joyfully into my pillow. How would I ever be able to go into the kitchen without the biggest smile on my face?

Fortunately, I was saved by Sean who came into the room carrying a cup of coffee.

"Finally awake?" He grinned. "You didn't move an inch all night. You were in a deeper sleep than a hibernating bear."

"But I feel like myself again," I said, accepting the coffee and a good-morning kiss. I wanted to put the cup down, pull him onto the bed, and kiss him some more, but I didn't want him to suspect I'd been eavesdropping. "Please tell me you got a confession. Tell me that Inspiration Valley can return to normal."

He sat on the edge of the bed. "It's over. The other chefs caught the first train out of Inspiration Valley. Ryan and his kids are gone, too. We have a signed confession and plenty of evidence to back it up."

"Thank the Lord," I said in relief. "Does it sound weird for me to admit that I feel sorry for Annie? Ryan and Klara used what was precious to her—her grandmother, her family recipes, and memories that belonged to her childhood. All Annie ever wanted was for Ryan to see her and to return the all-consuming love she felt for him, but she never existed in his eyes."

Sean looked thoughtful. "She chose to leave her family and her past behind based on an unhealthy obsession with a married man, Lila. And two people died because of that obsession. Annie was wronged. That much is true. But in actuality, she behaved like a spoiled child who didn't get her way. Instead of throwing a tantrum, she committed murder. Twice."

I nodded, unable to disagree. And as I considered his words, I thought of another young woman who had behaved like a spoiled child. "Sean, what about my slashed tires? Did anyone have a chance to informally question Zoe Bright?"

He leapt up, pulling the notepad from his pocket. "With all the goings-on surrounding Annie, I forgot to tell you. Vicky gave me Zoe's address and I went to see her myself. Apparently, the sight of a uniformed police officer at the door compelled her to confess to the vandalism before I even asked about it. She apologized profusely, and admitted acting in a fit of frustration because her attempts to rewrite her novel had failed and she had no one to lash out at except you."

I frowned. "That's a vicious way to vent her frustration. Should I be worried?"

He shook his head. "No. As a matter of fact, Zoe won't trouble you or the agency anymore. She's decided to give up on writing and plans to focus her energy on making jewelry. In any event, I charged her with vandalism for which she'll most likely do community service." He flipped pages. "She also offered to pay for the tire replacement and wanted you to pass her contact information on to the garage so they could send her the bill." He tore a slip of paper from the notepad and placed it on the bedside table.

"That's good news," I said, swinging my legs over the edge of the bed. "I'm sorry the writing didn't work out for her, but I have to say I'm glad I won't be seeing her again. Jewelry making is probably a better career path for her anyway. The necklace she crafted for me is actually quite beautiful."

Sean kissed me on the forehead and headed for the door. "I have to go. Don't make plans for dinner tonight, because now that things have quieted down, I'm going to arrange a special evening for us."

"That sounds wonderful," I said, bringing the coffee mug to my mouth in an attempt to hide my grin.

THE WALK TO work kindled my senses. Warm sunlight dappled the sidewalks, birds sang their morning songs, and the scent of lilacs and peonies permeated the air. Shop-keepers were opening their stores and there was a general atmosphere of buoyancy and joy around town. It was contagious, and I couldn't keep from smiling. There was no longer a murderer on the loose, the chefs had all left, and Sean was going to ask me to marry him. My feet barely touched the ground as I envisaged our romantic night together.

When I stopped in Espresso Yourself, Makayla waved me past a line of customers. "I've been waiting for you. I heard about what happened with Annie at your house last night, and I'm sorry you had to go through that kind of scare," she said, her green eyes sparkling. "But you're safe and our town is ours again, so nothing can dampen my mood. Ever since I danced with Jay by the fountain, I have been walking on sunshine."

"I can imagine," I said, thinking I was right there with her. I glanced at all the people in her café. "I have something to tell you, but not now. Can we have lunch today?"

"You bet." She handed me a cup. "Here's a caramel mocha latte to prepare you to read the magnificent, one-of-a-kind manuscript that's waiting in your email inbox."

A thrill of anticipation ran through me. "Did you finally send me your book?"

"Yes, ma'am. Now that things have calmed down around here, I figured it was time."

I HURRIED TO my desk and turned on the computer. Feeling giddy with anticipation, I opened Makayla's attachment and began to read.

Her book was a collection of interconnected short stories set in a coffee shop. *The Barista Diaries* recounted the lives of seven coffee shop customers as told by a sensitive young woman who'd gained an intimate glimpse of their hopes and setbacks by listening to them talk day after day. There were poignant tales of love, humorous narratives of mishaps and exploits, and moving family dramas. I was delighted to discover that Makayla was a skillful and talented writer. Her sincere voice transported the reader into the world of her fictional café and convinced me to care about each and every character.

After the third story, about an elderly man who discovers a happy secret while having coffee with his son, I sat back and took a sip of my latte, envisioning Makayla's book in print. I knew I could sell this book and mentally compiled a list of publishers who might be interested. A smile crept over my face. Despite all that had happened this weekend, I still loved my job. What could be more gratifying than making a writer's dreams come true?

Flora knocked on my door. "I've baked a special treat for everyone. We're all gathering in the kitchen," she said. "Come join us."

"Absolutely." I got up and eagerly followed her. "What did you make?"

"Some Dutch cookies from a recipe out of Klara's cookbook. I thought it would be nice to honor her this way." She sighed as we entered the kitchen, where Jude, Franklin, and Zach sat at the table, coffee mugs in hand. "Of course, that was before I found out she was a fraud and her recipes and stories had all been plagiarized. My, my, but it's all such a shame."

"The recipes are still good, aren't they?" Zach asked. "I hope so, because the Zachmeister's breakfast was hours ago."

"Yes, dear, they're wonderful. Annie's grandmother was the source of the recipes and I'm sure she was a great cook." Flora removed the lid from a round flowered tin, releasing the scent of cinnamon and almonds. "These are *jan hagel koekjes*. '*Koekjes*' means 'cookies,'" she explained.

The cookies were flat diamond shapes covered with toasted almonds. I bit into one of the crispy treats. The cookie's buttery sweetness, combined with cinnamon and nuts, was delectable. "It melts in your mouth," I said, taking another bite.

"They're baked as one big piece," Flora said. "After you spread out the dough on a cookie sheet, you sprinkle the almonds on top and bake the whole thing. When it's done, you cut the dough into diamonds and serve."

"These are totally amazing. I hope you made more than one batch!" Zach exclaimed as he chewed. "Klara may have been a crook, but there's nothing wrong with her cookbook."

Franklin took a sip of his coffee. "That's true. The book is very engaging. The stories about Annie's grandmother make it more than a simple book filled with photos and recipes. It's a snapshot of someone's memories." His eyebrows knit together. "Just not Klara's. How I wish I had known the truth about it all."

"I wonder if the sales will be affected when the news that Klara stole the material goes viral," said Flora as she poured hot water from the kettle over the teabag into her favorite mug.

"They'll probably go through the roof," said Jude. "Remember what happened with *A Million Little Pieces* by James Frey? He claimed he'd written a memoir and then people found out it wasn't true. The book sold like crazy. Even bad press is good for sales."

"Yes, but there might be legal ramifications as well." Franklin reached into the tin and took out another cookie. "Especially if Annie decides to sue Ryan and the publishers for rightful ownership."

I wiped crumbs from my hands. "I don't think she'll do that. Not as long as she's in love with Ryan."

"She may change her mind about that after spending time in prison," said Jude. He entwined his fingers behind his head and stretched back. "All I can say is that this stud of an agent is glad that it's over and we can get back to doing what we do best."

Franklin nodded his agreement. "I don't think I could survive another day with those chefs."

"And I, for one, would be happy if we don't have to organize another festival for a very long time," I said.

"Here, here," said Zach, toasting me with his coffee cup. "Well, people, Zachmeister's gotta run. Time is money." As he rushed out the door, he almost collided with Bentley. "Sorry, boss," he said and disappeared down the hall.

Bentley watched him go and then crossed the threshold. Flora held out the tin. "Would you like a cookie?"

"I'll take one to eat later," Bentley said as she reached her manicured fingers into the container. "Lila, Jude, what's the status on the Marlette sequel? Have you signed Jay Coleman as a client yet?"

"We're meeting with him this afternoon to do just that. His proposal is superb." Jude looked at me. "Jay emailed it to us last night. Have you had a chance to read it? I know you were somewhat preoccupied."

I shook my head. Jude was referring to my encounter with Annie, but in truth, I had been so wrapped up in Makayla's submission that I hadn't looked at anything else in my inbox. "It's next on my agenda. I can't wait."

"His plotline is tightly woven and complex. He's also managed to thoroughly replicate Marlette's voice." Jude turned back to Bentley. "We're confident that Marlette's remarkable characters will continue to live through Jay's writing. And I believe that the publishers will concur."

"Good. Let me know when it's all finalized." Bentley's departure spurred us to end our break. After a few more pleasantries, we all stood and dispersed.

At my desk, I enthusiastically focused on my computer. I clicked on Jay's proposal and its thousands of words and characters sprang onto my bright white screen. I wondered how many other queries and proposals were in line behind his, how many other fresh voices were just waiting to be discovered. Voices with powerful stories to tell, fascinating characters to bring to life, and intricate mysteries to solve.

Feeling utterly content, I settled in my chair and began to read.

Dear Reader,

Thank you for spending time in Inspiration Valley. I'm Ellery Adams. Sylvia May and I coauthor the Lucy Arlington mysteries, and I hope you enjoyed Lila's latest adventure. It's amazing what can happen in a pastoral small town, isn't it? After all the excitement, Lila is fortunate enough to be able to return to her office at Novel Idea and bury her nose in a book.

In the meantime, I'd like to introduce you to my newest mystery series: the Book Lovers' Resort Mysteries. These books take place at an exclusive resort called Storyton Hall. What's Storyton Hall, you ask? Picture a stately English manor house—a sprawling behemoth of a building—and then move it, stone by stone, to the Virginia countryside. Next, fill each room with books. Hundreds of books. Thousands of books. And then decorate each room so that it reminds you of a famous author. You'll end up with places like the Jane Austen Drawing Room, the Ian Fleming Lounge, and Shakespeare's Theater. Next, fill the many bedrooms with comfy chairs, soft bedding, fresh flowers, and boxes of complimentary chocolates. When all is ready, throw open the massive front doors, offer the guests a glass of champagne, and join them as they enter this readers' utopia.

But be warned. You're stepping into this haven for book lovers—this place of meandering garden paths, decadent afternoon teas, and secret passageways—at your own risk. For you see, a murderer has checked in along with you.

My friends, I invite you to take a brief sojourn into the delightful and occasionally deadly world of the Book Lovers' Resort Mysteries by offering the first chapter of

Murder in the Mystery Suite. *A word of caution, however. Once you visit Storyton Hall, you might be so captivated by the resort's beauty and charismatic staff that you may never want to leave.*

Yours,
Ellery Adams

THERE WERE BOOKS EVERYWHERE. HUNDREDS OF books. Thousands of books. There were books of every size, shape, and color. They lined the walls from floor to ceiling, standing straight and rigid as soldiers on the polished mahogany shelves, the gilt lettering on their worn spines glinting in the soft light, the scent of supple leather and aging paper filling the air.

To Jane Steward, there was no sweeter perfume on earth. Of all the libraries in Storyton Hall, this was her favorite. Unlike the other libraries, which were open to the hotel's paying guests, this was the personal reading room of her great uncle Aloysius and great aunt Octavia.

"Are you ready, Sinclair?" Jane mounted the rolling book ladder and looked back over her shoulder.

A small, portly man with a cloud of white hair and ruddy

cheeks wrung his hands together. "Oh, Miss Jane. I wish you wouldn't ask me to do this. It doesn't seem prudent."

Jane shrugged. "You heard what Gavin said at our last staff meeting. The greenhouse is in disrepair, the orchard needs pruning, the hedge maze is overgrown, the folly is hidden in brambles, and the roof above the staff quarters is rotting away. I have to come up with funds somehow. Lots of funds. What I need, Sinclair, is inspiration." She held out her arms as if she could embrace every book in the room. "What better place to find it than here?"

"Can't you just shut your eyes, reach out your hand, and choose a volume from the closest shelf?" Sinclair stuck a finger under his collar, loosening his bow tie. Unlike Storyton's other staff members, he didn't wear the hotel's royal blue and gold livery. As the resort's head librarian, he distinguished himself by dressing in tweed suits every day of the year. The only spot of color that appeared on his person came in the form of a striped, spotted, floral, or checkered bow tie. Today's was canary yellow with prim little brown dots.

Jane shook her head at the older gentleman she'd known since childhood. "You know that doesn't work, Sinclair. I have to lose all sense of where I am in the room. The book must choose me, not me it." She smiled down at him. "Ms. Pimpernel tells me that the rails have recently been oiled, so you should be able to push me around in circles with ease."

"In squares, you mean." Sinclair sighed in defeat. "Very well, Miss Jane. Kindly hold on."

Grinning like a little girl, Jane gripped the sides of the ladder and closed her eyes. Sinclair pushed on the ladder, hesitantly at first, until Jane encouraged him to go faster, faster.

"Are you quite muddled yet?" he asked after a minute or so.

Jane descended by two rungs but didn't open her eyes. "I think I'm still in the twentieth-century American authors section. If I'm right, we need to keep going."

Sinclair grunted. "It's getting harder and harder to confuse you, Miss Jane. You know where every book in this library is shelved."

"Just a few more spins around the room. Please?"

The ladder began to move once more. This time, however, Sinclair stopped and started without warning and changed direction more than once. Eventually, he succeeded in disorientating her.

"Excellent!" Jane exclaimed and reached out her right hand. Her fingertips touched cloth and leather. They traced the embossed letters marching up and down the spines for a few, brief seconds, before traveling to the next book. "Inspire me," she whispered.

But nothing spoke to her, so she shifted to the left side of the ladder, stretching her arm overhead until her hand brushed against a book that was smaller and shorter than its neighbors. "You're the one," she said and pulled it from the shelf.

Sinclair craned his neck as if he might be able to read the title from his vantage point on the ground. "Which one did you pick, Miss Jane?"

"A British mystery," she said, frowning. "But I don't see how—"

At that moment, two boys burst into the room, infusing the air with screams, scuffles, and shouts. The first, who had transformed himself into a knight using a stainless steel salad bowl helm and a T-shirt covered with silver duct tape, brandished a wooden yardstick. The second boy, who was identical to the first in every way except for his costume, wore a green raincoat. He had the hood pulled up and tied under his chin and carried two hand rakes. His lips were closed around a New Year's Eve party favor and every time he exhaled, its multicolored paper tongue would uncurl with a shrill squeak.

"Boys!" Jane called out to no effect. Her sons dashed around chairs and side tables, nearly overturning the coffee table and its collection of paperweights and framed family photos.

Sinclair tried to get between the knight and the dragon. "Saint George," he said in a voice that rang with authority, though it was no more than a whisper. "Might I suggest that you conquer this terrifying serpent outdoors? Things are likely to get broken in the fierce struggle between man and beast."

The first boy bowed gallantly and pointed his sword at Jane. "Fair maid, I've come to rescue you from your tower."

Jane giggled. "Thank you, Sir Fitz, but I am quite happy up here."

Refusing to be upstaged by his twin brother, the other boy growled and circled around a leather chair and ottoman, a writing desk, and a globe on a stand in order to position himself directly under the ladder. "If you don't give me all of your gold, then I'll eat you!" he snarled and held out his hand rakes.

Doing her best to appear frightened, Jane clutched at her chest. "Please, oh fearsome and powerful dragon. I have no gold. In fact, my castle is falling apart around me. I was just wishing for a fairy godmother to float down and—

"There aren't any fairies in this story!" the dragon interrupted crossly. "Fairies are for *girls.*"

"Yeah," the knight echoed indignantly.

Jane knew she had offended her six-year-old sons, but before she could make amends, her eye fell on the ruler in Fitz's hands and an idea struck her.

"Fitz, Hem, you are my heroes!" she cried, hurrying down the ladder.

The boys exchanged befuddled glances. "We are?" They spoke in unison, as they so often did.

"But I'm supposed to be a monster," Hem objected.

Jane touched his cheek. "And you've both been so convincing that you can go straight to the kitchen and tell Mrs. Hubbard that I've given my permission for each of you to have an extra piece of chocolate-dipped shortbread at tea this afternoon."

Their gray eyes grew round with delight, but then Fitz whispered something in Hem's ear. Pushing back his salad bowl helm, he gave his mother a mournful look. "Mrs. Hubbard won't believe us. She'll tell us that story about the boy who cried wolf again."

"I'll write a note," Jane said. The boys exchanged high fives as she scribbled a few lines on an index card.

"Shall I tuck this under one of your scales, Mister Dragon?" She shoved the note into the pocket of Hem's raincoat. "Now run along. Sinclair and I have a party to plan."

Sinclair waited for the boys to leave before seating himself at his desk chair. He uncapped a fountain pen and held it over a clean notepad. "A party, Miss Jane?"

Jane flounced in the chair across from him and rubbed

her palm over the cover of the small book in her hands. "This is Agatha Christie's *Death on the Nile*."

"Are we having a Halloween Party then?" Sinclair asked. "With pharaohs and mummies and such?" He furrowed his shaggy brows. "Did the boys' getups influence your decision?"

"Not just a costume party. Think bigger." Jane hugged the book to her chest with one hand and gestured theatrically with the other. "An entire week of murder and mayhem. We'll have a fancy dress ball and award prizes to those who most closely emulate their fictional detectives. Just think," she continued, warming to her idea. "We'll have Hercule Poirot, Sherlock Holmes, Sam Spade, Lord Peter Wimsey, Nick and Nora Charles, Brother Cadfael, Miss Marple, and so on. We'll have readings and skits and teas and banquets. We'll have mystery scavenger hunts and trivia games! Imagine it, Sinclair."

He grimaced. "I'm trying, Miss Jane, but it sounds like a great deal of hubbub and work. And for what purpose?"

"Money," Jane said simply. "Storyton Hall will be bursting at the seams with paying guests. They'll have the time of their lives and will go home and tell all of their friends how wonderful it was to stay at the nation's only resort catering specifically to readers. We need to let the world know that while we're a place of peace and tranquility, we also offer excitement and adventure."

Sinclair fidgeted with his bow tie again. "Miss Jane, forgive me for saying so, but I believe our guests are interested in three things: comfort, quiet, and good food. I'm not certain they're interested in adventure."

"Our readers aren't sedentary," Jane argued. "I've seen

them playing croquet and lawn tennis. I've met them on the hiking and horseback-riding trails. I've watched them row across the lake in our little skiffs and walk into Storyton Village. Why wouldn't they enjoy a weekend filled with mystery, glamour, and entertainment?"

The carriage clock on Sinclair's desk chimed three times. "Perhaps you should mention the proposal to your great aunt and uncle over tea?"

Jane nodded in agreement. "Brilliant idea. Aunt Octavia is most malleable when she has a plate piled high with scones and lemon cakes. Thank you, Sinclair." She stood up, walked around the desk, and kissed him lightly on the cheek.

He touched the spot where his skin had turned a rosy shade of pink. "You're welcome, Miss Jane, though I don't think I was of much help."

"You're a librarian," she said on her way out. "To me, that makes you a bigger hero than Saint George, Sir William Wallace, and all of the Knights of the Round Table put together."

"I love my job," Jane heard Sinclair say before she closed the door.

JANE TURNED IN the opposite direction of the main elevator and headed for the staircase at the other end of a long corridor carpeted in a lush crimson. She was accustomed to traveling a different route than the paying guests of Storyton Hall. Like the rest of the staff, Jane moved noiselessly through a maze of narrow passageways, underground tunnels, dim stairways, attic accesses, and hidden doors to keep herself as unobtrusive as possible.

Storyton had fifty bedrooms, eleven of which were on the main floor. And even though Jane's great aunt and uncle were in their late seventies, they preferred to remain in their third-story suite of apartments, which included their private library and cozy sitting room, where her aunt liked to spend her evenings reading.

Trotting down a flight of stairs, Jane paused to straighten her skirt before entering the main hallway. Along the wood-paneled walls hung with gilt-framed mirrors, gilt sconces, and massive oil paintings in ornate gilt frames, massive oak doors stood open, inviting guests to while away the hours reading in the Jane Austen Drawing Room, the Ian Fleming Lounge, the Isak Dinesen Safari Study, the Daphne Du Maurier Parlor, and so on. There was also a Beatrix Potter playroom for children, but that was located on the basement level as most of the guests preferred not to hear the shrieks and squeals of children when they were trying to lose themselves in a riveting story.

Jane greeted every guest with a hello and a smile though her mind was focused on other things. She made a mental checklist as she walked. *The door handles need polishing. A lightbulb's gone out by the entrance to Shakespeare's Theater. Eliza needs to stop putting goldenrod in the flower vases. There's pollen on all the tables and the guests are sneezing.*

She'd almost reached the sunporch when the tiny speakers mounted along the crown molding in the main hallway began to play a recording of bells chiming. Jane glanced at her watch. It was exactly three o'clock.

"Oh, it's teatime!" a woman examining a painting of cherry blossoms exclaimed. Taking the book from a man sitting in one of the dozens of wing chairs lining the hall, she gestured for him to get to his feet. "Come on, Bernard! I want to be get there first today."

Jane knew there was slim chance of that happening. Guests began congregating at the door of the Agatha Christie Tea Room at half past two. Bobbing her head at the eager pair, she walked past the chattering men, women, and children heading to tea and arrived at the back terrace to find her great aunt and uncle seated at a round table with the twins. The table was covered with a snowy white cloth, a vase stuffed with fuchsia peonies, and her aunt's Wedgwood tea set.

"There you are, dear!" Aunt Octavia lifted one of her massive arms and waved regally. Octavia was a very large, very formidable woman. She adored food and loathed exercise. As a result, she'd steadily grown in circumference over the decades and showed no predisposition toward changing her habits, much to her doctor's consternation.

"Hello, everyone," Jane said as she took a seat. This was the only time during the day in which she would sit in view of the guests. Very few people noticed the Steward family gathering for tea, being far too busy filling their plates with sandwiches, scones, cookies, and cakes inside the main house.

Fitz plucked her sleeve. "Mom, can I have another lemon cake?" He glanced at his brother. "Hem, too?"

"Fitzgerald Steward," Aunt Octavia said in a low growl. "You've already had enough for six boys. So has Hemingway. Let your mother pour herself some tea before you start demanding seconds. And you should say 'may I' not 'can I.'"

Nodding solemnly, Fitz sat up straight in his chair and cleared his throat. Doing his best to sound like an English aristocrat, he said, "Madam, may we please have another cake?"

This time, the question was directed at Aunt Octavia. Before she could answer, Hem piped up in a cockney accent. "Please, Mum. We're ever so 'ungry."

Aunt Octavia burst out laughing and passed the platter of sweets. "Incorrigible," she said and put a wrinkled hand over Jane's. "Are you going to the village after tea? Mabel called to say that my new dress is ready and I can't wait to see it. Hot pink with sequins and brown leopard spots. Can you imagine?"

Jane could. Her aunt wore voluminous housedresses fashioned from the most exotic prints and the boldest colors available. She ordered bolts of cloth from an assortment of catalogues and had Mabel Wimberly, a talented seamstress who lived in Storyton Village, sew the fabric into a garment she could slip over her head. Each dress had to come complete with several pockets as Aunt Octavia walked with the aid of a rhinestone-studded cane and liked to load her pockets with gum, hard candy, pens, a notepad, bookmarks, and nail clippers. Today, she wore a black and lime zebra-striped dress and a black sun hat decorated with ostrich feathers.

And while Aunt Octavia's attire was flamboyant, Uncle Aloysius dressed like the country gentleman he was. His slacks and shirt were perfectly pressed and he always had a handkerchief peeking from the pocket of his suit. The only deviation from this conservative ensemble was his hat. Aloysius wore his fishing hat, complete with hooks, baits, and flies, all day long. He even wore it to church and Aunt Octavia had to remind him to remove it once the service got under way. Some of the staff whispered that he wore it to bed as well, but Jane didn't believe it. After all, several of the hooks looked rather sharp.

"What sandwiches did Mrs. Hubbard make today?" she asked her great uncle.

He patted his flat stomach. Uncle Aloysius was as tall and slender as his wife was squat and round. He was all points and angles to her curves and rolls. Despite their contrasting physical appearances and the passage of multiple decades, the two were still very much in love. Jane's great uncle liked to tell people that he was on a fifty-five-year honeymoon. "My darling wife will tell you that the egg salad and chive is the best," he said. "I started with the Brie, watercress, and walnut." He handed Jane the plate of sandwiches and a pair of silver tongs. "That was lovely, but not as good as the fig and goat cheese."

"In that case, I'll have one of each." Jane helped herself to the diminutive sandwiches. "And a raisin scone." Her gaze alighted on the jar of preserves near Aunt Octavia's elbow. "Is that Mrs. Hubbard's blackberry jam?"

"Yes, and it's magnificent. But don't go looking for the Devonshire cream. The boys and I ate every last dollop." Her great aunt sat back in her chair, rested her tiny hands on her great belly, and studied Jane's face. "You've got a spark about you, my girl. Care to enlighten us as to why you have a skip in your step and a twinkle in your eye?"

Jane told her great aunt and uncle about her Murder and Mayhem Week idea.

Uncle Aloysius leaned forward and listened without interruption, nodding from time to time. Instantly bored by the topic, Fitz and Hem scooted back their chairs and resumed their knight and dragon personas by skirmishing a few feet from the table until Aunt Octavia shooed them off.

"Go paint some seashells green," she told Hem. "You

can't be a decent dragon without scales. We have an entire bucket of shells in the craft closet."

"What about me?" Fitz asked. "What else do I need to be a knight?"

Aunt Octavia examined him closely. "A proper knight needs a horse. Get a mop and paint a pair of eyes on the handle."

Without another word, the twins sprinted for the basement stairs. Jane saw their sandy heads disappear and grinned. Her aunt had encouraged her to play similar games when she was a child and it gave her a great deal of satisfaction to see her sons doing the same.

"Imagination is more important than knowledge," was Aunt Octavia's favorite quote and she repeated it often. She said it again now and then waved for Jane to continue.

Throughout the interruption, Uncle Aloysius hadn't taken his eyes off Jane once. When she finished outlining her plan, he rubbed the white whiskers on his chin and gazed out across the wide lawn. "I like your idea, my dear. I like it very much. We can charge our guests a special weekly rate. And by special, I mean higher. We'd have to ask a pretty penny for the additional events. I expect we'll need to hire extra help."

"But you think it will work?"

"I do indeed. It's splendid," he said, smiling at her. "It could be the start of a new tradition. Mystery buffs in October, Western readers in July, fantasy fans for May Day."

"A celebration of romance novels for Valentine's!" Aunt Octavia finished with a sweep of her arm.

Uncle Aloysius grabbed hold of his wife's hand and planted a kiss on her palm. "It's Valentine's Day all year long with you, my love."

Jane felt a familiar stab of pain. It was during moments like these that she missed her husband the most. She'd been a widow for six years and had never been able to think of William Elliot without a pang of sorrow and agony. Watching her great uncle and aunt murmur endearments to each other, she wondered if ten years would be enough time to completely heal the hole in her heart left by her husband's passing.

"Jane? Are you gathering wool?" Great Aunt Octavia asked.

Shaking off her melancholy, Jane reached for the teapot and poured herself a nice cup of Earl Grey. "I'm afraid I was. Sorry."

"No time for drifting off," Uncle Aloysius said. "There's much to be done to prepare for this Murder and Mayhem Week of yours. And might I say." He paused to collect himself and Jane knew that he was about to pay her a compliment. Her uncle was always very deliberate when it came to words of praise or criticism. "Your dedication to Storyton Hall does the Steward name proud. I couldn't have asked for a more devoted heir."

Jane thanked him, drank the rest of her tea, and went into the manor house through the kitchen. She tarried for a moment to tell the staff how delicious the tea service was and then walked down the former servant's passage to her small, windowless office.

Sitting behind her desk, Jane flexed her fingers over her computer keyboard and began to type a list of possible events, meals, and decorating ideas for the Murder and Mayhem week. Satisfied that Storyton Hall's future guests would have a wide range of activities and dining choices during the mystery week, she set about composing a newsletter announcing the dates and room rates. She made the special events appear even more enticing by inserting colorful stock photos of bubbling champagne glasses, people laughing, and couples dancing at a costume ball. She also included the book covers of some of Christie's best-known works as well as tantalizing photographs of Storyton's most impressive dinner and dessert buffets.

"They'll come in droves," she said to herself, absurdly pleased by the end result of the newsletter. "Uncle Aloysius is right. If this event is a resounding success, we can add on more and more over the course of the year. Then, we'll be able to fix this old pile of stones until it's just like it was when crazy Walter Egerton Steward had it dismantled, brick by brick, and shipped across the Atlantic. We'll restore the folly and the hedge maze and the orchards." Her eyes grew glassy and she gazed off into the middle distance. "It'll be as he dreamed it would be. An English estate hidden away in the wilds of the Virginia mountains. An oasis for book lovers. A reader's paradise amid the pines."

She reread the newsletter once more, searching for typos or grammatical errors, and, finding none, saved the document. She then opened a new email message and typed "newsletter recipients" in the address line. It gave her a little thrill to know that thousands of people would soon read about Storyton Hall's first annual Murder and Mayhem Week.

After composing a short email, Jane hit send, releasing her invitation into the world. Within seconds, former guests, future guests, and her newspaper and magazine contacts would catch a glimpse of what promised to be an unforgettable seven days. Tomorrow, she'd order print brochures to be mailed to the people on her contact list who preferred a more old-fashioned communication.

I'll have contacted thousands of people by the end of the week, Jane thought happily. *Thousands of potential guests. Thousands of lovely readers.*

But the lovely readers weren't the only ones who'd be receiving Jane Steward's invitation.

A murderer would get one, too.

DON'T MISS THE FIRST NOVEL IN
THE BOOKS BY THE BAY MYSTERIES FROM

ELLERY ADAMS

A Killer Plot

In the small coastal town of Oyster Bay, North Carolina, you'll find plenty of characters, ne'er-do-wells, and even a few celebs trying to duck the paparazzi. But when murder joins this curious community, writer Olivia Limoges and the Bayside Book Writers are determined to get the story before they meet their own surprise ending.